The Scorpion Signal

A PERILOUS RESCUE...

..."I'm not available. Listen, I came off the last thing two weeks ago. Didn't anyone tell you that? *Two weeks.*" My voice had risen a fraction and I didn't like that, but it might give him a clue to the condition I was in.

"I knew that, yes." He paused again. "You did rather well."

I left that one. Every word he said was a baited hook.

"A very great deal depends, you see, on whether we can do anything for this man. It touches all of us...."

My hands were frozen. I was afraid of what Croder was going, finally, to make me do, by pricking my conscience, or my pride. I listened to the rain beating at the row of narrow, sooty windows and wondered who the poor bastard was, and where.

"QUILLER IS IN TOP FORM THROUGHOUT."
—CHICAGO SUN-TIMES

"EXCITING, FULL OF TENSION..."
—THE NEW YORK TIMES BOOK REVIEW

The
Scorpion
Signal

By Adam Hall

PLAYBOY
PAPERBACKS

For Chris Holmes

CONTENTS

1 / SHAPIRO

I turned again, wheeling into the wind with the edge of the cliff a hundred feet below me. The air feathered against my face, numbing it, and tears crept back from the corners of my eyes, drying on the skin. A pale sun was turning the sea into hammered gold, below on my right side, and the waves were rolling in ice-blue arcs, hanging poised for an instant before they shattered along the shore.

It had been the twentieth turn: I'd been counting them. I was now half hypnotized by the sliding images of grass and cliff and sand and sea as they floated below my prone body, and by the periods of near-weightlessness as the wind gusts dropped me into the troughs and lifted me out again. A minute ago two gulls had come abreast of me and drifted alongside not far away, their sharp heads turned to watch me as they wondered what I was; inland I could see our three shadows gliding in perfect formation across the short brown grass of the cliff top, two small ones and the third much bigger but still the shape of a bird, not of a man. By a degree, however small, I was taking on their character, watching the land below and feeling the lie of the wind, the muscles compensating as evolution worked on my humanoid body and adapted its behavior to the needs of a bird.

I broke the next turn at ninety degrees and went downwind across the edge of the cliff to try out the air on the lee side. For a moment the car was directly below me and I saw Norton again, standing near it and gazing up. Another car was pulling in rather fast from the cliff road and bouncing over the grass, but I lost sight of it as the sail hit some turbulence. I worked on the bar, tilting it back to gain speed and pulling the nose up to get some more height; then I veered into the wind and crossed the cliff again, turning to drift parallel with it.

After the next turn I saw the other car had pulled up alongside Norton's MG. There were a couple of men in dark uniforms, and Norton started waving to me with wide urgent gestures. I checked the sail and rigging but couldn't see anything wrong. I didn't expect to: I had a rough idea of what had come up. At the end of the run I turned and moved inland again. All three of them were waving to me with flailing downward motions, putting a lot of expression into it; I could now see the white letters on the back of the second car. I didn't like it, any of it, because I'd been on leave only two weeks and my nerves were still trying to shake themselves out.

I made three more runs, trying to forget about them, but they began using the horns at me and a siren wailed into life and died again. They were still waving, so I compromised: I think I could have got enough height to come in and land on the grass and ask them what the hell they wanted, but I gave myself a final fling and put the nose down and swooped over their heads in a long arrowing dive across the cliff and the beach and the sea, wheeling against the beaten-gold reflection and moving into wind again, lowering, the trailing edge fluttering near stalling point a few feet above the ground; then I put the nose down and ran in with my feet plowing up the sand as I got the last of the wind out of the sail. I was still dismantling when Norton came sprinting along from the cliff path to help me.

"London," he said.

"I'm frozen stiff," I told him. "Look after this, will you?" I left him and ran hard for a mile, as far as the pier and back, feeling better because I'd worked a bit of the frustration out: there was absolutely no point in getting annoyed just because he'd mentioned London. They couldn't send me out again, not this soon.

"Police escort," Norton said as he strapped the spars together. "Not my fault."

"All I need," I said, "is a phone."

"And the best of luck."

"Oh for Christ's sake shut up."

I hated panic, and a police escort meant someone in London was panicking.

It was ten minutes before we got the kite up the steps in the cliff; the two cops helped us stow it on the rack of Norton's MG, asking a lot of silly questions, what did it feel like, wasn't it dangerous, so forth. They followed us to the hotel and I used the telephone and talked to three people, one of them Tilson; then I put the phone down and came back to the lobby and told Norton:

"You weren't joking."

He puffed out his cheeks. "Are you taking your car?"

"Yes. I'll need it to come back in, tomorrow."

He didn't make any comment. The two cops were

looking at us from the entrance doors and one of them called out:

"We were told to get a move on. It's up to you."

I went over to the desk to pay my bill.

"Give me a lift?" Norton asked me.

"Where to?" I was thinking of Helena.

"London."

I turned and looked at him. "Do they want you too?"

"They might."

I suppose he could have gone over to the telephone booth by the doors while I was calling London: the first line I'd tried had been engaged. Maybe they'd told him to make sure I got there.

"Look," I told the cashier, "there's a Helena Swinburn meeting me here in an hour from now. Give her this message and get the florist to bring round some gardenias, if not, orchids, if not, carnations, all right? Add twenty-five to the card to cover it. And I'm leaving my bags in the room."

He was making notes. "You'll be keeping the room, then, sir?"

"Yes. I'll be back tomorrow sometime."

I could hear Norton whistling under his breath. He'd caught some of the panic from London when he'd phoned, typical admin. reaction. I went over to the cops. "What's the form?"

"You follow us. If you can't keep up, just give a toot."

"Bloody cheek," I said, and went out to look for the Jag.

In the next ten minutes we cleared all the red lights in the town with the siren and flashers going and settled down into the nineties as soon as we got onto the motorway north, reaching Mitcham in seventy minutes flat.

"Chopper," Norton said. He hadn't spoken before.

I'd been watching it. The patrol car was slowing hard in front of us and taking us across the common, pulling up close to the spot where the helicopter was touching down on skis. It was a police machine with the coat of arms of the Royal Borough of Westminster on the side; I suppose they hadn't been able to get the Sussex constabulary to fly us in from the coast. Everyone had obviously been playing about with the radio and I began feeling depressed because this was fully-alert procedure and I was meant to be on leave.

The door slid back and a voice came above the sound of the blades. "No baggage?"

"No."

"Hop in."

Norton's foot slipped on the metal rung of the step as he swung up.

"Watch it."

They slammed the door and gunned up and lifted off with the first of the neon streetlights falling away below. Norton was still untalkative; he sat puffing his cheeks out, trying to get rid of the tension. He'd been with the Bureau nearly as long as I had and he knew the signs. This wasn't a mission they wanted me for: someone had blown a fuse and the whole network had gone out of whack. It had happened twice before, during my time: once when Fraser had been pulling a Polish intelligence colonel across the frontier at Szczecin and the checkpoint had shut down on them, and once when they'd hauled me out of Tokyo to look for some nerve gas some bloody fool had dropped all over the Sahara. Whatever they wanted me for this time it was no go.

London was coming up, a haze of light from horizon to horizon under the late January fog. Norton was rubbing his hands together, though it wasn't cold in the cabin; I felt sorry for him, with all that adrenaline sloshing about before he'd even started.

"Never mind," I said above the beat of the rotors, "it's probably some bloody fool in Signals getting his homework wrong."

"Oh shit," he said and swung to face me, and I realized he'd been startled out of his thoughts by the sound of my voice. I began wondering if he knew something that I didn't: something about the panic going on.

"Where are you putting down?" I asked the pilot.

"Battersea Heliport. All right?"

"It's your toy." We were lowering now, with the city lights swarming to meet us.

"You from the Yard, are you, sir?"

"That's right." We never mind what they think we are.

A signal was coming through and the navigator leaned toward me, the glow of the instrument panel on his face. "They want to know if our people can take your Jag to Sloane Street for you. They're off their beat already."

"Can you do that?"

"Easy." He talked into the headset and signaled out.

"Well," I asked him, "did you arrange it?"

"Yes, sir."

He could have told me.

Nerves.

There was a bump and we keeled even under slowing rotors while Norton hit his seat belt open and went down first and stood on the landing pad waiting to help me if I slipped on the rungs. Bloody little nurse-maid, they'd given him instructions to Bopeep me all the way home.

"Much obliged!" he called through the doorway,

and pulled his collar up against the icy draft. We jogged across to the door of the building as the rotors sped up and sent a gust of exhaust gas against our backs.

They'd got their liaison worked out: there was a squad car waiting at the curb when we went out through the front. Norton showed his card and they snapped the rear door open and got the flashers going the moment we turned out into the traffic stream, using the siren once or twice to get us some headway. Norton still didn't talk and by this time I didn't want him to. We tumbled out of the car across the slush of a recent thaw and slipped through the narrow doorway halfway down Whitehall and hit the lift button and waited, not looking at each other. Dirty water seeped from our shoes under the bleak security lights as I thought of Helena and wondered if I'd ever see her again.

Tilson met us as we got out of the lift.

"My dear fellow," he said, and held out his warm dry hand. "Long time no see."

"Two weeks. That's not long." Norton had gone quietly rushing off along the corridor: I suppose he'd been told to report somewhere the moment we got in.

"I know what you mean," Tilson said with a slow blink. He was trying hard to look amiable and comforting, since it was his role in life; but tonight he couldn't manage it; he just looked frightened to death, right at the back of his eyes. "What about a spot of tea?"

"What the hell are you talking about?"

"We've got a few minutes, you see." He guided me gently along the corridor as far as the Caff. "We're not quite set up for you yet."

"Look, Tilson, just give me a clue, will you?"

"It's not really for me to say, old horse." He shuffled

across the room in his carpet slippers to a corner table, one of the few left. Maggie saw us and came over and mopped up some spilled tea, and when she'd gone again he said with his lips hardly moving, "They've sent for Mr. Croder. He's on his way in from Rome."

"Croder?"

"He shouldn't be long."

I shut up for a minute. Croder was chief of the base directorate and handled the ultrasensitive operations and had a mortality rate for foreign actions higher than the rest of them put together, not because he wasn't brilliant but because he took on risks that most of the others shied at. I'd never worked for him, not even on the Sahara thing. I didn't want to.

I listened to Jessop and Wallis, sitting at the next table; but they weren't talking about the job: Jessop had bought a Piper three weeks ago and took one of his girl friends for a joyride and wrapped the thing round a power pylon and got away with it, except that she was suing him for five hundred thousand pounds for a new face before she could model again.

I listened to some people talking on the other side, but couldn't pick anything up. I was desperate for clues, because I knew I wouldn't get any from Tilson. He was just here to make sure I didn't get away.

"Tilson," I said evenly, "I've been on leave exactly two weeks and I'm due for eight and I'm not coming in yet, okay? No mission. Nix, *nyet, ninguno,* are you receiving me?"

He looked vaguely at the wall. "I don't think there's a mission on the board, old fruit. Not officially." The tea came and he began spooning sugar into it. He hadn't looked at me since he'd met me outside the lift and that wasn't like him: he's always been cagey but not this bad.

"What about unofficially?" I asked him.

"Nothing ever happens in this place"—he turned his bland pink face to me for the first time—"unofficially."

I held on hard. "I just want a clue, Tilson. Why has everyone started tearing up the pea patch?"

He began sipping his tea; it was too hot but he was just making a gesture and trying not to look scared. "You'll have to be a bit patient, old horse." He gave a wintry smile. "Not quite your forte, I know."

O'Rourke was coming toward us between the tables, his hands dug into the pockets of his mack and pulling it tight round his thighs so he wouldn't knock anyone's tea over. I thought he was coming to talk to Tilson but he dumped himself down between Jessop and Wallis at the next table. I heard him quite clearly. "They've lost Shapiro," he told them, and I saw Jessop going slowly white, and in a couple of seconds he got up and went out, bumping into a table on his way and not noticing.

"Dead?" I asked O'Rourke.

He looked up. "What?"

"Did they find him dead?"

"Who?"

"Shapiro."

"I don't know."

"Who found him?"

"I don't know."

I shut up. Tilson wasn't looking at either of us; he was just listening, with his face down over his tea. O'Rourke didn't know anything. Nobody in this place knows anything, because that's the official policy: the staff has to have an overall view of operations but there's always a handful of field executives hanging around between missions or waiting to be sent out, and the less we know of what's going on, the less we can tell the opposition if we make a mistake out there and they pull us in and throw us under the bright white light and keep us there till it burns through to the brain while they're asking us questions.

"You did a bit of work," Tilson said conversationally, "with Shapiro. Didn't you?"

"A couple of times." Cyprus, Tenerife.

He nodded and looked down and drank some more tea while I sat there trying not to think about Shapiro, trying not to remember him too well. There wasn't anything definite about that bit of news I'd just overheard; he could still be alive, and if he wasn't, there was nothing I could do about it. We come and go.

"I wonder if I can find anyone," Tilson said plaintively, "to look after you until Mr. Croder shows up. I don't like your having to hang about like this." He got up and wandered off and I noticed his tea wasn't finished; he just wanted to get me away from Wallis and O'Rourke before I overheard anything else. That suited me; the more we hear, up and down these bleak green-painted corridors, the more we become involved, the more we become exposed. We don't want that to happen. The Bureau doesn't exist, so we don't exist either, if we're wise. It's less painful like that, and infinitely less dangerous.

It was nearly nine in the evening before Tilson came and got me out of Monitoring, where I'd been passing the time listening to a lot of flak from one of our cells in Africa which was trying to pull itself out of the general bush fire that had gone up after the Kibombo massacre.

"Talk to you," Tilson asked from the doorway, "for a jiff?" It was terribly low-key, and I started worrying again. He took me along the corridor, with our footsteps echoing from the high arched ceiling; there's still no carpeting in this bloody place: they say the parquet's got woodworm in it and they have to keep a watch on it.

"We've got Mr. Croder for you," Tilson told me and hustled me into Signals. From that moment I began going cold. We can always refuse a mission and we don't have to give our reasons; some of the operations look strictly shut-ended during the planning stage and we reserve the right to go on living if we think the risk is too high. But we can't refuse to listen to a director if he's got something for us to do, and sometimes he'll prick our conscience or our pride and lever us into a tricky one before we know what's happening. My nerves were still out of condition from the last operation, although you'd think we'd get over it, one day, and learn to live with it; maybe some of them have, but I haven't, yet, and it's getting late.

There were only four people manning the room tonight, two of them handling separate missions at the main console with the code names *Flashpoint* and *Banjo* on the boards above their heads, and two others waiting for us at the unit nearer the door.

"Where is he?" I asked Tilson.

"Mr. Croder? He's in Geneva."

"He was flying from Rome, the last—"

"Never mind," Tilson said amiably, and looked at the big international clock.

"He's coming through on the hour," one of the operators said, "using the booster at Lausanne. Would you like to sit down?"

"No."

They waited quietly with their hands on their laps and the light of the panel on their faces.

I'll need a shield, a sharp voice came from the main console, *but you'll have to hurry.* It sounded like

Symes, but I didn't think they'd use him for an Asian job: both missions were designated *Far East* alongside the code names and he was a Latin-country specialist, you could smell the garlic the minute he came in for debriefing.

The operator flicked the switch for direct contact with the base director and started talking, but I didn't hear the rest because a light started winking on our unit and the man with the chewing gum opened the signal and set to scramble and clarify.

"A-Alpha. Channel 3. Clarifying."

We waited. The light went on winking.

"Croder." There was a long pause. "The weather's closing down everywhere, and the London flight was laid off." His voice was thin and precise, the scrambler giving it a metallic echo. "Have you brought Quiller in?"

"Yes, sir." The operator slipped out of the padded chair and motioned me to take it.

I sat down. "This is Quiller."

"Ah, yes." A couple of seconds went by. "You were on leave, I understand."

"I still am."

There was a much longer pause. "Yes. I am on leave too. But I want you to listen very carefully. I don't think I can reach London with any immediate predictability, since a lot of flights are either being canceled or diverted. But I can reach Berlin before midnight, according to current reports. I would like you to meet me there, as soon as you can get a plane."

In a moment I said: "Look, I'm still on leave and I need to relax. It's too soon."

I felt Tilson move an inch, beside me.

"I understand that," the thin, precise voice came from the speaker. "But something rather exceptional has happened, and we've got to deal with it as soon as we can. Or if you prefer, *I've* got to deal with it. I was rather hoping you'd agree to help me, but—what can I say? You are on leave."

The silence was so long that I thought he'd gone off the air again, like some kind of ghost, fading and reappearing. I was very cold now, and sat with my hands folded into my arms and my neck hunched into my coat. There was something weird about this whole thing: Croder was sitting on some sort of time bomb and was having to use an awful lot of control in the way he handled me. He wasn't used to that. Finally I couldn't stand the silence any more.

"Is it a mission?" I asked him.

"It is a rescue mission. We—I have to get someone out."

I waited for more, but he'd stopped. I didn't ask him "Out of where?" because that didn't make a lot of difference. He meant out of trouble.

The air in the room seemed to shiver suddenly as the sharp voice came from the main console across from us: *I tell you we can't hope to go in without a shield.*

Tilson moved again beside me, unnerved. He's normally a stoic type and can keep as still as a lizard for hours.

I said to Croder: "Why can't someone else do it?"

He came back a little faster this time. "Of those people available, I think you stand the best chance. If there's a chance at all."

"I'm not available. Listen, I came off the last thing two weeks ago, didn't anyone tell you that? *Two weeks.*" My voice had risen a fraction and I didn't like that, but it might give him a clue as to the condition I was in.

"I knew that, yes." He paused again. "You did rather well."

I left that one. Every word he said was a baited hook.

"A very great deal depends, you see, on whether we can do anything for this man. It touches all of us."

He was being as specific as he could, on the air. It was no use asking him to spell anything out: he couldn't. He was trying to get me to read between the lines and I wasn't interested. *I didn't want to know.*

The operator with the chewing gum was on my other side, opposite Tilson, and I swung my head up. "Would you go and spit that bloody stuff out, for Christ's sake? I can't stand the smell."

My hands were frozen. I was afraid of what Croder was going, finally, to make me do, by pricking my conscience, or my pride. I listened to the rain beating at the row of narrow sooty windows and wondered who the poor bastard was, and where. *We have to get someone out.* He couldn't be done for, yet; he was lying on a rooftop somewhere in the pouring rain with the patrol lights sweeping the streets, waiting till he had to show himself; or hunched between rocks in a frontier zone like a wild dog with a broken leg and no hope of food or shelter or mercy when they found him; or sitting in a basement propped in an upright chair with the bright light probing into his eyes till he couldn't see them any more, could only hear what they were asking him, feel what they were doing when he didn't answer. *It touches all of us.*

The man with the chewing gum had moved away but I could still smell the stuff, like toothpaste.

I spoke into the console. "Is it Shapiro?"

Tilson moved again.

"Yes," Croder said. I could tell by his tone that I wasn't meant to know. I wanted to say, well what about

O'Rourke and Wallis and Jessop, shouting the bloody odds all over the Caff down there? Security stank, in this place, always did, half the staff trying to keep the lid on things and the other half yelling their heads off.

Shapiro. A small quiet man with sharp pointed ears and a passion for chess and a girl in Brighton and a scar the length of his forearm where the knife had got him before I could throw the rest of them off and reach him in time, glass all over the place from the explosion and the sirens coming in, Tenerife, with a full moon and the night temperature still in the nineties and Rosita sobbing her heart out in the bar at the end of the jetty because they'd got Templer, nothing we could do. "I'll take this one," he'd told me the night before; "they know you, but they don't know me." But it was just that he'd been frightened, and wanted to prove he wasn't. We've got a few things in common.

So he wasn't dead.

"What theater?" I asked Croder.

"Europe."

That was all I'd get. There wasn't anything more I could ask him. He could have switched to selective code but he obviously wasn't prepared to. In a couple of seconds he said:

"You know him quite well, I understand."

Shapiro.

"Not too well. But I know him."

The bloody thing had been ticking all the time and he'd stood looking at it with his small gnome's head on one side. "The best thing'd be to disarm it, don't you think, take it apart, before it can do any harm." He'd worked at it for nearly three hours without a break, his pale gray eyes wide open staring at God all the time while his nicotine-stained fingers stroked and caressed the mat-black metal components and the sweat ran off his face and dripped onto the bare boards where I sat waiting, hunched into my own ghost and unable to look away. "I think that's it," he'd said at last, and pulled the detonator clear and reached for a cigarette and put it into his mouth with fingers that shook so badly now that he knocked the flame out and I had to strike another match for him.

Shapiro.

Say this much: he was a professional.

"You know his work, at least," Croder's voice came insistently.

"Yes."

"What would be your opinion of him"—in slow and reasonable tones—"as an executive in the field?"

I felt Tilson listening, beside me. I thought of lying, then realized I didn't have to. In the end I could refuse, I could refuse, repeat it like a litany, I could refuse.

"First class."

"Quite so. You wouldn't," Croder said with a certain silkiness, "consider him expendable."

Like a dog with a broken leg.

"No."

Stonewall the bastard, don't give him any rope.

"All I would ask is that you would at least meet me in Berlin, so that I can give you the details." Three seconds, four. "That is all I would ask, for him."

The lights glowed on the console. I could hear the voice of the man in the field coming faintly across the room, where they were running *Flashpoint*. Tilson hadn't moved. The smell of peppermint had gone now, or I was getting used to it. I leaned forward toward the console so that Croder would hear me clearly, and know by my tone that I meant what I said.

"I'm on leave. I haven't got my nerve back yet—it was close to the crunch, that time, and I'm lucky to be here. So you'll have to find someone else, because I refuse."

I got out of the chair and went past Tilson without looking at him and opened the door and threw it shut behind me and walked down the green-painted corridor to the lift and pressed the button for down.

It was a deluge outside and there was a traffic block near Hyde Park Corner and I sat waiting for fifteen minutes before I took the phone off the clip and got Tilson and told him I wanted a police car to get me out of this mess and I wanted a flight to Berlin, the first he could find for me. And tell Croder.

2 / TEMPELHOF

Blinding sleet and the runway lights floating up from the dark as the wheels hit and we bounced and they hit again and we bounced again with the airframe shuddering.

"Was, zum Teufel, macht der Pilot?"

A few uneasy laughs but at least we were down.

"Bitte behalten Sie ihren sicherheits Gürtel an."

A fat man sat leaning forward with his face white and his head down; I hoped he'd found the bag. Sleet washed past the windows in a bow wave.

"Mon Dieu, il est impossible même de voir la tour d'observation!"

"Espérons que nous n'allons pas s'enfoncer contre elle!"

Reverse thrust and we sat feeling the drag.

"Are you all right, Audrey?" someone asked.

"Sort of." A breathless giggle, then she lit a cigarette and blew out a noisy sigh. In the rear of the plane a child had started crying.

Tempelhof was packed.

"Excuse me, but do you know where the information desk is?"

"In the middle of that crowd over there," I said, and she went hurrying off, trailing a flight bag with a broken strap. There were puddles everywhere, with people bringing slush in from the front of the building.

"Haben Sie etwas zu deklarieren?"

"Gar nichts."

"Keine Rauchwaren, keine Alkohol?"

"Nein."

He didn't bloody well believe me, went right through my bag.

"We were meant to land at Tegel," a man with an astrakhan coat said to me, "but there was too much stuff in the circuit." I wondered if he'd got any other useless information.

In the main hall people were milling around looking for friends, children, baggage, a porter to help them out of the chaos. Three North Africans carrying skis edged their way through the crowd, clouting people every time they turned round to look for what they'd lost.

"Entschuldigen, sind Sie Herr Wolsieffer?"

"Nein," I told him.

A party of Chinese trotted past toward the main exit, their leader waving a little red flag to guide them.

"Pardon, monsieur. Vous êtes de Paris?"

"Non, mademoiselle, c'est le vol de Londres."

She went across to the information desk. Pretty legs.

"Not a very nice evening."

"Not very," I said.

"What sort of flight?"

"Bloody awful." We started walking, looking for somewhere we could talk. "Been waiting long?"

"Half an hour," he said.

"Did what I could. London was a mess."

"Let's go over there," Croder said.

"All right." There was a lot of water on the floor below one of the big windows, which had sprung a leak, and we stood there with our backs to the dark glass watching the people near us. I didn't know whether he'd got here without any tags on him; as a rule the London directors aren't too good in the field. He stood with his hands in the pockets of the big military coat he was wearing, its buttons plain now and the marks still showing where the insignia had been taken off. It looked too big for him: he was a slight man, thin-boned and pallid, with a head like a skull and the hands of a skeleton and only the eyes alive, brooding in his face as if they were trapped there under the taut parched skin, their black luminescence shadowed by heavy lids. He hadn't looked at me yet.

"Good of you to come," he said formally. "I was surprised when they said you'd changed your mind."

"So was I."

He made a smile with his small teeth, like a rat nibbling. "We nearly missed each other. They had to get back to me through Interpol." It was a reprimand.

"Where's Shapiro?" I asked him.

He didn't answer for a moment. There was a lot of noise from a bunch of people over by the doors, and Croder gazed at them steadily. "East Germans," he said. "They were going into Schönefeld but an engine was out, so they came into Tempelhof instead." His small teeth made a token smile. "Half of them are demanding asylum. Wouldn't you? We don't know where Shapiro is," he said without looking away from the group. "His cover name is Schrenk. Forget Shapiro. Schrenk." He spelled it for me. "He was in Moscow for two months, working very well, then they uncovered him and put him through interrogation in Lubyanka. Then he escaped."

For the first time he turned and looked at me with his black contemplative eyes and I thought Christ Almighty, only Shapiro could have got out of Lubyanka by the midnight express. Only Schrenk. "He got as far as West Germany," Croder said, "and we had him put straight into a clinic. I don't think he would have made it as far as London—he was in a pretty bad way."

"Were you running him?"

I didn't think he'd answer that.

He looked back at the group of East Germans. "It doesn't matter who was running him. He was in the clinic for nearly three months, and recovering steadily. They were going to discharge him before long, as soon as he was fit enough to stand up to debriefing. But the K got him again, and one report says he's back in Lubyanka."

There was a chill coming into the air; I felt it against my skin: possibly the sweat was starting to creep, setting up refrigeration. I have never been inside Lubyanka, but I've talked to people who have. There aren't many of them at liberty. North had got back from there, the night he blew his brains out at Connie's place.

Croder was gazing across the hall in silence, and I asked him: "What's our timing on this?"

"There's a flight for Hannover in forty minutes, and there's a seat booked for you."

"In case I want one."

He ignored that. "Schrenk carried a capsule. It was part of the contract, on that particular mission. Obviously he didn't use it." He turned away from the group of people and stood facing me, hunched into his big coat and saying with muted force: "He would have saved us an immense amount of trouble if he had used it. An immense amount of trouble." He waited for the message to sink in. "Because what we have on our hands now is a potential disaster—unless we can somehow prevent it. Schrenk prided himself on his ability to survive the most grueling interrogation by the use of practiced and convincing disinformation; he had three or four different scenarios worked out and he rehearsed them every day of his life, in series. We know that. We had him tested at Norfolk, a year ago, and even hypnosis couldn't break him down, because he'd used auto-hypnosis himself, to move his scenarios down into the subconscious. *That* is the kind of man he is." The heavy lids were lowered for a moment. "But Norfolk isn't Lubyanka. We do not *know,* you see, how bad the position is, because we don't know how much he gave away."

He withdrew into himself again, staring at nothing, or maybe at Schrenk's insubstantial image, lost somewhere in the wastes of Soviet Russia. The sleet outside was turning to water on the window, and the light from the tall gooseneck lamps threw its translucent delineations against his face, so that his skin crept with rivulets.

"What has he got," I asked him, "to give away?"

"I'm sorry?" He swung to look at me.

"You said you didn't know how much he gave away. You mean something specific?"

His sharp teeth bit at the air again. "Yes. The Leningrad cell."

Mother of God.

This was why Norton had been showing his nerves today, and why Tilson had looked scared behind the eyes. The Leningrad cell had taken eleven years to build up, and once established and running it had given us the Sholokof Project and the submarine dispersal pattern and the tactical analysis for the buried-weapons system for transmission to NATO and the CIA, plus satellite scanning, plus laser progress in the military-application laboratories, plus the whole of the missile-testing program including the ultra-classified global-range ICBMs from X-9 to the city-heat guidance Marathon 1000. That was the Leningrad cell.

"But he couldn't have known," I said hopelessly, "much about it."

"He worked there for two years, before he was seconded to the field-executive branch. He knows *everything* about it."

I didn't understand. "But who could have let him—"

"That is not your concern." Spittle came against his lower lip, and in a moment he licked it away and said more slowly: "For your information, it wasn't I."

I let it go. Someone had blundered, and disastrously, because once you're with a cell you stay there till your time's up: you don't go anywhere else and you don't get seconded to the field-executive pool, because you know too much of value and they won't risk sending you into the field where the opposition can pick you up and drag you in and take your brain apart. But someone had done that with Schrenk.

"Your only concern," Croder said with a lot of control, "is to find him and pull him out—if indeed you're prepared to do that for us." The need for control worried me, because this man was known for his cool and he'd lost it, and in front of the executive he was desperate to recruit. My nerves were jumping again. "You would receive intensive support, I need hardly say."

"In Moscow?"

"Right in the target area, wherever that may be. Cut-outs, backups, shields—"

"No shields."

He shrugged. "You may be glad—"

"I said no shields." My own control wasn't too good and I waited and counted three. "I make my own decisions and my own mistakes and I won't involve anyone else." Shields were dangerous; they could get in your way, and when the crunch came they'd save themselves, not you. "What about the director in the field? If the timing's that close you can't—"

"Bracken," he said.

"Bracken's in Singapore."

"We called him in." He moved his eyes to the clock over the information desk. "He is at present airborne with BOAC, arriving Moscow at noon tomorrow, local time." He waited.

"I've never worked with him."

"He's first class, you know that. He directed Fenton in Cairo last year. He got Matthews out of Peking. First class."

There were thirty minutes left on the clock, and I thought of something else. "When did you find out Schrenk was back in Moscow?"

"Early this morning."

"Then you haven't had time to set up. I'm not—"

"It was ready to run before I called base from Geneva. You have a director, a safe house, contacts, sleepers, signal availability and Embassy liaison." His thin mouth was contemptuous. "What more do you want, for God's sake?"

"Access. I'm on their files and I'd never get through the airport."

"You have access by road into East Germany."

"Overt?"

"Of course not."

"What are you talking about, a bloody farm cart or something?"

"A closed truck will take you across the frontier at Zellerfeld, in the Harz Mountains, with no questions asked."

He was blocking me every time. I was his last hope, I knew that now. He'd tried half a dozen other people and drawn blank, because this was a suicide trip and he didn't pretend it was anything else.

"What about access into Moscow?"

"By commercial airline: Aeroflot. We have a seat for you on the morning flight from Leipzig, where the truck will drop you. It's perfectly straightforward."

I took a slow breath. "Cover?"

"Transit papers, East German national."

It was beginning to sound like a trap and I stopped thinking about it for a minute, watching the people in the group by the main doors. A man was shouting his head off now and so was his wife: he wanted asylum but his wife said it would mean leaving her mother behind, and the secret police would take reprisals. A younger man, possibly their son, was trying to make them shut up. Two more policemen were marching toward them, unbuttoning their holsters to make an effect. A crowd was collecting.

Fluggäste für Flug nummer 903 für Hannover bitte kommen Sie sofort zum Eingang nummer 2.

I looked at the clock.

"Is that the flight you booked for me?" I asked Croder.

"Yes."

"Then there's no time for briefing."

"You'll be briefed on the access in Hannover, and fully briefed in Moscow."

"By Bracken?"

"Yes."

"Who's our man in Hannover?"

"He's an agent-in-place."

"I want to know who he is."

"All you want," Croder said with his mouth tight, "is just one good reason for getting the next plane back to London with what's left of your conscience, and the problem is that you won't find one because we've been hard at it setting the whole thing up, and it works, it really does. The odds, of course," he said without looking away from my face, "are not in your favor, and I'd quite understand it if you didn't feel up to the task. Your nerves, as you say, are still—"

"My nerves are my business." A lot of the heat came out and his black eyes flickered. "You know bloody well you've got me hooked or I wouldn't be here in this stinking hole, would I?" Control, get control. "It's just that I want—" But the anger ran out and we stood facing each other without another word, while the shadows of the rain crept down his neon-gray face and his eyes looked into mine and waited to know whether I would do the job that had to be done or whether I was too old, at last, for this game, or too scared.

When I was ready I said: "Who else did you ask?"

"I told you before. I went straight for you."

His eyes went on waiting.

I only had one more question, and it was difficult, because I thought I knew what he'd say, what he'd *have* to say. "What happens if I find him, but can't get him out?"

He didn't hesitate. "That would make things easier for you. All we want is his silence."

3 / JUMP

It had been snowing in Hannover; the roofs were white with it under a full moon when we touched down.

He was waiting on the other side of the gate, a short man with a deerstalker hat and a long green woolen scarf wound several times round his neck. He was rubbing his hands and blowing into them, watching me as I came through.

"From the office?" he asked me.

"Who are you?"

"Floderus. Have you got any baggage?"

"No."

"Okay. I've got a car here." He led the way with short energetic steps, his hands in his coat pockets now.

"I want to see the clinic," I said when we got outside. "Did he tell you?"

"Yes. I only just caught the doc there: he's off on vacation first thing in the morning." We got into the Mercedes.

It was the only condition I'd made to Corder: I wanted to know everything I could about Schrenk, if I were going to do anything for him.

"What was it like in London?" Floderus asked.

"Pissing down."

"I should've known."

He got off the autobahn at the Hannover-Herrenhausen exit and drove south on Route 6 as far as the river.

"Are you expecting any problems?" I asked him.

"What? No." He did it again. "Why?"

"Fond of the mirror."

"Oh. Habit."

I supposed he could have been in from the field; sleepers and a-i-p's aren't normally so nervous. "What's this man's name?" I asked him.

"What man?"

"The doctor."

"Oh. Steinberg." Along Dorfstrasse he turned right and began slowing. The clinic was just after the church, a long white building with a board with gold letters. Floderus pulled up.

Steinberg opened the door to us himself, tall, stooping, wrapped in a dressing gown with cigarette burns on it, a man who worked too late. He took us straight into a consulting room and I let Floderus stay. We spoke in German.

"You wish to know about your patient here, I understand."

"Yes. I want to know his state of mind."

He considered this, staring at the top of his desk through thick round glasses. "I know nothing at all about his *present* state of mind, of course. He was abducted in violent fashion, and that would have induced further shock. I have no means of knowing what has happened to him since, in terms of his state of mind."

"What was he like just before the abduction?"

He lit a cigarette and squinted through the smoke. "At that time he was quite alert, quite normal. The nightmares had stopped, and he did very well in tests. Still rather bitter toward those people, understandably. We felt he—"

"Bitter?"

He glanced up quickly. "He harbored a grudge against them. Don't you feel that was understandable, Herr Matthöfer?"

"I suppose so," I said. It was as far as I could go; he didn't know who we were. But something was odd: we don't harbor grudges against the opposition, whatever they do to us; there's nothing personal: it's dog eat dog. I didn't see why Schrenk should have been "bitter."

"He put up quite a struggle," the doctor said. "The place was in a mess, with blood on the carpet and some glass from a broken syringe. One of my staff ran into the street after them, but they didn't stop."

"You called the police?"

"Immediately. We are not used to that sort of affair in my clinic. It was very disturbing."

"What did they do to him?"

"They took him away." He looked at me quizzically. "I told you, they—"

"I mean before. Before he was brought here."

"Ah. That." He screwed his face against the smoke and pulled a drawer open, putting a thick file onto the desk and opening it. "I have had some experience with these things, you understand. I am a member of Amnesty International and the World Medical Association. We study these phenomena." I looked at my watch and he noticed, but didn't hurry. Floderus sat snuffling in his handkerchief. "We questioned the patient, and his answers were consistent with the trauma we noted on his body." He studied the file. "He was subjected to the 'wet canvas' treatment. Do you know what that is?"

"Yes." But they wouldn't have started off with that one. They risk losing you, that way, because panic sets in.

"They used *falanga,* and we found extensive ecchymoses and edema, with some degree of irreversible ischemic changes in the intermetatarsal areas of the foot. There were—"

"What was he walking like, before they took him away?"

"His feet were still rather painful. He tended to hobble."

"All right. What else?"

He looked at the file again. "He said they had suspended him from the arms for prolonged periods, but we found no evidence of cervical dislocations. We took X rays, of course. He could use his arms perfectly well, after about eight weeks. We found hematuria and some bleeding from the ears, but again we were able to treat these symptoms successfully. This kind of thing is found extensively in Chile, by the way, and Uruguay."

"You'll find it everywhere," I said.

I heard Floderus swallowing saliva.

"So we are beginning to discover." Steinberg nodded and dropped ash onto his dressing gown. "There was, in Herr Schrenk's case, local infiltration of anesthetics into the eyelids."

Floderus was leaning forward. "What for?" he asked the doctor.

"I beg your pardon?"

"So that he couldn't shut his eyes," I told him, "against the light." I wished I hadn't let him stay; he was getting on my nerves. "Did they use drugs?" I asked Steinberg.

"He described certain phases of mental disorientation, including hallucination, but of no great significance. It might have been induced by reaction to the physical trauma. If they used drugs, they may have used thiopental or one of the amphetamines; he exhibited no lasting evidence of this." He closed the file and put it in the drawer.

"Can you tell me anything else?"

He drew on his cigarette, leaving a shred of tobacco on his lip. "I think that is all I can give you. As to his present state of mind, it depends upon how they have treated him since they took him away." He spread his thick white hands. "We can only hope that by some good fortune . . ."

"Did he tell you he'd revealed any information?"

"I heard nothing about that."

"Would you have heard?"

"It would be in the records."

"Taped records?"

"We record conversations with patients, yes. It is routine, an essential part of the therapy."

"Can I hear some of the tapes?"

"That is quite out of the question. Such matters are strictly confidential. We—"

"Did he mention any names? Names of people in Moscow?"

"I cannot say. It would be in the records." He began fidgeting with a penholder.

"Did he scream any names in his nightmares?"

"Herr Matthöfer, I am not at liberty to—"

"Did he make any threats?"

"Of what nature?"

"Any nature. Any threats against anyone at all." I

got up and walked past his desk to the window and back. "You said he was bitter, and bore a grudge. Against whom?"

"There was nothing specific." He stubbed out his cigarette, annoyed by the way things were going. He was the topkick in this place and he'd found me on the doorstep washed up by the night.

"You mean he was bitter *in general?* What made you think he bore someone a grudge?"

He stood up and came from behind his desk, drawing the dressing gown around him. "Surely you can understand that a man in his condition should bear a grudge against those responsible for it?"

"Or did you just *expect* him to feel like that?"

It was important and he didn't realize it and I couldn't explain.

"You will have to excuse me, Herr Matthöfer. I agreed to receiving you in the middle of the night in order to discuss this patient's case for a few minutes, but not to submit to an interrogation. I am leaving Hannover at nine o'clock and I need some sleep." He jerked the chain of the desk lamp and went over to the door. Floderus got up. I asked Steinberg:

"Did the police find any clues?"

"Not to my knowledge."

"They came here to ask questions?"

"But of course."

"Did anyone see the car these people used?"

"No, they did not. I would have been told. Now I will say good night, gentlemen." He opened the front door for us.

Floderus started blowing into his hands again the minute we were in the street.

"Haven't you got any gloves, for God's sake?"

"I lost them," he said irritably.

"Haven't you got any others?"

"Why was it so important," he asked me, "about Schrenk being bitter?" He swung the Mercedes in a full turn and headed north by the river.

"It's right out of character. What time's our rendezvous?"

"Three-thirty at Zellerfeld. He should be there by now."

"Why so early?"

"I didn't know you wanted to see Steinberg first."

"Couldn't you signal him?"

"Look," he said, "we're all doing our best, okay?" He got onto the autobahn at Hannover-Flughafen and drove east, moving into the eighties before turning south at the cloverleaf with the Hildesheim sign coming up. "Your stuff's in the glove pocket if you want to start looking it over."

I found the thick envelope. It had the single word *Scorpion* written in pencil at the top left corner. "Where else did they take him," I asked Floderus as I pulled out the papers, "apart from Lubyanka?"

"We think he was at the Serbsky Institute of Forensic Medicine in Moscow, and the mental hospital in Chernyakhovsk. London's still checking with our people in Moscow and you'll be briefed when you get there."

"Is that all you know?"

"I'm just contact and relay, sorry."

I checked the stuff over: transit cover in the name of Hans Matthöfer, East German representative for Plastischen Fabriken; visa and travel permit, Moscow only; record of previous visits; stated purpose of present visit; advance hotel booking and proposed itinerary (including a visit to the Bolshoi Theater on the evening of February 23, unaccompanied); currency vouchers; a batch of sheets in a file with photographs of plastic moldings and three letters of introduction, one of them to the Ministry of Labor. My photograph was recognizable, with fur hat.

"Have you got any clothes for me?"

"In the back. Coat, hat, fur-lined boots and gloves; it's twenty below in Moskers, rather you than me."

We drove for two hours, through Hildesheim and over roads covered with snow when we reached the mountains, while I thought of Croder and Schrenk and Steinberg and tried to think why Schrenk should feel "bitter" about what they'd done to him. It didn't fit with the pattern and I kept on worrying it because these are the little things that can take you off course if you're not watching. I'd done two missions with Schrenk and in two missions you learn a lot about a man; Schrenk knew the score, all the way along the line, and he wouldn't bear a grudge against the KGB any more than he'd bear a grudge against a snake that had bitten him, *because there's nothing personal about these things.*

Floderus was slowing, and I tore off the top left corner of the envelope and put the papers back.

"Where are we?"

"The other side of Zellerfeld. I made a loop." He drove slowly for another half mile and pulled up on a snow-covered patch alongside the road, dousing the head lamps. The moonlight brightened gradually.

"Is this the place?"

"Yes."

"Where is he?"

"He should be here."

"What's the landmark?"

"That sign over there." Einbeck.

I began worrying. "How far is it to the checkpoint?"

"Four kilometers." He began blowing into his hands and I reached over to the back seat and rummaged about and found the gloves and dropped them onto his lap.

"For Christ's sake put these on."

"You'll need them when—"

"Put them on *till then*." A slight break in the tone, inadmissible in the pre-jump phase but my nerves were only just under the surface and small things were picking at them because this is the phase when you're stone cold and your mind is clear and you know you're putting your life on the line and you know you've done it before and got away with it but this time it's different and you're scared again, and swallowing and alert to the signs and portents that are suddenly in every sound and every shadow, till you can't stand a man blowing into his hands because the repetition drives you up the wall.

Not good. Not at all propitious. Better to get to a telephone and pull Tilson out of bed and tell him to find Croder: *Tell him I was right, I'm not ready, he'll have to get someone else.*

". . . Gunther."

"What?"

"His name's Gunther," said Floderus again. "The man with the truck."

I wound the window down and listened. The air was perfectly still and the snow had brought its own peculiar silence; a jet was moving at altitude, lost in the brightness of the moon, its thin whine threading the night. I could hear other sounds, distant and muffled by the terrain.

"Dogs?"

"What? Yes. At the checkpoint."

"Where else?"

"Nowhere else, in this area."

I don't like dogs.

"You want a gun?"

"What for?"

He looked at me in the pale light, sniffing a drip off his nose. "For the mission."

"No. Is this meant to be clearance?"

"Sort of."

I wanted to laugh. Clearance and briefing normally takes hours and you see a dozen people and sign a dozen forms and make half a dozen declarations because that's all that's going to be left of you if you muck it up out there: a record of what you were. It makes you feel you're important to somebody, if only to the computer clerks. But this trip I was being kicked across the frontier by a junior a-i-p with a drip on his nose and only just enough control over himself to keep him from telling me I shouldn't have got him out of bed in the first place.

"You'd better sign this." He sniffed again and got out a crumpled handkerchief, taking off one of my gloves to use it. "Is that your own code?"

I looked at the form. "My own what?"

" 'Five hundred roses for Moira.' "

I didn't want to talk about that, so I got a pen and signed the form, no next of kin, no dependents, nothing saved up to leave to anyone, just enough for the roses. *What was she doing now? When did she last think of me?*

"Where the hell is that man Gunther?"

Floderus looked at his watch in the moonlight. "He'll be here." He put the glove back on.

"How big's the truck?"

"It's a ten-tonner."

"What's it carrying?"

"You."

"Come on for Christ sake I want briefing!" He jerked

back and stared at me. "I want to know what else that truck's carrying and where it's going and why he's got a free run across the frontier. I want information, is that too much to ask?"

He pulled himself round on his seat and said a bit shakily: "Look, I haven't been told all that much. You're being briefed in Moscow, they said. All I'm here for is—"

"*Information,* don't you know what it means? About the *truck.*"

"Oh. Well"—he gave a long riffling sniff—"it's taking luxury goods across for the black market in Leipzig, a regular run, scotch and perfume and American goods, jazz records and cassettes and stuff like—"

"Who runs this?"

"The Party, if you want to go right to the top. It's for them and their wives, the same thing that goes on in Moscow. They—"

"How often does this truck go across?"

"About every month. It varies."

"Just the driver, no one with him?"

"No. He—"

"Is he Russian? East German? West German?"

"He's from Hamburg."

"Has he ever been turned back?"

"Only once. He—"

"*Only once?*"

He caught his breath and said in a moment, "There was a new guard commander, and he wasn't tipped off. He was changed again."

I didn't want to know any more. This was Russian roulette they'd got me playing: either we'd get across the frontier or we wouldn't. Either I'd find Schrenk or I wouldn't. All I could do was to stop thinking and let

the strain off and leave it to Croder and try to believe
he knew what he was doing.

I shut my eyes for a while, until I heard the faint
clinking of snow chains and the throb of a diesel
engine. There was light flushing across the road behind
us.

"Is this Gunther?"

"Yes. He said he'd—"

"How do you know it's not someone else?"

"There shouldn't be anyone else up here, this time of
night."

"Shouldn't? Jesus Christ." I wished Ferris were here,
or someone who didn't leave everything to chance.

"It's okay," Floderus said, "he's flashing us."

"What sort of terrain is there," I asked him wearily,
"between here and the checkpoint?"

"What? Oh, just rocks, and a few trees."

"Why doesn't he just give a blast on the horns?"

He stared at me. "They'd hear it from the frontier."

Some kind of laughter came out of me, maybe panic
in disguise. The truck came alongside and I waited for
Floderus to check the driver before I got out and
opened the rear door of the car and changed coats and
put on the fur hat; at least London had got this much
right, pulling the tailor out of bed as well, to check on
the size.

"Gloves," I said.

"Oh." He gave them to me. "This is Gunther," he
said in German.

A thick-shouldered man in a reefer jacket and
woolen hat, his flat square face half buried in a scarf.
"Everything is in order," he said.

"Why were you late?"

"There was snow." He pulled open the rear doors of
the truck and jumped up. "In here."

Most of the stuff on the floor was scotch, in cases of a dozen bottles, and he had to shift four of them before he could drag the lid of the recess upward and swing it to one side. The compartment was lined with felt. He stood clear of it to let the roof light shine down.

"What's underneath?"

"Nothing," he said. "The road. But it is thick, and there are steel brackets."

"Do you bring people across in this, the other way?"

"I have brought seven, in the past three months. Seventy thousand U.S. dollars. Not for me. For them." His breath clouded under the roof light.

"How much do you get?"

"One thousand. I get one for you." His small brown eyes moved over me. "It's the first time I've taken anyone *east*."

"Are you going to move those cases back over the trap when I'm inside?"

"Yes."

"How many of them?"

"These here. Four. Maybe five."

"How much do they weigh? Each?"

"Seventeen kilos."

I dropped into the recess facedown and told him to shut the lid; then I humped my back until my spine made contact. There weren't more than a few inches of leverage, but it might be enough to shift five cases of scotch because I'd only have to do it if I got trapped and if I got trapped there'd be a lot of adrenaline to help me. I told him to open the lid.

"On your back," he said, "is best."

"That's the way you put people in coffins." I looked at Floderus, standing out there at the back of the truck with his hands tucked under his arms. "Is there anything else?"

"This," he said, and gave me a small red metal box. Normally I refuse it but on this trip I didn't think much of my chances and if they caught up with me in Moscow and pulled me in I might want to opt out rather than finish up like Schrenk, *his feet were still rather painful, he tended to hobble.* I put the box in my pocket. "Send a signal," I told Floderus, "as soon as you can get to a telephone. Understood?"

"Okay."

I dropped into the recess again and told Gunther to shut the lid. The time by my watch was 03:37.

First there was just one man, talking to Gunther; then a second one came up and told him to open the rear doors of the truck. I could hear those bloody dogs again, not far away now. I was lying in total darkness, with only aural data coming in. When the doors banged back the voices were much clearer.

What is in these boxes? What is in those packages over there? So forth.

Sweat was running on my face because there weren't enough ventilation holes in this thing and *they shouldn't be asking all those questions out there:* Gunther had said there wouldn't be any trouble at the checkpoint, he'd drive straight through as soon as they recognized him.

How many cases are there?

Their boots grated on the floorboards just above me. I lay with my eyes shut to keep the sweat from running into them.

Does the Kommandant know about this consignment?

There was grit under their boots and it sounded like static, immediately above my head. Of course the Kommandant knew about it, Gunther told them. I thought his voice was too loud, too blustering.

A dog barked again and my scalp shrank, because this wasn't the end phase of the mission with the blood up and the nerves singing and the target in sight; this was the jump phase and the sweat was cold on me and I wasn't ready for them to tell Gunther to pull up the floorboard here, this loose one.

Wait here. I shall have to wake the Kommandant.

They'd be in trouble, Gunther told them, if they woke him for nothing. He'd have their hide.

We shall see about that, the man said, and his boots thudded on the roadway as he dropped from the truck.

I listened to the ticking sounds of the exhaust pipe contracting as it cooled. Light showed faintly through some of the ventilation holes and a door slammed somewhere on the right of the truck. Voices came again, Gunther's the loudest and with panic in it. They didn't listen to him.

Move your vehicle over here. It's in the way.

His boots loudened again and the doors at the rear slammed shut like an explosion. I listened to him going forward and climbing into the cab, pulling the door shut. Exhaust gas seeped in through the ventilation holes as he started the engine, and I began shallow breathing as we started to roll. I waited to feel the movement as he turned the wheel but it didn't come: my feet were being pushed against the end of the recess as he gunned up in first gear and botched into second and kept his foot down as a man began shouting somewhere behind us. The roar of the exhaust drowned everything out until the truck hit something head on and began dragging the debris with it, possibly the barrier, though I tried to believe that Gunther knew he wouldn't have a chance in hell of putting a ten-tonner through a checkpoint and getting away with it.

There were more shouts now and I could see light flashing in the ventilation holes; then the noise fell away and we seemed to be clear of the debris as Gunther forced a fast change into third gear and flattened the throttle again. A lot of vibration started and I braced my hands forward in case we hit something else.

When the first shots came I humped my back and heaved upward against the trapdoor, feeling the weight of the cases and heaving again till they were forced clear. There was some rapid fire now and I crawled out of the recess and lurched forward, getting most of the cargo between my body and the rear doors as a bottle was hit and glass exploded inside one of the cases. The truck was swaying as we took a curve, and some of the load went over, bursting open and shattering against the doors. I thought I could hear Gunther shouting in the cab, but couldn't make out any words. A bullet came through at an angle, deflected by the cargo and crumping into the timber close to my head. I lay face-down, my body in line with the longitudinal axis of the truck, feet toward the rear doors.

Light was showing from somewhere, bright light from behind us, filtering through the gaps where the hinges were. The shots were lower now, clanging into the chassis below the tailboard; one of them ripped a hole in the muffler and a sustained roaring started up; I heard a tire burst but there were twin wheels at the rear getting louder as a vehicle closed in, its light silvering the dark through the cracks in the rear doors; the next volley smashed into a case and sent glass fluting through the air. Then they were shooting low again and two more tires burst and the truck lurched over, right-ing itself and lurching again and starting a long slow zigzag on the rear wheel rims.

Then everything went. I felt a final lurch and then a brief period of weightlessness as the truck left the road and began floating into the drop, tilting to one side and staying like that, then tilting right over before it hit the rock face and started bouncing. Orientation was down to near zero now: I was inside a rolling barrel and the cargo had gone wild and all I could do was squeeze under the rear shelf and try to hang on but it wasn't easy because the noise had reached a crescendo: I was trapped inside a thunderstorm and couldn't think my way out.

Glass shattered, raining against me, and I kept my face down, my head hunched between my shoulders. A period of weightlessness came again—two seconds, three, four, five—as the truck found a sheer drop and floated free, turning slowly and bringing a kind of calm as the rotational speed of the cargo matched the speed of the truck itself. It was the eye of the storm, and I waited. Seven seconds, eight, nine—then we struck rock and smashed down again and the storm burst as it had burst before, a crash coming as the rear doors were forced open, one of them dragging itself off the hinges with a scream of metal on stone. Then the truck veered at right angles and the rolling stopped. We hit the floor of the slope head on and I was flung backwards with the rest of the cargo, keeping my head in my arms and going with it, something dragging against my thigh and ripping the coat away and tearing the flesh, a shower of glass whining across my head through the open doors, a last case toppling and smashing down as the truck shuddered and rolled again, slowly, and rocked to stillness.

I made for where I could smell the air and see the

moon. The senses were partially numbed and the organism was working with instinct, but I could smell fuel oil and I worked in a frenzy to get clear, feeling the snow under my hands as the first flame burst and took hold. The split tank coughed into life and black smoke began pouring across the rock face as I pitched forward and got up and staggered, straightening and going on down the mountainside away from the fierce white light that had started blazing from the roadway above the ravine. The truck was a mass of flames and I kept low, lurching and rolling among the snow-covered boulders and keeping the fire between me and the fierce white light. Twice I saw my shadow in front of me and dropped flat, waiting to know if they'd seen me, waiting for the shot.

4 / MOSCOW

I sat waiting.

The night was perfectly quiet, with no movement in the air. The moon neared its zenith, toward the south.

I shifted my position again and the nerves in my right thigh reacted; the tissues had only just begun healing. I didn't know if I could run yet, if I had to. There was nothing else wrong with me, except for the lingering effects of the shock: unexpected sounds made my head jerk, as if they were shots.

It was freezing cold.

"What held you up?"

Another trolleybus went past the end of the street, along Ckalova ulica, a No. 10. It was the seventh I'd counted. There had been a dozen cars during the same period; it was eleven o'clock and traffic was light.

"We crashed the truck," I told him.

He started the engine again to blow some more air through the heater. It was a Pobeda, stinking of oil and stale cigarette smoke. We couldn't run the engine all the time because it'd be noticed: we were parked by the river, close to the intersection, and four militia patrols had gone past in the last fifty minutes, one of them slowing to look at us. I didn't like it, any of it; my scalp crept too easily, and I was breathing too fast. I'd got close to being wiped out in that truck and the organism remembered.

"We thought we'd lost you," the contact said. His speech was indistinct, as if his mouth were bruised. "There was a complete blackout on you after Floderus signaled from Hannover."

"It was close."

"What happened to the driver?"

"The truck went up." I didn't want to talk about it.

He turned the engine off and the cold began creeping through the cracks again from outside the car.

"What else?" he asked me.

It was his job to find out. This was Moscow and in Moscow you live from one minute to the next because there's no building that isn't bugged and no street that isn't surveyed and no hope of getting away with sloppy security or a doubtful drop or inadequate cover. They could stop, the next time around, and poke their torches in here and ask for our papers and pull us in if everything wasn't exactly right. Or even if it was.

So he had to find out what I'd been doing, because in five minutes from now I might not be able to tell anyone. I said: "I got as far as Aschersleben in a shepherd's Volkswagen and asked for some medical attention and bought a new coat. That was this morning. There wasn't a plane till thirteen-twenty Leipzig time. Then—"

"What medical attention?" He turned to look at me, and the oblique light shadowed the scar that ran from one ear along the jawline. A lot of them look a bit creased in one way or another when they've come in from the field.

"Torn leg," I said.

"Is that all?"

"And screw you too."

He laughed without any sound at all, laying his head back and giving a little shake. "As long as you're fit for work."

"I'm as fit as I'll ever be. Where the *hell* is Bracken?"

He began watching the intersection again. Through a gap in the buildings I could see a curve of floodlit gold, one of the domes in the Kremlin. "It's difficult," he said in that soft-slipper voice of his. "Since the trial started we can't make a move without drawing a tag. There's a lot of foreign journalists in town and the K don't like it."

"How did Bracken get in?"

"Diplomatic cover. It was last-minute stuff: they had to fake a case of hepatitis in the Embassy and send a man home, with Bracken to replace him."

My nerves reacted again, shrinking the scalp. Most of the field directors come in like that, but not so fast: London would prepare the ground a month ahead to avoid any fuss. But this wasn't a planned operation; it was a last-ditch emergency job, and the man they'd thrown me as director in the field was trying to shake off the ticks before he got close to me and blew me sky high at the first rendezvous.

I began taking slow breaths, working on the nerves.

"Bracken's all right," the contact said. "He knows his Moscow, don't worry."

"It won't help him. Not at night." Bracken would have left the Embassy in a car with diplomatic plates and the tags would have fallen in behind: it was routine KGB procedure when someone new joined the staff. And he couldn't drive clear of them by putting his foot down because he wasn't going to ground: he was going back to the Embassy sooner or later and they'd ask an awful lot of questions. There's not much traffic at night in this city and you'd wake the dead if you hit the tit and left rubber all over the road. All he could do was to try getting a truck or a bus or something between them and himself and ease off into a side street while their view was blocked. And the best of luck.

"Have you worked here before?" the contact asked me.

"No. I was trained here for Curtain operations."

"Are you fluent?"

"Yes. Local accent."

"When were you here last?" he asked me, watching the intersection.

"Three years ago." Another militia patrol went past, in one of their small snub-nosed Volgas. A face was turned toward us. The car didn't slow.

"That's a long time," the contact said. "Things are changing fast over here. You'll have to be careful."

"Oh for Christ's sake d'you think I need telling?"

His head moved a fraction to watch my reflection in the windscreen. "Sorry, old boy."

I slowed my breathing, counting the breaths. I'd have to do better than this, a hell of a lot better. Otherwise I was going to blow up when the heat came on. Three, four, five. "They pulled me in from leave," I said more quietly, "two weeks after the last lot."

"Bastards, aren't they?"

We watched the car.

"I could have refused."

"Why didn't you?"

"Vanity."

He laughed again soundlessly, but didn't take his eyes off the car. It was moving into better light now, turning off Ckalova ulica toward us and speeding up a little. It was a black Humber with CD plates.

"You're driving this one," the contact said, "all right?"

I said yes, and watched the Humber. There was nothing behind it but there was still plenty of time: we were parked less than a hundred yards from the intersection. It came on, slowing as it neared. Another bus went past along the ring road, then a private car, going quite fast.

"Cutting it fine," the contact said.

The Humber was nearly abreast of us now and slowing under full brakes, the driver's door coming open an instant before it stopped. A man got out and came across to us as the contact hit the door open and left the wheel to me. I slid behind it as the other man got in and said, "You'd better hurry."

A squeal came as the contact took the Humber away with the engine racing in low gear before the change. I hit the stick shift and did a tight U-turn and found a side street and swung into it with my eyes on the mirror. There was nothing.

"You'd better go south," the man said. "Get onto the ring road as soon as you can." He sat back, stretching his legs out. "But I think we're all right. I'm Bracken."

"Quiller." I made two right turns, watching the mirror.

"This is the car you'll use," Bracken told me. "The papers are in the glove pocket. I was getting worried about you."

"We had problems." At each turn the streetlights threw his reflection onto the windscreen and filled in what I remembered of him. He was a shut-faced man with a tight mouth and eyes that never came to rest on anything for more than a second: he was looking around him now with brief jerks of his head. He couldn't keep his feet still either; he kept on shuffling them against the floorboards. Maybe he wasn't always like that; he could be worried at the moment because he'd been cutting things fine. If they'd turned off the ring road after him he would have driven straight past us but there's always a risk and he could have come close to blowing me. I didn't know much about him, only a few things I'd heard over cups of tea in the Caff between missions; someone had said he'd been thrown out of an instructor's job at Norfolk because he'd used a live charge to demonstrate his de-arming techniques, and someone else had told me he'd murdered his mistress and been acquitted because the Bureau had suppressed some of the evidence; I didn't necessarily believe either story but the truth was probably somewhere there in the background. There's usually something a bit touched about the field directors: look at Ferris, always strangling mice.

"What sort of problems?" Bracken wanted to know.

"Access. Croder's not as good as they say."

His blunt head turned quickly. "Croder is *very* good. It couldn't have been his fault."

"He took a hell of a risk."

"Quite possibly. He takes on things that other people won't touch. So do you. That's why he wanted you for this one. Did you fly in?"

"Yes."

"Where did you land?"

"Domodedovo."

"What hotel?"

"The Aeroflot."

"Are we still in the clear?"

"Yes." I'd been using the mirror at five-second intervals.

He stopped shuffling his feet. "Did you leave your passport with Immigration?"

"Yes."

"I want you to ask for it back in the prescribed two days and then go to ground and come up as a Soviet citizen." He took an envelope from his coat and put it into the glove compartment. "Everything's there." He talked for ten minutes without stopping except to answer questions; we covered liaison, contacts, signals, the safe house, and possible exit procedures. "I want you to know that you'll receive every support from the people here in the field and of course from London. I'm not trying to boost your morale. We want Schrenk, badly, and we think you can pull him out for us."

"Where is he?"

"We don't know. We've—"

"You don't know?"

He waited three seconds. "We are looking for him very hard. We have a man inside Lubyanka, watching for Schrenk to come in. At the moment we can't understand why he wasn't taken straight there from Hannover. We're therefore watching a lot of other places: the Serbsky Institute here in Moscow and the facilities they run in the Urals, the Komi Republic, Murmansk, the Potma Complex, and of course"—with the slightest pause—"in Leningrad."

"They might have gone to Hannover to kill him." I made another turn and got onto the ring road going south. The mirror was clear except for a trolleybus in the distance.

"Not without trying again to break him, and they couldn't do that in Hannover. It's going to take time, and a lot of personnel. We know that."

"What about Leningrad?"

His speech became slightly faster, pushed by his nerves. "The cell is still intact. Obviously Schrenk hasn't been broken yet. Of course they might have gone too far: he might be dead. But we've got to *know*."

"What are their plans, if he breaks?"

He said in a moment, "Some of them will try making a run for it, but they won't get across any of the frontiers because the guard posts will be alerted, and so will the airports. They can't quietly leave their jobs before the balloon goes up because most of them are entrenched very deeply into official positions and they'd expose the whole network. One or two have elected to take capsules if they have to, rather than face interrogation and the labor camps." He took some kind of inhaler from his pocket and started using it; it smelled like Vicks.

"How many people are there?"

"Fifteen."

Headlights came into the mirror and I watched them.

"Can't *any* of them get clear?" Comstock was in Leningrad, and so was Whitman. I'd worked with both of them.

"Not without putting everyone else at risk." He'd begun shuffling his feet again. "Incidentally the CIA is furious with us about Schrenk. They know Leningrad could blow."

"They've done all right for eleven years."

"That's why they're furious." He inhaled again and then screwed the cap on. The whole car was reeking of menthol.

"The papers for this car," I asked him, "are for which cover?"

"You've got both."

"Get them out, will you? Put the East German

papers in your pocket. These too." I pulled out the credentials Floderus had given me. "Start reading the Russian cover, do you mind?"

"Aloud?"

"Yes."

He didn't turn his head. "Have we picked someone up?"

"I don't know yet. It's just some headlights."

His hands began working busily, transferring the papers. "Don't you trust the German cover?"

"I'd rather be a local citizen if I'm going to be found with a foreign embassy man. Just a slight edge." But I wasn't happy, because every minute we were together we risked being picked up and questioned. The whole operation was balanced on a knife edge and we had to keep very still.

"Kapista Mikhail Kirov," Bracken began reading, "age forty-two, born Moscow, October 29, 1937, the Kuncevo district." He paused briefly. "Height, weight, and description are all yours precisely. The—"

"Faster." The lights in the mirror were getting bright now.

"Father, now deceased, Valery Kapista, died in an industrial accident, Troice-Lykovo district, 1976. Mother also deceased—"

I took a right turn and gunned up with the tires just this side of the squealing point and passed three parked trucks and crossed some lights at red and turned right again. Glare filled the mirror and died away.

"This car's perfectly all right," Bracken said.

"They've picked up a radio call and they're sniffing out the area where you slipped them. They started calling the minute they lost you." I turned off all the lights and waited as long as possible before I put the Pobeda into a side street a hundred yards before the next major intersection. There was a whole line of trucks parked along one side of the street and I gunned up again and found a gap and hit the brakes and pushed the stick into reverse and got a brief whimper from the rear tires as the power dragged us against the curb. I cut the engine and sat waiting.

"Read more?" Bracken asked.

"No time."

He sat with his feet perfectly still, his head turned slightly to the left, where he could pick up echoes and reflections from the buildings opposite. The wheel was locked hard over and I left it like that because they might be stupid enough to leave a gap if they came past and saw us and stopped: there was just a chance we could get out fast enough to confuse them before they could open fire. If they saw us and pulled up and blocked the gap I could try making a break on foot: the trucks gave a lot of cover and there was no snow on the ground. It would depend on what Bracken wanted me to do.

"Instructions," I said.

He waited two seconds. We both had to listen. "If you can drive us out of it," he said evenly, "do that." We listened again, and heard the distant sound of a car. "But not unless the chances are good."

"All right." The sound of the car was loudening. It was accelerating very hard in one of the indirect gears. "Where do I drop you, if I can get clear?"

"Any cab rank. I'm going back to the Embassy."

We listened again. The car had changed into top and was traveling flat out. Echoes were coming in now from the buildings at the intersection and they made it difficult to hear what was happening. I thought I was picking up a second car somewhere, also accelerating. I wasn't sure.

"If I can't drive us out?" I asked Bracken.

"Run."

"All right." I sat listening again. Bracken wouldn't have a lot of trouble: they couldn't search him and they couldn't arrest him and at the moment they didn't have anything on him to justify kicking him out of the country. But if they caught me they'd question me, and a Soviet citizen shouldn't make contact with any foreigners, least of all members of a diplomatic mission. The cover wouldn't stand up, if they wanted to put it under the light.

"Two?"

"What?"

"Two cars?"

We listened again.

"Yes." The first one was close now; the second one was still piling up the speed in an indirect gear, somewhere in the distance. "What is there in the envelope," I asked Bracken, "on Schrenk?"

"Quite a lot. Everything you ought to have."

"Local friends, movements, contacts?"

"Everything. Croder instructed me."

"Fair enough."

We sat waiting. Light swept suddenly across the face of the buildings opposite, brightening and going dark as the first car crossed the intersection flat out with its echoes drumming and fading over the next few seconds.

"One."

"Yes."

Tires started howling and light came again on the buildings as the second car turned at the intersection and sped up toward us with a gear botching and the power coming on and the exhaust sending out a hollow rising roar until the gears shifted and the power came on again. I got comfortable in my seat and moved the stick into low and kept my foot down on the clutch and put my fingers against the starter key and watched the light flood brightly across the buildings as I waited to know if the trap we were sitting in was going to spring shut.

5 / NATALYA

"Good evening, little mother."

Her head came up sharply. She was sitting with her back to the wall of the hallway, her cracked black shoes resting on the edge of a slow-combustion stove, the naked bulb throwing light on her white hair. Some mauve knitting was on her lap, and she had been nibbling at a sausage when I'd come in.

"What do you want, comrade?" Her small eyes were narrowed, focusing on my face.

"I want to see the *upravdom*. Is he here?"

She eyed me up and down again, noting my clothes, needing to find a pigeonhole for me in the infinitely varied strata of Moscow society. "I will see," she said, and took another small bite at the sausage.

I waited while she reached and took a brass bell from the shelf of her vestibule, and swung it three times. I was standing halfway between the stairs and the entrance doors, with the street exposed to my peripheral vision. This was just routine: I'd left Bracken at a taxi rank along Narodnaya ulica ten minutes ago and got here clean. The second militia patrol had gone hound-

ing straight past us and I'd used the back streets toward
the ring road, working my way out of the search area.
"Reach me through the Embassy," he'd told me. "I
shall be in signals with London direct. We're on the
board as 'Scorpion' and you'll use that in paroles and
countersigns." I'd had to ask him for my East German
papers back: he hadn't thought of it first. Not a good
sign: he was here to direct me in the field and the
field was dangerous and already he'd missed a trick
because the brush with the militia patrols had unnerved him.

I felt vulnerable and exposed.

Footsteps sounded on the stone stairway. "I am Yuri
Gorsky." A fleshy man with watchful eyes and a shock
of stiff graying hair, his worn suit smelling of black
tobacco. His hand was steady and strong.

"Kirov," I said.

He led me upstairs to a room at the end of the
passage on the third floor and showed me in. It was
small, cluttered and stifling, with the fumes of a charcoal heater sharp on the air. One door, one window,
one light bulb and one narrow bed. No telephone.

"I have been expecting you," Gorsky said in a low
voice. He stood waiting.

I was looking for signs everywhere, signs of something wrong, of a hundred things wrong. He understood
this, and I could feel his understanding as we waited
the time out, unsure of each other. That was on the air,
too, as strong as the charcoal fumes: the scent of crea-
tures met by night, their hairs lifted and their eyes
watching at the edge of vision, their breath held and
their muscles tensed by the knowledge of where they
stood—on dangerous ground.

Bracken had said he was totally reliable, but I didn't

trust that. I trusted my own feelings. "Is this the top floor?" I asked him.

"Yes." He closed the door quietly and went to the window, lifting the lower sash so easily that I knew the wooden frame must have been soaped. He beckoned to me.

The freezing air came into my lungs as I leaned and looked down, tracing the skeletonic pattern of the fire escape downward to the ground, where a streetlamp stood. There was nothing running upward, against the wall; the guttering passed across the top of the window, two feet higher; it looked strong but that meant nothing.

"It's the best room," Gorsky said, and I believed him. People from the other rooms on this floor would have to run the length of the iron balcony before they reached the fire escape. The lower floors were more dangerous: they would be searched first, if anyone came. "Don't worry," he said in his low voice, "about the little *dezhurnaya* in the hallway. She has a grandson in the labor camps. But give her money if you want to. Not too much."

"How long has she been in this building?"

"Nearly seven years. As long as I have."

I slid the window shut. "Was Schrenk here?"

"Yes." He offered me a black-and-yellow packet and I shook my head.

"When?"

"Before they arrested him." He took a cigarette and lit it, throwing the match into the charcoal heater. I went absolutely still, and he sensed it. "Don't worry," he said, "they arrested him in the street, nowhere near here. They wouldn't have been interested in where he came from; they would have been interested in what he was doing. If they had wanted to know where he came from, they would have asked him, and if he had told them, they would have come here." He drew the cigarette to a bright red glow, and then blew the smoke out in a slow cloud, watching me through it. "So don't worry. You will be safe here."

I looked at the bed, and the cracked handbasin, and the flimsy bookshelves, one end wired to the wall where a calendar was pinned, two years out of date and with a portrait of Lenin on the yellowed paper.

"Was he here in this actual room?"

"Yes," said Gorsky. "He was comfortable." Gorsky was responsible for the safe house, not for people who got arrested in the street.

"Telephone?" I said.

"You must not use the one in the building. I cannot send messages, either. You must use the telephone box in the street, at the first corner. The light in it doesn't work, but if you need it, screw the bulb in tighter." He drew deeply on the black tobacco. "Will you have visitors?"

"No."

"That is better. I won't write your name in the residence record, of course. We shall agree, if it is ever necessary, that I forgot." He gave a faint smile. "Though it would be too late for excuses, by then. Tell me," he said as he moved to the door, "if there is anything you need. There is an alleyway, quite narrow, not far from the building; you go past the telephone box and turn to the right, and you will see it. It is useful."

When he'd gone I looked round the room again, at the armchair with the stuffing out and the cracked mirror askew over the handbasin and the pile of dog-eared magazines on the floor by the window. Schrenk had been here, then, before they'd arrested him. I was that close. And that far.

I had the new cover by heart in thirty minutes: Kapista Mikhail Kirov, Moscow representative for the state factory complex in the Ukraine, plastics and allied products. Current Moscow visa for three months, schedule of meetings at the Ministry of Labor; references, employment card, food and lodging vouchers, transport allowance rates per day; members of family and next of kin; Party membership card, Izmailovo chapter.

There were voices and I listened. They were a man's and a woman's, nearing along the corridor. A door opened and closed and the voices went on, muffled now. I would have to get to know the voices here, so that one day if strangers came I'd be warned. I trusted Gorsky, but he was human and therefore fallible. A safe house is a safe house until it's blown.

There was a dossier on Helmut Schrenk, with photographs and a description; I didn't think he'd look much like that now. He was described in his cover as a demolition worker, which was typically close to reality: he'd been trained at Norfolk in explosives. It said that four months ago when he'd been doing a low-key penetration job in Moscow he'd applied for a post as agent-in-place. *Why had he done that?* I went over the material again: in the last three years he'd completed seven successful missions, apart from his "liaison work in the north"—Leningrad. At the age of thirty-five he had a lot of steam left and he wasn't the type to sit at a desk and play about with microdots: there was a tremendous amount of latent aggression in the man and he used his executive work as a safety valve; I'd seen him in action.

I'd have to ask Bracken. It was the second thing that

didn't fit Schrenk's character; the first had been Dr. Steinberg's reference to his bearing a grudge against his interrogators in Lubyanka.

I laid the destruct material on top of the charcoal until it caught fire and then held it at the mouth of the galvanized chimney so that all the smoke would go out. Then I put the East German cover and car papers inside the third magazine from the bottom of the left-hand pile and went down to talk to Gorsky again. It was then that he told me about Natalya.

"She's over there."

The café was crowded.

They were mostly young people, perched along the benches with newspapers opened on the tables among the dark bread and bowls of soup—*Komsomolskaya Pravda, Sovetsky Sport, Literaturnaya Gazeta.* At one table they were arguing loudly, and passing separate sheets from their newspapers for the others to read. They were talking about the Borodinski trial. I looked across the room.

"Which one?"

"With the fair hair, next to the man with the beard."

I pushed my way between the tables; some of the men looked up at me, noting my clothes and looking away again. I assumed they'd seen the man sitting alone near the doors and talking to no one. They must have.

"Natalya?"

She looked up at me through the tobacco smoke. So did the bearded man.

"Which Natalya?" he asked me, straightening.

"Natalya Fyodorova."

She went on staring at me without answering, her ice-blue eyes showing nothing at all.

"Who are you?" the bearded man asked me. I went

on watching the girl. The man said: "She doesn't want to talk to you."

I leaned over the table and spoke close to the girl, on the other side from the man. "I'm a friend of Helmut's."

Her hands were on the table in front of her, and I saw them move slightly, coming together. As I straightened up she looked at the man. I thought she was wondering if he'd heard what I'd said.

"She doesn't want to talk to you," he told me. "Are you deaf or something?" He pushed his bowl of soup farther away from him, as if to give himself room.

The girl looked up at me. "Who are you?" Her eyes were still cool, but she was watchful now, involved.

"A friend of his. I'm trying to find him."

The sound level around me went down suddenly as some of the people stopped talking. I looked into the mirror above the brass samovar and saw two men coming in. They didn't greet anyone, but took up a position on the far side of the room, talking to each other but looking around them. In a minute the sound level went up again, but it wasn't as loud as before.

I looked down from the mirror.

"Whose friend?" the bearded man asked me. He was leaning back, ready to get up if he had to. The girl was quite pretty, and I understood his reactions. I wondered if she'd noticed that he hadn't heard the first thing I'd said to her. It could be important.

"The trial's fixed," said a young Jew at the same table. *"They're all fixed, we know that. All of them!"*

"Shhhh!" a girl said, gripping his arm.

"To hell with them," he said loudly, and looked across at the two men who'd just come in. The noise level dipped again and recovered. A woman laughed

about something, to show that she didn't care. In the mirror I saw the two men watching her.

Natalya stood up suddenly, taking her sealskin hat from the table, knocking against a bowl of soup; the man caught it in time. "I remember him now," she told him, "he's in my office. This is work." She came round the table, shaking her hair back and putting her fur hat on, glancing into the mirror through the haze of smoke.

"This isn't the time to work!" the man said, and got to his feet.

"Stay there, Ivan. I'm coming back. And get me some more *solyanka*." As we moved away she asked me, "What's your name?"

"We'll talk outside." The two security men weren't watching us specifically but I didn't want to give them time to take an interest; in this city the faceless live longest.

The militiamen were still at the junction of the two streets when we went outside, stamping their feet in the cold; their breath clouded in front of them as they turned to watch us leaving the café. A black Volga was parked halfway along the block with its lights out. It hadn't been there before.

The girl asked my name again but I said, "It wouldn't mean anything to you." She wanted to stop, but I kept going and she had to come with me; men on surveillance get bored and they'll question anyone in sight. We turned the corner and kept walking; this street was clean and the Pobeda was parked in shadow between two of the lamps.

"How did you find me?" She kept swinging her head to look at me, frightened because I knew her and she didn't know me. I took her arm so that she'd keep walking; the two militiamen would be watching us, simply because we were something that moved in a static environment.

"Gorsky told me where to look."

"I don't know any Gorsky." She tried to hold back and I tightened her arm in mine.

"Do you want to see Helmut again?"

"Yes," she said on a breath. "But they—"

"Then trust me, and do as I tell you. We've got to keep walking." She quickened her step. "You do know Gorsky. He's the *upravdom* at the building in Vojtovica ulica."

She was beside herself, Gorsky had told me, *when she heard he'd been arrested. She kept coming back every day, asking if I had any more news.* This was another thing right out of character with Schrenk: when you're in the field you do *not* take a girl to the safe house; you don't take *anyone.* I'd been worried about his state of mind after they'd interrogated him but now I was worried about the things he'd been doing before his arrest. It was as if there were two people: Schrenk and this other man who'd been breaking all the rules.

"Do they always watch that café?" I asked the girl. She was keeping up with me now, and I could feel the tension in her, because I'd talked about Helmut.

"Not always. Tonight it's because of the trial; they think we might demonstrate, or make trouble. Most of the people who go there are Jews, and they want Borodinski released. It would be symbolic."

"Of what?"

"Of the power of the dissidents. There've been many demonstrations all over the city. Don't you know that?" I felt a slight tug on my arm as she held back again, not trusting me, not knowing who I was, and not wanting to cause any harm to Helmut.

She wasn't his type. His women had been dark, simmering, sensual. Corinne, Rebecca, Toni Alvirez. I couldn't see him with this fair-haired girl full of her fears and her extrovert dreams, the symbolic power of the dissidents, the effectiveness of demonstrations. Not his type: it was inconsistent again.

"What's your job?" I asked her.

"I'm a senior clerk, in the Kremlin."

Connection.

"Who's the man you were talking to?"

"Ivan? He's an engineer."

"Did he know Helmut?"

"No. I don't understand," she said tightly, "you said you were looking for him. But he was arrested, didn't you know that?"

"He escaped."

"Escaped?" Life came into her and her hand dug into my arm. "You mean he's free?"

"I don't know."

Two more.

"I don't *understand,"* she said anxiously. "If he escaped then he must be—"

"He managed to reach West Germany. Then they found him again. I think he's in Moscow."

Two more militiamen.

"You mean in prison?"

"I don't know." I began slowing our pace a fraction. "If he is, there are certain friends who'll be trying to get him out."

"By demonstrating?"

It was all they could think about. They thought they could get Borodinski off a life sentence or a death sentence, just as they'd thought they could get Ginzburg off, and Pektus, and Shcharansky; but all they could ever get by demonstrating was a night in the cells and a roughing up and a new entry on their records in the KGB files.

"No," I said. "Not by demonstrating."

They were coming toward us from the other end of the street on this side. The Pobeda was on the opposite side and the distance at the moment was about the same. I could turn round now and take the girl with me and get her into the car and drive off but I didn't think I could do it without hurrying, without being *seen* to hurry. I might have done it alone, measuring my steps, walking indiscernibly faster and with a longer stride, getting my keys ready; but I couldn't do it with the girl: she was still frightened of me, frightened *for him,* because whatever I said to her it wouldn't convince her that I wasn't in the police and hunting for Schrenk and hoping she could lead me to him.

"Who was his best friend," I asked her. "You?"

"I love him." Her voice faltered on it. It was over three months since she'd last seen him and she'd been starting to get over it and now I'd brought it all back. "I'd do anything to see him again."

"Then keep hoping. And trust me."

The two militiamen were close now. There was no reason why they should stop us but there was always a risk and it worried me because yesterday I'd been hang-gliding over the Sussex cliffs trying to shake off the tensions of the last operation and then Croder had thrown me out here and this was alien soil, hostile and dangerous and unpredictable, and I didn't feel ready to take the risks and beat the odds and stay this side of survival. I wasn't sure of my cover or my accent: to be word-perfect in the safe house was different from being put to the test in the street. Above all I wasn't sure of the essential steadiness of nerve I was going to need if they lifted a hand and said *Propusk.* Papers.

"What other friends did he have?" I asked her. There wasn't much time now; we might get separated.

"He didn't have many friends."

"Give me one of them. Two of them. Trust me."

They carried walkie-talkies. So if I turned round and took the girl with me and began hurrying they didn't even have to shout to us to stop: they just had to press a button and tell the other two to *stop that car when it reaches you, and check it out.* And there'd be no hope this time of keeping enough distance between them and the number plate: they'd see it and alert the Volga and bring in the radio networks and it wouldn't matter how fast I drove or how far.

I could feel the blood leaving my face and going to the muscles, and the quickening of the pulse as the adrenaline started to flow. I was that bad, to that degree unready even for a routine encounter with a couple of half-trained young militiamen: an exercise the training directors put the novices through on their first trip behind the Curtain. *So what was it going to be like when Bracken called me and said yes, he's inside Lubyanka after all, we want you to go and get him out?*

"Ignatov," the girl said.

"Other name?"

She hesitated again because she didn't know that she wasn't putting Ignatov in danger. Or Helmut.

I watched the militiamen coming.

"Pyotr," she said, half holding it back.

"Who else?"

"I don't remember anyone else."

She thought she'd gone too far. "Natalya," I said, "is your identity card in order?"

She swung her head. "Yes. Why?"

"These two here," I said. "If they question us, don't

mention Helmut, or Pyotr Ignatov. We're just recent acquaintances, you understand?"

"Yes."

They were watching us now. Peaked caps, batons, sidearms, radio sets. They were walking in step.

"You don't know anything about me," I told her. "Just my name. My name is Kapista Kirov. But we both like music. Classical music."

Close now. Briskly in step. They were young men, conscious of their uniforms and their heady power. They might stop us simply because they decided they'd like to talk to a pretty girl, watching her ice-blue eyes while they went through the routine questions.

"I'll step off the pavement," I told her. "We'll make room for them. The whole problem with Prokofiev, it seems to me, isn't in his music at all. It's simply that he's overrated by the critics. The result is that a lot of his work sounds disappointing, after all the eulogies and the acclaim." Their eyes in the shadow of their peaked caps, watching us. "His music is just as good as it always was, and we should listen to it as if we've never heard of him before. Otherwise we shall miss a lot of what he was trying to convey." Briskly in step. "Nikolai doesn't agree with me, I know, but—"

"*Propusk,*" one of them said as they stopped.

6 / IGNATOV

Two kopecks.

"Is Sergei there?"

"Who?"

"Sergei Panov."

"I'm sorry, there's nobody here by that name. This is the British Embassy."

"Oh, excuse me. I must have asked for the wrong number."

"That's quite all right."

Every line to the Embassy was tapped and radio was out of the question and protracted speech code was a slow-burn fuse because they'd go straight through the exchange and trace the call and raid the place within minutes, so I'd had to ask for a cutout.

"Sergei" was for Taganskaya Metro station and I got there in fourteen minutes, feeling nervy again because in this city there wasn't much traffic at night and I was vulnerable. It had been bad enough half an hour ago.

Have you been to the café? the younger one had asked.

Yes, she'd said before I could stop her.

I see. And were you talking about the trial there? About the traitor Borodinski? His eyes going over my papers again, turning them to the light, looking for the wrong weave, the wrong coloration, the wrong serial number, looking at the photograph and then at my face, then back at the photograph.

We were talking about Prokofiev, I said before she could answer. She could get us arrested: they were trying to provoke us into saying something wrong.

Prokofiev, or Borodin-ski? A little joke, his tone amused, a young man who knew his composers.

He wasn't playing a game of his own. Since the trial had begun, the standing orders for the police were to show these dissidents that it was useless protesting and demonstrating and thumping the café tables. Comrade Borodinski would be tried in the court, not in the streets. A night in the cell would remind them of that.

If we call him a traitor before he's tried—

It simply means, I cut in on her again, *that it's how we regard him.* With a short laugh, squeezing her arm: *Ask Helmut—he says we ought to raid the courthouse and string him up from a lamppost outside.*

Who is Helmut? His eyes watching her, watching me.

A friend of ours, I told him. *He feels rather strongly about traitors.*

The other man stamped his feet, feeling the cold, getting bored. I was waiting for Natalya to say something, ready to cut in on her at once; but she was quiet now, because of my warning.

Where are you two going now?

Home, I said.

He looked down at the papers again. *But you live in opposite directions from here.*

I'm seeing my friend home first.

His head came up. *Why? Are you saying the streets
are dangerous?*

Of course not. It's just that I'm enjoying her company.

A thin smile. *Let's hope she's enjoying yours.* He
passed my papers back, slapping them onto my hand.
*It's late for people to be out on the streets. It disturbs
the more respectable citizens who are trying to sleep.*

Quite bad enough.

The cutout came up the escalator of the Metro station, dropping his thin little cigar into the sand bin at
the fourth pace from the moving stairs and sliding both
hands into the pockets of his coat, thumbs hooked out.
He wasn't too quick on the parole and countersign
and I put him through a variation before I took him
across to the car and drove five blocks and stopped
between two trucks parked on the wasteground alongside a building site where a crew was working the night
shift. It was a new apartment block and a crane was
swinging an entire prefabricated wall into place with
four window apertures in it; sparks flew in a fountain
from a welder's torch on the floor below.

"Have they found Schrenk yet?"

"Not yet," he said. "You'd have been told."

"I was absent from base."

"Oh." He gave me the tape recorder and took something else from the glove pocket and sat clutching it in
his bare hands.

"What's that?"

"This? Hand warmer. Burns charcoal. I can't stand
this bloody cold, look at these chilblains."

I began talking onto the tape. *2/2 12:09. I need all
info on Natalya Fyodorova, senior clerk, Kremlin
office, companion of subject before arrest. Also all info*

on Pyotr Ignatov, Party member, often in subject's
company, no other details known.

She'd told me I would find him at a meeting of the
Izmailovo chapter at ten o'clock tomorrow morning
and I was going to be there if I could make it. This
wasn't for the tape because Bracken might decide to
send someone else in to watch Ignatov and I wanted to
work solo: the man could be ultrasensitive about
Schrenk's arrest and they could frighten him off.

I need to know how the subject was arrested: in a
street or where? What street, what place? Had he made
a mistake? Bad security? Was he blown? Need to know
why he applied for post as a-i-p: this is important. I'm
finding inconsistencies in his behavior prior to arrest.

Condensation was forming on the windscreen and the
crane swung its skeletonic arm through the floodlights
insubstantially, like a back projection on frosted glass.
The welder's torch flared with an acid radiance and I
looked away from it to protect my night vision.

Should I stress the importance of Natalya Fyodorova? She probably knew more about Schrenk than
anyone else in Moscow, more than Bracken's team
could find out in a month. But I was seeing her again
tomorrow: leave it at that and don't risk over-surveil-
lance. She could be frightened off as easily as Ignatov.

I suggest messages by hand direct to base in di-
graphic square, key 5. When absent I'll report hourly
at the hour plus 15, Extension 7, silent line. Signal ends.

I sat thinking for another five minutes. There was a
lot more I wanted to ask but I wasn't going to put it
on the tape because I didn't want to show my hand at
this stage: I didn't know how Bracken normally worked
but I knew he was the key man in a crisis and he might
react differently; once he knew my line of inquiry he

might throw in contacts and tags and shields and the whole bloody bazaar. I didn't want anyone in my way.

"Who does this go to?" I asked the man beside me.

"Winfield."

"Who's he?"

"One of our a-i-p's."

"Where's his base?"

"Didn't anybody tell you anything? We—"

"Where's his base?"

Low threshold.

"The airport." His head was turned to watch me now.

"Oh come on, *which one?"*

"Sheremetyevo. It's—"

"For Christ's sake," I said, "you don't go all the way out there every time?"

"No. We use a drop."

"Mobile?"

"Yes, the Aeroflot ferry bus."

Desperate times. Bracken was keeping himself strictly in the shadows while he tried to dig himself in and set up an untapped phone line and signals facilities somewhere outside the Embassy and it wouldn't be easy to do but he'd have to do it because all I'd wanted was a brief squawk on the tape and this man had taken twenty minutes to make the rendezvous and so had I. You'll receive every possible support, Croder had said, Bracken had said, both of them lying, this wasn't support, it was bloody musical chairs. Or was this what they'd meant by *possible?* Was this all they'd got me for?

"We're trying to put someone into your sector," the cutout was saying, rubbing his hands on the charcoal thing. "I mean really close, you know, five minutes away. Make things a lot easier. Of course it's always getting a phone that's the trouble, I mean a clean one."

I dropped the tape recorder onto his lap and started the engine and wiped the stuff off the windscreen. "Who's my director?" I asked him.

"I don't know."

Strictly in the shadows. But that was all right; it was what a cutout was for: to protect both ends of the signal.

"I'm going to put you back on the Metro at Proletarskaya," I told him.

"Is that closer?"

"No, but I don't like doubling on my tracks. The trains don't stop running till one o'clock, you've got enough time." I got into gear and swung the headlight beams across the low relief of the wasteground.

"What's he done?" he asked me in a moment.

"Who?"

"Schrenk."

I got fed up again: he hadn't been fully trained. The executive asks all the questions and it's a strictly one-way conversation because otherwise it's dangerous: once in the field you don't look for non-brief information any more than you look for a gas leak with a match and they ought to have told him that.

"He's disappeared," I said.

"I know, but—"

"And it's all you need to know."

It began snowing the next morning not long after first light, a few big flakes drifting down from a lead-gray sky. I'd slept for three hours, with the foot of the bed jammed against the door and the castors out and the window raised a few inches from the bottom with the lid of the samovar hanging from one edge of the frame, a fat lot of good against a full-scale raid but it'd give me five or six seconds to trigger the organism and I was here in this city now with the morning light in my eyes because more than once, somewhere along the line in Berlin or Bangkok or Hong Kong, there'd been five or six seconds to spare on my side instead of on theirs.

He took me right across the Jauza from the place in Izmailovskiy Prospekt where they'd held the Party meeting, and it was difficult at first because he'd walked for two blocks to where he'd left his car, and his flat heavy features and his dark fur coat and hat made him look like most of the other men in the street. I'd had to tag him in the Pobeda, moving at a crawl and stopping when I could, in case he got onto a tram. I wasn't even certain he was the right man: at the meeting they'd addressed him as Comrade Ignatov but it was a common enough name and there might have been more than one of them there.

He was driving a small mud-colored Syrena, taking his time and going westward across the river into the Baumanskaya district. The snow was still falling steadily but the sky wasn't thick with it; this looked like the edge of a cloud formation that was moving in from the north at slow speed. The road surface wasn't affected yet and there were no sand trucks on the move. Along Baumanskaya the Syrena turned right and stopped just after the intersection, so that I had to drive past and pull up a hundred yards further on, using a parked van for cover. I was out of the car and walking toward the apartment block just as Ignatov was going up the steps and I kept moving because if he lived here I could get his number from the *upravdom* and if he didn't live here there'd be no way of tagging him inside the building without the risk of a confrontation on Schrenk's movements before the arrest but I might learn more

by watching him than by asking questions and it might
be safer that way: Schrenk could have been blown by
one of the people he'd been running with and it could
have been Ignatov.

The building was red brick with the single word
Pavillon in corroded aluminum over the entrance: four
stories, eighteen windows along the front, and no other
doorway into the street. I made one circuit and found
a yard with a dozen cars parked in it and room for a
dozen more; Ignatov would have used this if he'd
lived here. Then I went back and moved the Pobeda
into deeper cover but left it facing the same direction
and used the mirror and the rear window, focusing on
the Syrena.

He was in the building for an hour and he came out
alone. I'd got his walk now: he leaned backward
slightly and his feet were splayed, the walk of a heavy
man with somewhere to go. *Where was he going?* His
time and travel pattern might be repetitive and I noted
11:39 on my watch as he got into the Syrena and
started up and drove past me without turning his head.

He took me west again, this time along Karl Marx
ulica and across the ring road. Traffic was light and I
kept well back, leaving a truck and a VW between us
and pulling ahead only when there was no street to the
right at the lights to take up the slack if he went through
close to the yellow: I didn't want to lose him.

At 11:52 he stopped near Plevna Metro and went
across to the telephone box by the cigar store, looking
at his watch. I noted this because the people of this
city are not punctual and he wasn't going to call anyone to say he'd be late, because he hadn't been hurrying. I didn't like it.

There was a slot by the curb and I put the Pobeda
into it and sat scanning the environment and doing it

carefully. He shouldn't have looked at his watch like that. When I'd picked him up at the Party meeting he'd walked to his car without any hurry and he'd driven at a normal speed to the Pavillon building and driven away from it at the same speed and suddenly he wanted to know the time.

Nerves: the alarm threshold was still too low.

Ten private cars parked, and a light van unloading cardboard cases near the intersection. A No. 41 trolleybus moving in to the curb and putting down four passengers, taking on seven. A militiaman standing not far from the cigar store, hands behind his back, his feet feeling the cold. Other people on the pavement, most of them hurrying a little because the snow was going to get worse. Nothing in the environment to worry me. Nothing. But the hairs had begun rising on the backs of my hands and my breathing had quickened.

Ignore.

The trolleybus pulled away and I could see the whole of the environment again, as it had been before. Nothing had changed. Ignatov was still in the telephone box, the pale blur of his face showing through the condensation on the glass. A woman in a muskrat coat came up and started waiting for the phone, a child with her, both of them eating ice creams from the stall on the other side of the cigar store. In Moscow the people eat ice cream in all weathers, even in the depth of winter. In Moscow the people are not punctual, and should not look at the time.

The cold was creeping into the car again but I didn't switch the heater on because it would mean running the engine, and I didn't want to do that till I was ready to drive away because the militiaman would catch the sound and turn his head. *The ideal to aim at in a potentially hostile environment,* they tell us repeatedly at

Norfolk, *is to become or remain invisible, inaudible and unfindable.* Noted.

A black Zil limousine with Central Committee MOC number plates and its rear windows curtained and its headlights on came hounding down the Chaika lane and I watched the policeman at the intersection jumping into the roadway with his illuminated baton raised to halt the cross traffic, his whistle shrilling as the Zil went through on the red, heading westward toward the Kremlin.

The woman was still standing there eating her ice cream. The small boy was waving his in the air, trying to make a snowflake settle on it. The woman laughed, and began doing the same thing.

11:55. Ignatov had been in the phone box for three minutes.

My legs were getting chilled because of the cold air coming into the car through the gaps round the doors, and because of the nerves. Three minutes was a long time. In three minutes the environment had changed considerably: most of the people who'd been on the pavement when I'd arrived here had gone, and as many others had taken their place. But the woman and the child were still there, and the militiaman had moved a few paces to stand watching them, smiling as the boy caught a snowflake at last on his ice cream. In Moscow everyone loves children.

The light flashed across the glass door of the telephone box as it opened and Ignatov came out. In the warmth of the box he had loosened his dark coat, and now he buttoned it up and pulled his woolen scarf straight, tucking it in. Without looking around him he stopped to talk to the militiaman, halfway across to his car, taking something out of his wallet and showing it to him briefly and getting a salute and putting the wallet away as he went on talking, standing quite close. In a moment the militiaman unclipped the radio from his belt and began speaking into it, looking up and down the street.

I waited, watching them. It was all I could do, or needed to do: I had no information. The militiaman was gazing up the street now, also waiting; then he began walking into the roadway, taking his time as he raised his baton to halt the line of traffic on the side where I was parked. In my mirror the line was slowing to a stop, except for a low black van with lights on its roof, a police vehicle coming up fast and overtaking the other traffic until the militiaman swung his baton and pointed it straight at my car and I thought *Oh Christ it's a trap.*

The police van was still slowing hard under the brakes and veering across the front of the traffic line when I hit the starter and botched the gears in and wheels spun into motion with the tires squawking and the flashlight on the windscreen ledge sliding across and smashing against the pillar as I locked the wheel over and heeled into the roadway and straightened up, clouting the front end of the van and ripping my rear wing away: I heard it clatter behind me, a jangle of metal on tarmac as the whine of the siren came in and someone shouted.

On the conscious level the visual and aural experience was mostly a kaleidoscope of shapes and a medley of sound: the militiaman leaping clear and the siren wailing and a faint thin whine starting from the rear end of the Pobeda where a wing bracket was gouging the tire, a face on the pavement—*Ignatov's*—and a small boy hunched in surprise and the lights at the intersection changing to red and the siren still howling as the van closed up and smashed into my rear bumper and

bounced back with its reflection rocking in the mirror.
The traffic policeman tried to get in my way but I kept
going and he jumped back with the shrill of his whistle
breaking off. A truck had started across and I touched
the wheel and used the only space I had and ripped the
rear door across his front end before I was clear and
moving faster with the engine at peak revs in second
gear. The mirror was vibrating but I could see the truck
slewing to a stop and the front of the police van nosing
round it with the rear end swinging as it struggled for
traction.

This was Kuibysheva ulica and the street was wide
but I needed obstacles for cover because if I kept
straight on I'd be plumb in their sights so I took the
first right turn with the tires sliding on the thin wet
film left by the snow and the whine of the wing bracket
descending in tone and then yipping suddenly as the
rear wheels spun under the acceleration. I was driving
by instinct: the organism was in shock and trying to
survive, but nearer the conscious level I knew there
wasn't a chance because these were the streets that
fanned out from the Kremlin and there were people
along the pavements and a militia patrol at every corner
and it was full daylight, strictly no go but I wasn't going
to stop before I had to.

Mirror. The van was there with its roof lights flashing. The siren died away and a voice came over the
bullhorn: *Stop—you are ordered to stop.*

There wasn't a chance because they'd be sending this
out on their radio and asking for a converging movement, a routine trap that would put me into the center
of a closing net and hold me there while they slid to a
stop and the doors swung open and they came for me
on foot, not hurrying.

I could drive this thing through any gap they left for

me and run it into the ground if I had to but I'd need clear streets and there weren't any: if I kept on going I'd risk losing control and plowing into the people on the pavements, this was a dead end, a bottleneck. There were sirens ahead of me now, echoing from the face of the building at the intersection while the surrealistic voice squawked from the bullhorn behind me: *Stop— you are ordered to stop.* The mirror was shivering, the black rectangular image jerking in it like an old film. I couldn't judge the distance between us but on this surface I could spin the Pobeda full circle without losing control and take it from there and hope for confusion —enough confusion to give me the five or six seconds I'd need to work in if I came out of the wreckage and there were anything I could do.

Another siren was cutting in: the whole city was wailing and the echoes were washing the sound back in undulating waves. I was still accelerating but the break-off point was close now and if I didn't shut down the speed I'd lose the surface and slide into the intersection with the wheels locked and no hope of any control. The nearest threat was still the vehicle behind me and if I could knock it out there was a chance of getting clear before the others turned into the street ahead of me. The surface was touchy and nothing much happened when I swung the wheel hard over and left it there and waited; then we found a drier patch and the Pobeda began spinning with one side lifting off the springs and a howl rising from the nearside wing brackets as they shaved the tires while the street went swinging round against my eyes and the black rectangle came closer, curving away on the next swing and coming closer again, curving for the third time and suddenly filling the vision field as we met and hit and bounced and hit again as the van's momentum carried us locked to-

gether across the wet surface before a tire burst and
was wrenched off and the wheel buckled and dug into
the roadway and the van swung hard and lifted, rolling
over and slamming down with the Pobeda half looping
and then tumbling against it with a shrilling of metal
and flying glass.

The sirens were closing in.

7 / SEPULCHER

A city is a warren and the nearest hole I could see was one of the dark arched doorways of the GUM department store and I went for that, headlong across the roadway and the pavement and through the people as a man tried to trip me and someone shouted, whistles blowing and the last of the glass still tinkling among the wreckage as the doors were forced open, the whole street shocked and full of sound and stilled movement for the two seconds it took me to reach the arch, another man with his hands going down to tackle me but not fast enough as I hit the doors and pitched through into the bright lamplit interior and swerved at right angles and broke through a group of people, faces opening in surprise, someone running to the glass doors to see what was happening outside in the street, *stop thief* someone was calling out, it was a trap in here but worse in the open, *keep running it's all you can do.*

Glass doors, arches, windows and a stairway, everywhere crowded, wrought-iron bridges crossing the cathedral form of the building, a bell ringing somewhere, then more shouting as doors crashed open behind me

and to my left, *keep running and find a door,* a man's
hand swinging out and his arm hooking round my
throat but I used a face claw and spun clear and hit
the door and went through, a woman screaming and a
table going over with buttons everywhere, a thousand
of them and reels of cotton rolling and a box of scarlet
plumes falling and exploding through the air, my hand
on a brass handle and the inner door slamming back
against shelves as I went through and saw the long narrow window and got there and used a packing case as
a springboard and rolled, breaking the iron latch and
falling, the woman screaming again.

It was a corridor and I ran hard for the door at the
end, slowing and going through at a quick walk, shutting it behind me. I was back in the main building
again with a lot of commotion at the Kuibysheva entrance where I'd come in. I began walking the other
way, a little faster when I reached the big central fountain, not too fast, watch it, everyone's looking the other
way and I'm nót, I'm on the move, *become or remain
invisible, inaudible, and unfindable,* an old woman in
black watching me, *question* it, and now a man, *why?*
Watching my face and I touched it, blood, and got out
my handkerchief as someone began shouting, a lot of
them looking at me now, so I went low and broke and
ran again, dodging a group of children, the whistles
blowing behind me and a foot darting out and sending
me pitching against a man whose lined gray face
loomed and stared straight into mine before I spun
away and went full tilt at the big glass doors at the end,
stop thief, a full rising roar as I hit the door on the
left and swung through and found the street, *slow down,*
the snow filling the dark sky and the pavement slippery
with it, *slow down,* the sound of sirens on the air again,
directionless and echoing from everywhere, a black pa-

trol car slewing in to the curb with uniformed men getting out of it, uncertain where they should go.

I began walking faster because people had started staring at my face again and I kept on using the handkerchief but it was soaked by now and I put it away and broke into a run as far as the corner and saw two militiamen and swerved away and found a doorway as they shouted behind me and I knocked someone down, running hard, a room on the left and a girl with her face opening in shock and starting to scream as I kept going and found a corridor *empty* and ran hard to the end, the word MEN on a door and I went in and the bloodied face met me in the mirror as I stopped dead, no wonder she'd screamed.

Water gushing and a rolled paper towel: it was a long gash from the cheekbone to the chin and I could feel glass fragments moving in it as I went to work. Blood on my hands, on my coat: I used more water, swabbing at the astrakhan, listening for sounds outside, a door thudding and someone shouting. I ripped off some more of the towel and made a wad and held it against my face as I went out and climbed three steps and found the street again.

Slow. Slow down. Get the breathing under control, head down and watching the wet pavement like everyone else, breathe deep and breathe slow and don't look up, don't look round. The noise was behind me: a staccato medley of voices, and further away a siren dying and the slam of a car door. I was on the east side of Red Square now with the walls of the Kremlin opposite. I went that way, crossing the open space with the knowledge that if they found me here there wouldn't be any cover except for the long queue of people reaching from below Spassky Gate to Lenin's tomb. I kept walking, my head down and the snow drifting across the ground, beginning to settle.

Three men walked together toward the line of people, and I moved nearer them to make a group. Others were crossing Red Square toward the walls of the Kremlin, hurrying because of the snow and because the queue was lengthening. One of the sirens was still wailing through the streets behind me, and I could hear a car moving at high speed with its engine racing. I didn't look back; I walked with the three men in black through the drifting snow. The wad of paper was pressed hard against my face; if I could stop the blood flow I could regain something like a normal image. I didn't know whether the paper was white or red; it would make a difference when I reached the queue of people. They were facing toward us, all of them, wrapped tight in their fur coats and hats and head-scarves, staring across the square.

"What's happening over there?"

"Was there an accident?"

We walked steadily toward them, joining the line near Spassky Gate. It was four deep and I took up my position on the far side, away from the department store.

"Do you have toothache?"

"Yes," I said.

"What's happening across the square there?"

"I don't know."

I counted seven police cars, one of them moving slowly round the cathedral and another one turning and accelerating in the opposite direction, but both keeping close to the square.

"Tch! There's blood on your face. Are you hurt?"

"It's nothing much. I slipped on the snow."

"You need medical attention."

"It will heal."

A body of militiamen was moving away from the thick of the patrol cars and spreading out along the edge of the square, facing this way. One of the cars had dropped two men off not far from Nikolsky Gate, and they were walking steadily past the museum toward the queue of mourners. They looked closely at everyone they passed. I turned away from the queue but saw a police van slowing to a halt opposite Nabatny Tower; a dozen men got out of it and began forming a group facing this way. I turned back.

"Do you live in Moscow?"

"Yes," I said.

"We are from Abramtsevo." She was a motherly woman half buried in black shawls, her bright eyes watching me. "This is my son, Viktorovich. He would like to live in Moscow, but he can't get a visa. He's a sewage engineer, an apprentice."

I nodded to him. "You must keep trying. You know how it is, when you want something from them."

When I looked behind me again I saw the group of police spreading out and moving slowly toward the queue, stopping a man here and there and questioning him. I turned again and looked toward Spassky Gate, where two sentries stood.

"Have you visited the Mausoleum before?" asked the woman.

"No. I've been wanting to see it for a long time."

The sentries would certainly see me and probably stop me: they were aware that every male in the square was being scrutinized. The three lines of police and militiamen were moving steadily in from the other three sides.

"We have been twice already," she said. "Every time I see the sepulcher, I have tears." She rocked gently, nodding with the whole of her round shawled body. "Every day we have fifteen thousand people here to see it. But you will know this, since you live in Moscow."

The snow was falling thickly now; the sky overhead was storm-dark and the air was heavy. We shuffled forward, watched by the police guards.

"The last time we came," the woman said, "the queue reached right round to Kutafya Tower! Of course it was summer then." She peered up at me with her bright eyes. "Do you have influence in Moscow?"

"No," I said. "But your son should keep on trying. It wears them down in the end."

A man and a woman broke from the queue not far away, and a police guard called to them. "Return to the line, please! Get back into line!"

"But we can't wait any longer. My wife has a cold."

"Very well."

We shuffled forward again.

The militiamen were halfway across the square by now, one of them stopping the man to question him while his wife waited, puzzled. When I turned round I saw two of the police unit reach the end of the queue and start moving along it, scrutinizing the men. Ahead of us people were breaking away to put their cameras and parcels into a locker room, coming back to their places and shuffling forward again. The militiamen were moving steadily in our direction.

There wasn't any way out. If I tried running they'd head me off and if I stayed where I was they'd question me: *What have you done to your face? Why is your coat torn like this? Were you in an accident?*

"The snow is already thick, in Abramtsevo. The chickens can hardly find the grain." She moved forward with her son.

There was no way out but I had a choice. *Schrenk*

carried a capsule, Croder had said. *He would have saved us an immense amount of trouble if he had used it.* The small box was in a pocket on the inside of my waistband and in it was the capsule, cushioned in silica-gel desiccant. They might not search me immediately, not for anything small; but they'd see me if I tried to reach it and in any case they'd make a detailed search as soon as we got to Lubyanka and that wasn't far from here, four minutes in a police car.

It depended on how much he'd told them. Ignatov. *He didn't know who I was.* He was a total stranger and he hadn't looked at me once in the meeting hall or when I'd followed him to his car, not once. *But he'd told them to pick me up.*

We moved forward again and the woman's son took his camera across to the locker room and came back. The police guards were watching us closely now, their caps jutting and their bonewhite faces reflecting the snow.

Natalya? She might have told Ignatov, *he said that if Helmut was in Moscow there were certain friends who'd try to get him out of prison.* Natalya, possibly. I didn't think so; she hadn't enough guile. Who else, if not Natalya? There was no one who knew me.

"Keep close in line." Their eyes moved over our faces.

We shuffled forward again and climbed the steps between the guards of honor, going inside. It was quiet now except for the movement of feet across the wooden platform. People had stopped talking, and the men were taking off their hats. Guards with fixed bayonets stood watching us as we climbed the steps to the tomb.

It would depend on what Ignatov had told them. If he'd said I was a dissident trying to provoke others last night in the Star Café, a dissident with certain friends who would try getting Schrenk out of prison, I could manage what they would do to me. But if the inconceivable had happened and Ignatov had told them I was an agent from London then they'd take me through the full routine as they'd taken Schrenk, and I didn't know for certain if I could stand up to it as he'd managed to do, because I wasn't fresh in the field and the tensions of the last operation were still flickering in the nerves. I could break and if I broke I could blow London, the whole of what I knew.

"There . . ." said the woman in front of me, and leaned forward in her black shawls to gaze at the bright glass coffin with the exhibit inside it, either the preserved body or an effigy, it was impossible to tell. She began weeping quietly, but the line wouldn't stop for anyone and I had to nudge her, as the man behind was nudging me. We went down the steps and made for the huge rectangle of the doorway, passing between the guards and reaching daylight. The snow fell softly over the square and over the dark moving figures, bringing its silence to the scene. I stayed with a group, talking to the woman and her son; she was still weeping quietly but he took no notice. The nearest policemen were fifty yards away; I could hear their voices under the dark sky.

"When do you expect to get your license," I asked Viktorovich, "in sewage engineering?" I steered the two of them to the left, toward the history museum, keeping my head down to talk to the boy and holding the paper wad against the wound with my hand covering most of it, because the blood must have soaked through by this time.

"When they give it to me," the boy said. "I've passed my exams. It's a question of time." He looked around him at the huge museum and the gilded domes. "One

day I'm going to live here, you know that? But you
need a visa, and you can't get a visa without a job here,
and you can't get a job here without a visa." He kicked
at the snow, thrusting his bare knuckly hands into his
pockets.

The woman stopped weeping and gave a sigh, fum-
bling among her shawls for a handkerchief. "It was
beautiful," she said, "beautiful."

I held her arm, keeping her in a straight line for the
museum through the gap between the two policemen. I
watched the ground.

"Look at this snow," the boy said. "I forgot to cover
the tractor before we left this morning."

The policeman on the left was questioning someone:
I could hear his voice. It was the other one, on the
right, who came suddenly across to us, the leather of his
new boots creaking.

"You," he said. "Papers."

8 / VADER

Within a minute there were five or six of them round me, forming a circle.

"His face," they kept telling each other. The first one had raised his arm and held it like that until a captain came up, the heels of his polished black boots clinking on the hard surface: I think they were iron-capped.

"His face, Captain," the first one said.

"What have you done to your face?" The captain pulled my hand away and stared at the wound.

"I slipped on the snow. I was carrying a mirror."

"When?" His breath steamed against my face.

"An hour ago, when—"

"An *hour* ago. Did you have an accident?"

"Yes, I slipped on the snow—"

"Did you have an accident in your *car?*"

Others came up. Behind them I caught a glimpse of the woman in the shawls, staring at me with her bright eyes, shocked.

"When did he have the accident?" It was another captain.

"He's lying."

"How did he tear his coat?"

"Papers. Show me your papers."

I could feel blood trickling on my chin: the wound had opened when the captain had pulled my hand away.

"Kapista Kirov. That tells us nothing." They came closer, gathering round like boys who'd found an injured animal.

More of them came, and one of them said: "He is the man I saw running away from the car."

"Are you sure?"

"I was there! Of course I'm sure."

They all started talking at once.

Capsule.

"Take him along. Four of you."

"March!"

People stood perfectly still in the falling snow, watching us as we walked past them toward the roadway. Three Black Ravens had already pulled up alongside the curb; their engines were still running. The rear doors of the nearest one swung open with a bang and I got to it when they hustled me inside: it was in my hand by the time I sat down on the padded bench.

The rear doors slammed and the steel bar was dropped across outside. Four of them sat with me, watching me but not talking.

"I don't understand," I told the captain. "I slipped on the snow, and broke the mirror. You're making a mistake."

"Perhaps."

I went on talking to him, explaining that I wasn't the man they wanted. He shrugged at intervals. The box was in my hand but I hadn't decided yet. I couldn't get the capsule out while I was sitting here: they were watching me the whole time.

Dzerzhinsky Square, through the barred windows, and the Children's World department store. Then, just opposite, Lubyanka.

I had no information. The choice was simply heads or tails, black or white. Ignatov had known I was an agent and had told them so, or he hadn't. If he had known, and had told them, then I risked betraying London when they brought the pressure on and my system began overloading. If I wanted to avoid that risk, I would have to take the capsule within the next few seconds, and blow the fuse.

"You can open up!" the captain called out.

Hands hit the steel bar upward against the rear doors.

Once inside Lubyanka I would be closely watched and meticulously searched, if they were doing their job. They would know there were two critical points at which an active intelligence agent is liable to take his capsule: within minutes of his arrest, and when the interrogation began breaking him. Woodison had done it; so had Racklaw; so had Fane. The pressure had got too much: not just the pressure of their last arrest and interrogation but of all the other arrests and interrogations they'd been through since they'd first gone eagerly into the field as younger men, brandishing their unbruised innocence. The pressure is cumulative.

"Out!" the captain told me. Two of the men dropped from the rear of the van and two stayed behind. A dozen more were waiting for me outside, and two patrol cars swung through the heavy gates, pulling up alongside and spilling their crews.

There was another decision I had to make, within the next few seconds. If I didn't take the capsule I must get rid of it.

"Was he driving that Pobeda?"

"He says he slipped on the snow."

"Get Orlov here. He was in the van that crashed."

"Come on, out! March!"

I dropped to the ground and made my first decision. If I became certain, three days from now, four days, five, that I couldn't protect London, I would use the other method of blowing the fuse.

"Orlov! Is this the man you saw running from the Pobeda?"

"Yes, Captain!" His face peered into mine. "This is the one!"

Bloody fool, I'd come out of the smash like a bat out of hell and he didn't have time to take anything in because the van had rolled over. He wanted the kudos.

"Get him inside!"

There was a drain grid at one side of the steps and I let it drop and waited to hear if it made any sound, metal on metal, that would be audible above the tramp of their boots.

"Captain," I said loudly, exasperated, "you're making a mistake."

"I don't think so. But we shall see."

Green-painted walls, passages, doorways, uniformed clerks, a smell of leather, black tobacco, gun oil, and the ancient smells that breathe from the walls of old buildings.

"Search him in there and then bring him to my office. Is Colonel Vader in the building?"

"Yes, Captain."

"Tell him we have the suspect in Room 9."

Barred windows, and the smell of sweat and damp uniforms and my own fear.

"Good evening. My name is Vader."

"Good evening, Colonel. Kapista Kirov."

He was in uniform but without a cap.

"Would you like to smoke?"

I shook my head and he put the packet away. He was a short square man with red hair on his head, in his nostrils and on the backs of his hands. His face was heavily freckled and his eyes were honey-colored, a luminous amber. His hands were square and spadelike, and moved when he spoke, spreading out on the table or pushing at its edge; his nails were short and well trimmed, and there were no nicotine stains on his finger-tips. I found I was interested in him, because he was probably going to be the man who would force me to decide, in three days from now, four days, five, whether I must kill myself.

He tilted his chair back, and the light cast the shadows of his brows against his face, so that he looked as if he were frowning suddenly; but I don't think he was; he had an amiable face, well composed, contemplative. He looked the kind of man I could have soldiered with, in a different world; but there was the risk here of deceiving myself: I was also dangerous, and had been known to kill.

This wasn't his office we were sitting in; it was one of the interrogation rooms. There are photographs of them in London, overprinted to show where the microphone is, and giving all the dimensions: floor area, height of the small barred window, width of the door, so forth. The furniture is also featured: table, two upright chairs, single overhead lamp, nothing else. The lamp is angled rather more on the face of the man being interrogated, but this one wasn't blinding or even uncomfortable: this wasn't where they would bring the pressure on. They'd probably do that at the Serbsky Institute if I proved difficult. The London photographs are not meant to help us plan some kind of escape: things aren't so boyish inside Lubyanka. They're just meant to give us information we might need one day, on the principle that to be informed about one's environment is to give one confidence, because it's the unknown that makes people most afraid. I remembered looking at those photographs before I was sent out here for training in the Soviet theater three years ago. None of us likes having to look at them, as a required part of the briefing. We make a little joke and say we prefer the ones in *Playboy*.

"How do you feel?" the colonel asked me.

"Fine."

"Did they get all the glass out?"

"She did a good job." A large and efficient woman, smelling of antiseptic and perspiration, talking all the time behind her cotton-gauze mask as she put the stitches in.

He smiled with his square even teeth. "That was quite a crash."

"It wasn't a crash. I was carrying a mirror."

He smiled again.

The microphone was built into the lamp, invisible in the glare. The other man would be in the next room, working the tape recorder. On the wall behind me was the opaque screen, for flashing directions on the closed circuit; Vader was First Chief Directorate, counterespionage, but I didn't know whether he was handling this session himself or whether a superior would be using the screen to guide his questions.

"We don't want to waste each other's time," he said briefly, his hands pushing at the table. "Your name is not Kirov, and your papers are false. We've been through the main computer. Kapista Mikhail Kirov, born in Skvira in the Ukraine, died at the age of seven

months, of pneumonia. You should have bought some
better shoes." He smiled comfortably.

They too had their little jokes. "Shoes" meant walking papers, i.e. passport. But my papers weren't forged:
they were false, and he knew that. London doesn't forge
anything if it can get the real thing and put a photograph on it: it saves all the fussing about with sized
safety paper and fugitive dyes and watermarks and per-
forations and date-coded numerals. But the problem
with using genuine papers is that a good computer can
dig through the historical records and find the grave.

"Requiescat in pace," I said.

"M'm? Oh." He smiled dutifully.

The thing was, I couldn't lie and I couldn't tell the
truth. I had to say nothing.

In the silence I noticed the marks on the table: narrow parallel striations. I wondered what they were.

"I'd like you to tell me," Vader said, "about yourself."

He was different. I began listening.

"There's not much to tell," I said.

"All the same, I'd like to hear it."

"Well, I slipped on the snow, and broke the mirror.
Your people picked me up, thinking I was someone
else. That wasn't my fault."

He watched me with his head slightly on one side,
like an amiable ginger cat. "Very well, you slipped on
the snow and hurt yourself. But what are you doing
with false papers? What is your real identity?"

"I can't tell you that, Colonel. It would mean letting
someone down."

"Letting someone down?" In Russian the idiom is
perhaps ambiguous.

"Betraying them."

It was as far as I could go. He knew I wasn't Kapista Mikhail Kirov and he knew I was the man who'd come out of that crash and run for cover. But that was all he must know.

"Yes," he said easily, "I understand that. But we want to know all about you, and we shall succeed in doing that, as I'm sure you are aware. But I thought we might start like this, with just the two of us talking around a table." He leaned forward slightly, and his leather belt creaked. "I don't consider this a waste of time; I regard it as a gesture of hospitality. We are a hospitable people." He leaned back again.

"I appreciate that," I said.

He hadn't looked behind me yet, at the little screen. He was handling this on his own, so far. There wasn't a lot I could do to change the pattern. He was going to give me a chance of talking freely; then, if I chose not to, he was going to force me, or have me forced. I could speed things up or delay them, but not by much. It wasn't that I hadn't been prepared for this. Croder had pitched me into the field with light cover at short notice and I'd known what to expect if I got caught. This.

"Talking of hospitality," Vader said, "would you like a drink? A little vodka?"

"Not now."

"I would be happy to join you."

"You go ahead, if you'd like something yourself."

He shook his head, smiling. "I'm rather too fond of it," he said in a stage whisper, and the smile became a chuckle.

There was no point in speeding things up, but there was a point in delaying things: there might, somewhere in the next few days, be a chance of getting out of this alive, just a chance in a thousand. But it wasn't going to be fun, delaying things, because it would give me a lot more time to anticipate what they would finally do to me if that chance never came.

"Which intelligence branch are you in?" Vader asked with polite interest.

"What makes you think I'm in intelligence?"

"Oh, false papers, an attempt at surveillance, an attempt to avoid arrest, a reluctance to betray your cell. Good heavens, I've been through all that myself, plenty of times." The smile relaxed. "London, are you?"

"The problem," I said, "with security people is that they see everything from their own specialized point of view. I suppose that's true of most people. What I mean is, betrayal isn't confined to the intelligence services. One can betray a friend."

"Oh. Agreed. Also, of course, oneself." He pushed his red-haired hands across the surface of the table, watching them. "As a human creature, for example, you've no wish to suffer pain, but if the ego decides you shall submit to it, that would be a kind of betrayal. Wouldn't you say?" His hands stopped moving.

I supposed by this time Bracken would have started worrying. Extension 7 would have reported no signal at eight-fifteen, nine-fifteen, ten-fifteen, so forth. I wondered when he'd tell London. Shapiro gone, Quiller gone, not really their day. The red lamp over the board for Scorpion would still be on, but one day they'd have to switch it off. That man who'd been on the stool would reach up and flick the lever and go on sucking his bloody chewing gum, and Tilson would go padding quietly back to the Caff in his plaid slippers and bury his face in a cup of tea. *We got this from the Foreign Office just now. D16 have located Q in one of the Potma Complex camps, no trial, twenty years.* Better put out the light.

"We're getting into philosophy," I told Vader. "If I decide to go the whole way, rather than let down my friend, that's what I'll finish up doing."

For a few seconds we watched each other across the table; then he leaned back, tilting the chair under him. "As you know, intelligence agents feel a certain degree of—what shall we say?—sympathy for one another. Especially for their opposite numbers. A grudging regard, m'm? That's understandable, surely—we share the same kind of experience. So I'm inclined to put myself in your place, at the moment, because I've actually been there, once or twice." He looked up at me apologetically. "Though I have to admit that I was never in your exact predicament. What I want you to understand is that I dislike the idea of your having to submit to indignities, even though you may choose to let it happen. I really do dislike it very *much*." He leaned forward again, and spoke earnestly. "I'd see myself there, in your place. That is why I'm offering you this chance of doing all the talking around a table. You see?"

He really wanted an answer.

"Of course," I said. "I'd feel the same way myself."

"I'm sure." He smoothed the surface of the table. "I'm quite sure." Like the walls and the door, the table was green, with the wood grain showing through in places, especially where the long narrow striations had formed. "Also," he said, "I want you to know that I'm a family man. I have a charming wife and two pretty daughters, ten and twelve years old. With red hair—did you guess?" He threw back his head and laughed about this. "So you see, underneath the uniform there's just an ordinary man like yourself, with very human instincts. This is another reason why I hope you'll save us both a lot of misery. Surely you understand?"

"Yes," I said, "I understand."

"Then let's make a fresh start." He tilted his head in curiosity. "Who are you?"

This was the first phase.

"Who are you?" he screamed, and brought the flat of his hand crashing against the table. *"Who are you?"*

"I can't tell you!" The chair toppled and hit the floor as I got up and faced him: his rage had got me onto my feet because he was towering over me and I thought he might lash out and I had to be ready—in this mood he could half kill me if I let him.

"Your identity! Your *identity!* I demand to know your *identity!"* The amber eyes burned in his face.

This was the second phase and I'd been expecting it because it was a classic procedure and he'd been so bloody cozy the first time that I knew he was going to do this the next time we met, but it still took some handling because his rage wasn't spurious: he wasn't a man who liked being blocked.

"Are you English?" His hand hit the table again. "Are you from London? Answer me!" The table was rocking. I moved away from it, wary. He'd be strong and fast and well trained and I didn't know his breaking point, the point when he'd lose his control—he was working for Mother Russia and for Mother Russia he'd smash a million Englishmen against the wall.

"Answer me!"

The blood had left my face: I could feel it. It had gone to the muscles and the adrenaline was ready: the organism was triggered and what I had to do now was watch him, watch his every move in case he lost control and wanted blood for the sake of blood.

"Tell me who you are! Tell me!"

His wide leather belt came off so fast that I was into a *kokutsudachi* stance but he brought it down across the flat top of the table with a sound that cracked through the confines of the small bare room and I reacted: the edge of my hand was lined up with the carotid nerve of his neck and the mental rehearsal was already over and the hand was ready to lift and strike with the accuracy of an automaton.

"You were carrying false papers and you were following one of our citizens and you tried to avoid arrest and now you refuse to explain your actions!" He took two paces toward me and I sank an inch lower, solidifying the stance. "Do you know how many years that would get you in a forced-labor camp? *Do you?*"

I would let him take one more step. If I let him come closer than that he could do some damage. The element of surprise was on his side: when you don't know *when* the opponent is going to attack there's no real problem—you just have to wait; but when you don't know *if* he's going to attack it can be very difficult because you're liable to let the hairspring off the hook and get to him first and it might not be necessary. I didn't want to break his clavicle or paralyze him by going in too fast: they wouldn't like me for that.

He started shouting again, bringing the belt cracking down for emphasis, stopping to glare at me with his eyes narrowed to slits and his teeth bared. "How do we know what harm you might not be planning against our country? How do we know what appalling danger you might not be placing our citizens in? This man you were following—did you intend to kill him? *Did you?*"

The belt snaked down and left another weal across the top of the table. The sweat was bright on his face under the white light, trickling to the edge of his collar. He was following the prescribed routine but he also believed in what he was saying: this was his city, his country, and I was an unknown danger. I could see his point of view.

"Who was this man you were following?"

When I heard that, I didn't believe it.

"Who was he?" His rage was genuine and he couldn't think clearly enough to use subterfuge, yet he couldn't be serious about this. I just didn't believe it.

"Answer me!"

The belt sent a sliver of wood flying from the table.

"I don't know," I said.

It was the first time I'd spoken and the sound of someone else's voice got through to him and he stood still and stared at me. "What are you standing like that for?" he asked with suspicion. "Are you thinking of attacking me?" His wide chest heaved under his uniform as his lungs worked to recover oxygen. "Do—you —know—what they would do to you for attacking a colonel of the *Komitet Gosudarstvennoy Bezopasnost?* For attacking him physically in his own headquarters? *They—would—have—you—shot!"*

He was being very Russian. Anyone who can read a newspaper knows that once you're inside the headquarters of the *Komitet Gosudarstvennoy Bezopasnost* on the wrong end of the banana you're not going to come out looking all that fit. But I wasn't interested in that. I was getting terribly interested in this thing about the man I'd been following, because Vader didn't seem to know his name. Or mine.

It was unbelievable. The first time he'd asked me who I was I knew I'd have to start listening because this was a different approach: they usually want you to feel they know *everything* about you. What I couldn't believe was that Ignatov had made a phone call in the street and told them to pick me up and they'd done that

*but they didn't know his name and they didn't know
mine.*

Something wrong there.

"Of course I'd get shot," I told him, and turned
away and folded my arms. "But what d'you think I'm
going to do if you start putting that fucking belt of
yours across me—just stand there?"

He dropped it onto the table and started walking
from one wall to the other, his square-toed boots landing flat on the floor with no spring in them, his arms
held slightly forward like a bear's, as if he were looking for something to break, for some kind of life to
crush out. He was my height and heavier and all muscle
and he could kill me in an even match but I didn't
think it was even because they're exceptionally fussy at
Norfolk: they don't send you into the field unless you
can take on a tank and get the tracks off without a lot
of deeping breathing.

"Who were you following?" He swung round, hitting
a fist into a palm.

Back on that tack.

Fascinating.

"How the hell should I know?" I asked him. "I was
following him to find out who he was!"

"I don't have to accept that!"

You bloody well do.

He started walking again, from wall to wall. He must
have seen a lot of this place, look at that table. "Why
did you want to find out who he was? Who put you on
to him?"

It was difficult because we didn't really have a topic
for conversation. He knew I was some kind of agent
because we get to recognize the signs in one another:
my behavior in this room, confined with a KGB colonel

who was ready to flay me alive, was totally different from the behavior of an innocent tourist who'd slipped on the snow and got snatched by mistake because he'd injured his face—*you can't do this to me, I want my lawyer here, I'll have you charged with wrongful arrest,* so forth. This man knew I was an agent but as an agent I couldn't tell him anything and he understood that, and he was annoyed because he was trying to build a reputation as a red-hot interrogator who could get information out of anyone they sent to him and without having to throw him to the clowns to work over, because that takes a lot of time if you want to go after *all* the information he's got in his brain: you can't rush things, it's no good just poking a red-hot needle into his urethra and saying *now talk* because he'll either pass out or scream unintelligible things and the most you can do is to get one word out of him at a time, one name, one target, one key to one code; you've got to spend days at it, with some of them.

Vader stopped walking and picked up the belt. He'd lost a lot of his color and the sweat was drying on him and there was foam at the corners of his mouth. "I will ask you one more time. *Who are you?*"

"Kapista Kirov. I told you, the computers have gone on the blink."

It wasn't a lie and it wasn't the truth and he knew that; it was all I was going to tell him, nothing, like saying it looks as if we're going to get some more rain again.

"Very well!" The belt hit the table and the sound went round the walls like an explosion. "You realize we shall get this information from you in the end, don't you? Of course you do. We shall use every method

available to us, every technique, every refinement. *We shall show you no mercy.* You understand me?"

"Yes."

"Very well."

Bring on the clowns.

9 / RAINBOWS

The rat sat preening its whiskers.

I watched it.

It sat with its rear paws spread on the ground, their tips visible at the edge of the gray fur body. The front paws worked rhythmically, pulling each fine whisker through the toes from the root to the tip.

It hadn't seen the snake.

I watched the snake. It was rock-still, coiled in a perfect ring with the angular head slightly lifted and pointing in the direction of the rat. The distance between them was about three feet. The snake was large, and I could see that its length was quite sufficient to carry the jaws that far when it struck.

The rat was facing at right angles to the snake. Its round black eye reflected the environment in miniature. I think it saw the snake, in terms of light reception by the retina, but didn't know what it was: the brain interpreted it as a rock formation, or just a pattern of light and shade. Otherwise it wouldn't be sitting there.

I detected movement now in the snake, though it was so slow that it was almost an illusion: the pointed head was drawing back, millimeter by millimeter, across the coils, the neck flexing to keep the head pointing directly at the rat. At the same time the coils were tensing, as the muscular energy gathered and flowed, preparing for the whiplash speed of the strike.

The rat was oblivious of this movement. Once, it turned its head for an instant, but away from the snake, catching some small sound that escaped me. Then it went on preening.

I watched quietly, wondering if—*then the snake struck like a whip and the rat*—

"*Wake up!*"

The rat tried to leap but—

"*Wake up! Wake up!*"

I swung my head up and opened my eyes and called out: "All right, I'm awake now, why don't you bugger off?"

Blinding light.

"Are you awake?"

"Yes. Bugger off!"

The light was above the door and angled downward, a flood bulb in it so that there was nowhere in the cell where I could get away from it. The glare hid the small sliding panel immediately below the light, so that I couldn't see him watching me. It was the third time he'd woken me up. Third, or fourth? It didn't matter, but I'd have to start counting things like that because some of them would be important. Call it the third time and start counting from there.

Bloody snake. I'd dreamed about that before; I suppose it was that long leather belt whipping through the air at the table. Where was Vader now? Sleeping? They'd taken my watch and there wasn't a window, only a ventilation grille near the ceiling, clamped across a square of darkness. That didn't mean it was night, necessarily: this was a close-confinement chamber for sleep deprivation and disorientation, so they would have fixed the grille accordingly. The metabolic clock pulsing in my system told me it was midnight, give or take an hour; but that wasn't reliable because I'd fallen asleep three times. Three, or four? Three. Yes.

A man screamed suddenly from somewhere close, and I sat listening to him with the sweat springing on my skin.

Ignore. Ignore and do some work.

Of course they'd started with an advantage. Today was Wednes—no, yes, Wednesday, and on Monday I'd still been in England hang-gliding over the cliffs, and from the time when Norton had escorted me to London that bastard Croder had had me on a pinball table— Berlin, Hannover, Leipzig, Moscow—and the only sleep I'd had was a couple of hours on the mountainside after the truck had crashed and a few hours at the safe house last night—five or six hours in sixty-four, not enough, and if I'd known the rat was going to sit there I would have—*look out it's going to strike again*—

"Wake up!"

"I *am* awake! Can't you tell when someone's asleep or awake, for Christ's sake?"

"You were falling asleep!"

"Go and screw yourself."

Then the man started screaming again next door and I had to listen to it until it was cut off abruptly, and all I could hear was my own breath releasing.

Bastards. Do some work.

Oh yes, well, the terribly interesting thing is this: they don't know my name, and they don't know Ignatov's. Unbelievable. I mean, what did he say when he phoned them: there's a man in a Pobeda tagging me, pick him up? That wouldn't have been enough to trigger all that action—a whole fleet of police cars and militia. They'd have asked him who I was, and why it was so important. *But Ignatov hadn't known.* He didn't know anything about me. So what had he told them? What information had he given them, to persuade them to throw all that action at me? *He didn't have any information.*

Sweating. I was starting to sweat, because of the cerebration and the heat of the floodlight. All right, that's one thing. Take the other. These people here don't know Ignatov's name either, or anything about him, except that he made a phone call from a public box. What had he shown that militiaman, to get a salute? What name had he given, over the phone? He couldn't have given them any name, or Vader would know it—and believe me, he wouldn't have asked me for that man's name unless he'd wanted it: it wasn't part of the technique or a feint question because he was in a rage at the time, piping hot. So there you are: an unknown man rings up the security forces and tells them to pick up another unknown man and that is precisely what they do, in full force and with no questions asked. Unbelievable.

I suppose that was why Vader was so bloody annoyed.

But don't forget one thing, old boy. This isn't so funny. It looks like a Judas operation. A Judas somewhere in Bracken's team. Out to blow me. Successfully.

Not funny.

Bracken ought to be told. Vader, old horse, can I use your phone?

"Turn round!"

"What?"

"Turn round. Face the light."

"Why don't you buzz off?" You come in here, my

son, and I'll go for your throat and you'll never know your eyes popped out before you snuffed. I'm getting cross.

"*I'm getting cross!*" I yelled at the light.

"Repeat that."

Watch it. Watch it. Did I use English then?

I am a Russian citizen. I speak only Russian. I will—

"*Repeat that.*"

"Oh shut up, will you?" Yes, I'd said it in English and the bastard had caught it. He might not recognize English but he'd heard something foreign. This was getting dangerous.

Perhaps it was time to blow the fuse.

I had the whole of London in my head, inside this sweating brightly illuminated skull: names, duties, operations, D16 liaison 9, signals, codes, the whole thing. It was time to think about the fuse. But before I did that I ought to tell Bracken he had a Judas in Moscow who'd blown me, just as he'd blown Schrenk, a Judas working through Ignatov.

Footsteps.

Or it could be Ignatov himself. That'd shake them, by God. *I need all info on Natalya Fyodorova, senior clerk, Kremlin office, companion of subject before arrest. Also all info on Pyotr Ignatov, Party member, often in subject's company, no other details known.* Shake them rigid.

Was Bracken trying to get a signal to me, while I was sitting here in this bloody place? *Re info requested: Ignatov is one of our people. State reason for request.*

No reason, really, except that I don't like being blasted off the street. Nor did Schrenk. Signal ends.

Query: if Ignatov is a Judas working inside Bracken's operation, why don't the KGB know about him? That's a nasty one. He'd been coming out of the telephone box, not looking around him in the beginning, beginning to snow, with the ice cream waving about in air, the air, trying to catch, *watch it—*

"Wake up! Wake up!"

I got onto my feet and threw a side kick at the door, controlling it enough to make a noise without hurting my foot.

"Does that sound as if I'm asleep?"

"Keep away from the door!"

Voices. They were talking. I'd forgotten about the footsteps. I backed away from the door because this could be interesting, it could be someone else wanting to talk to me and I felt murderous and I might decide to take someone with me, a half fist into the thyroid with enough force to kill, a matter of .5 second and nothing they could do in time to save him.

Watch that too. Emotion was dangerous because they'd got a red lamp over a board marked Scorpion in London and the executive in the field for the operation was holed up in a disorientation cell in Lubyanka prison and he'd have to get out and if he couldn't even control his emotions he'd never make it, *so start thinking with the brain instead of the gut, this is life or death.*

Bolts drawing back.

Two men.

One of them beckoned. "You will come with us."

They walked on each side of me along the green-painted corridor, and stopped outside a door halfway along.

Assume clowns now.

"Won't you sit down?"

Different room.

"I'd rather stand. I need some exercise."

Id est: I am not sleepy.

Different room *or just a different table,* this one with a plain surface with no belt marks on it. Need to observe more efficiently: I ought to know whether this is a different room or only a different table.

"I expect you do," he said apologetically. "I'm not responsible for everything that goes on here, you must understand. Otherwise"—he spread out his hand—"your accommodation would be different."

He waited for me to say something, but I couldn't think of anything. I had to detach myself from him and work out my own game plan while he worked out his, making contact only when I needed information. I had to start thinking, and if possible, acting. The emotional phase was over: they'd taken me quite a long way into sleep deprivation and produced an initial reaction—childishness, the urge to attack them. They were probably going to take me much deeper: they hadn't started using this particular technique with the intention of stopping halfway. But from now on I would have to work out the necessary defenses.

"I'm afraid I rather lost my temper," Colonel Vader said. "I do hope you'll forgive me." He paused but I didn't say anything. "We people have too lively a sense of the dramatic, perhaps—make a lot of noise"—with a rueful laugh—"let off a lot of steam, m'm? Look at our music, look at our grand opera, you see what I mean?"

He stepped rhythmically from wall to wall, declining to sit down, since I wouldn't. He had manners, give him that. I began pacing too, for the exercise and because it would express freedom of movement; but I went from left to right, while he went from right to left: it would look ridiculous if both of us went the same way.

"Prince Igor," I said. "Always admired it. Lot of fire."

"That's exactly what I mean!" he said in relief, and turned to me with a laugh of understanding. "As a matter of fact I don't remember much about what I said to you, and all I hope is that it was nothing too offensive." He spread his hand again. "Put it down to an unseemly outburst of Russian temperament, m'm?"

As if speaking to a non-Russian. Noted.

"Bit hard on the table," I said, and he laughed boy-ishly, deep from the chest. We went on walking, like two prisoners in an exercise yard, talking to each other across an invisible wall. He walked neatly with his hands folded behind his back and his polished boots clumping down solidly on the parquet floor, heel and toe together.

"It's difficult for you," he said, and stopped suddenly, swinging the chair on his side halfway round and resting one boot on it, facing me with his intelligent amber eyes. "And quite frankly, you know, it's difficult for me too."

I went on walking, but turned to look at him from time to time. He was being quite civilized, and that quiet murderous rage I'd felt in the detention cell had evaporated.

"Why don't you make it easier?" I asked him, not meaning to be funny. A full colonel must carry quite a lot of clout in this place.

"My dear fellow, I only wish I could. I say that quite sincerely." He'd lowered his voice, and I had to stop walking to listen. I had the strange urge to swing my chair halfway round and rest one foot on it, but that too would be ridiculous, as if there were only one of us here, and a mirror. "The problem," he said quietly, "is that I would need your cooperation. And you're proving—how shall I put it?—rather hesitant."

I compromised and swung the chair round and sat on it with my arms folded along its back, so that I could face him. His smile was tentative as he waited for me to comment on that, and his expression was perfectly genuine. It occurred to me that if I admitted what he already suspected—that I was in fact from London, he might reciprocate by—*you're falling asleep, you're not thinking straight, he's not perfectly genuine and he's not being civilized and he doesn't have any manners and if you admit you're from London you're right in the shit, so start waking up.*

He'd begun to blur in front of me, swaying back and then forward. I got into focus again and he stopped. This was one of the classic techniques: interrogation sessions alternating between friendliness and hostility to get you so confused you started blurting things out. *And you always believe it'll never work because you're too bloody smart.*

"That," he said with quiet charm, "is the problem."

"Problem?"

"We would require your cooperation, if we were to make things easier for you." He stood away from the chair and took a pace or two, deliberating, coming back. "If you could overcome your hesitation, you see, we might arrange something to our mutual advantage." Another rueful laugh. "I'm sorry to have to beat about the bush like this, but I can't trust you until you trust me." He sat on the chair backward, just as I was sitting, as if in sympathy.

Not in sympathy.

"Arrangement?" I asked him.

Kept having to refocus.

"Yes." His honey-colored eyes played directly onto

my own for a moment as he deliberated again. "You know what I'm going to do? I'm going to take a risk, to show we can be just as sincere as I know you would really like to be. I'm going to trust you." He sat back a little, regarding me with open candor. "Now how does that sound?"

I allowed an appropriate period of hesitation before I spoke.

"Generous."

He sat back and slapped his big square hands together, pleased as a boy. "I'm delighted you think so, I really am delighted. Yes, I'm being generous, I freely admit it." With his head tilted slightly, as if he'd suddenly seen me in a new light: "You know, I was certain we'd find a way of putting our heads together, if we tried. Now this arrangement . . ." He hesitated a fraction, then went on: "I'm going to put it to you quite frankly. There's someone we want to find, very badly, and if you were able to tell us where he is, we'd bring him in and exchange him for you. We'd let you go." He leaned forward confidentially. "His name is Schrenk."

I tilted my chair back, watching him. He was waiting for me to say something, but I didn't want to commit myself without thinking it over, and he got impatient and stood up and whirled his saber. *"Slovo o polku Igoreve!* You said you always admired it, remember?" He threw out his chest and began singing, his voice—

"Wake up! Wake up!"

I jerked my head back.

"Sorry."

Blinding light.

"You must stay awake."

"Yes. I'll do that."

I sat up straighter on the stool and let my head go

back against the wall. He knew what I was doing, but it was all right because I had to keep my eyes open, so he'd know if I dozed off again. With my head back, the light was fierce, a burning disk that wavered at the rim, as if I were staring into the sun; but at the same time I could slip into a kind of half sleep, somewhere between the alpha and theta waves, without losing too much awareness. They'd let me take off my jacket, and I was sitting with my arms resting on my thighs, with the sweat trickling down to the elbows: I was soaked with it, because of the lamp's heat and the stress going on in the organism. My head was a ball floating in the sea of light, drifting and bobbing, with the images going on inside it.

His name is Schrenk. That threw me, yes. Threw me completely. So they hadn't got him. So where was he? I think it was okay, the way I reacted, I mean by not reacting. Shook my head, don't know him. But threw me, really. Bracken ought to know. Vader, old boy, mind if I use your blower?

No idea of what time now, day, night, anything. Maybe night now, it seemed worse, diurnal rhythms very slow, cortical vigilance down, way down, down—

"Wake up! Wake up!"

Shouting in the glare.

"Sorry. Wake now."

Reticular formation lagging, yes, the process thoroughly understood, tell you everything you need to know at Norfolk, bloody place, wish I, was wish I, was there. Dogs barking somewhere, hate those bloody things. I'd begun hearing them same time when I'd seen the fish swimming in the light, all colors of rainbow, swimming round and round and round and—

"Wake up! Wake up!"

Oh shit.

I straightened up again and felt for the wall with the back of my head and then took it off again because I had to do some thinking. I was leaving it late now. I knew they'd got me. They were going to trot me along to Vader again and I wouldn't be able to take any more, I'd just go to sleep and they'd keep on waking me up and finally they'd bring on the clowns and I'd start talking without even knowing what I was doing, blow London, no go.

Capsule.

But that was down the drain, so I'd have to do it the other way, bite through the median cubital artery and wait sixty seconds, *finis,* Lorenz had done it in Chile when the terror squads had strung him upside down from a swing in a children's playground, he didn't want to play any more, messy but then he wasn't going to have to clear it up, *finito.* One little problem though: they never left me alone. Even when I asked for the lav they stood there with the door open in case I shoved my head in. Never left me alone. Watching me now, man up there with his eyes in the hole behind the hot bright light, *bastards,* lea' me alone, lea' me alone, you *bastards,* all I want is sixty seconds, bite and then spurt, spurt, spurt and London safe.

Man screaming next door. Me screaming? No. Other man.

Shuddup screaming, can't stand it.

Sweet Jesus I want to sleep.

Wake up and think. Think about London, it's the last chance. But they won't lea' me alone, watching me all the time, I could do it in sixty seconds but they keep going round and round and rainbows round and—

"Wake up! Wake up!"

"Yes. Yes. Wake now."

Sleep. Softly go . . . sleep.

London.

What? Yes, all right, do it in the room with the table. Only the two of us. Vader and me. Energy of rage and finish him off and then bite the artery, bite, bite before anyone comes, can do that, yes, can do that.

"Wake up!"

"Yes. Wake up, yes."

Remember London.

10 / RAGE

So this was the place was it.

I'd thought it was going to be some other place, so often: the street outside the Hotel Africa in Tunis when the car had gone up, or ten fathoms down at Longitude 114° and Latitude 22° in the waters off Hong Kong, or in that stinking room on the Amazon when she'd found me there and gone on squeezing the trigger. No. Not in any of those places.

Here. In a city under snow, in a bleak green-painted room twelve feet by fourteen with a door two feet eleven inches wide and a window five feet three inches high and nothing in it but a lamp and two chairs and a table and the man: the last man I would ever see, the man who didn't know I was the last man he himself would ever see. We had a lot in common.

I don't want to die.

Oh it's you is it. Sniveling little organism starting to panic. Shut up, it won't hurt.

We can get out of here if we try.

Oh really.

The light shone down. This wasn't the table with the

smooth top; it was the one with the narrow marks on it. The two guards had only just gone out, shutting the door. Vader was standing under the window, watching me with the blank stare of the predator that contemplates the prey without emotion, his honey-colored eyes unblinking and his big square hands hanging by his sides, his booted feet set in a balanced stance ready for instant movement. He was a strong man, and young for his rank. The room was so quiet that I could hear the faint rustling creak of his leather belt as he breathed.

"My patience is exhausted!" All on one note and with the words drawn out, his mouth moving like a trap. The sound went into my head and beat there, hammering. I hadn't been ready for it, and my nerves weren't too good: it made me blink and he noticed it, I saw it in his eyes, the satisfaction of the victor in the presence of the vanquished.

Sleep. Don't take any—

London. Remember London.

My head came up a fraction and I was warned: it had been dropping, degree by degree, as the soporific wave had crept over me despite the shock of his voice. London, yes.

"Do you understand?"

The voice of a bull, roaring out of the barrel chest and drumming in the room.

Think about what has to be done. It has to be done in the next sixty seconds, or I won't have the strength left.

I don't want to die.

Shuddup.

I had to take him down, and I had to do it with all the speed I could manage, and with all the force. Standing here thinking about it, I could believe I would never do it; but I knew from experience what the mind can make the body do, if enough depends on it. I wasn't worried about that. Vader was mine, unless he'd had my specific style of training. The enemy was in myself, in my emotions, in the undisciplined tides of feeling released by the knowledge of imminent death.

Moira.

Is that your own code?

Five hundred roses for Moira. To be delivered only after she has been informed by the Bureau.

Where was she now?

The tides of feeling, yes, that would have to be ignored, because they were irrelevant, and dangerous.

Take him down, and with as little force as necessary, so that I would find the strength. Let him come close first.

"I have given you every possible chance of cooperating! And you have refused!" He began walking, dropping his boots squarely on the worn parquet, walking toward me. "Do you happen to *enjoy* the kind of interrogation you will receive at the Serbsky Institute? M'm?" He stopped within three feet of me. It wasn't close enough. "Are you a masochist?"

Sleep. Dear God let me sleep.

He was blurring again in front of me, his thick body swaying gently backward and forward, sending me to— *wake up, come on, wake up.*

"Answer me!"

Yes. Keep him talking. Keep him close.

"I can't think straight, that's all. Too tired." I heard the words slurring, couldn't quite recognize the voice.

"Too *tired!* And you think that is all that's going to happen to you? *Do you?"*

Rehearse. A preliminary *shankutsu,* my left foot behind his right heel, with a spinning *nagashi* at the *jodan* level, my right fingers hooking for the eyes. Then the knife edge to the throat, half an inch above the khaki serge collar. Then the work on myself, at the median cubital artery. Rehearse.

"No. I know what's going to happen to me."

Rehearse. *Shankutsu, nagashi,* eyes and the knife edge.

"Then why do you refuse to cooperate?"

Shouting at me as if I were fifty yards away, his voice roaring inside my skull.

"Told you," I said. "I'd betray a friend."

"Friend!" He pulled one of the chairs away from the table and sent it crashing into a corner of the room, one of its legs flying off and hitting the barred window. *"What friend?"* He came closer, his amber eyes staring into my face. *"You mean Schrenk?"* He came right up to me. *"Do you mean your friend Schrenk?"*

He was close enough and I shifted my left foot and got the *nagashi* spinning and in the next tenth of a second I saw surprise beginning in his eyes as he started pitching back with my foot blocking his heel before I formed the claw hand and raked at his face. He wasn't off balance yet but his arm swung up and he lost the last of his equilibrium and the strike missed my head and he fell hard, harder than I was ready for, with my fingers too far from his eyes and my hand forming the knife edge to bridge the gap and swing down for the throat with enough force to kill, but something crashed and I was on top of him and striking much too short as the door hit the wall and they took me from behind, pulling my arms back and locking them so that I had to stop moving, no go, it was no go.

Rage burning inside my skull. Rage and the hot bright light.

My head had been dropping onto my chest and at

first I had pulled it up again from habit to avoid that bloody man's voice up there where the light was; then I had let it rest there, my head, and nothing had happened, he hadn't yelled at me to wake up. I might even have slept, but I didn't know for how long. Not long: the urge to drop my head again and sleep and go on sleeping was overwhelming, but I couldn't do that: I had to work.

Rage against myself, of course, for getting it wrong, for not thinking, for not realizing they must have a closed-circuit television camera behind the dark glass of the window: they wouldn't be so stupid as to leave one of their colonels in there with people who might not like him.

They'd been worried about him but he'd just said I'm all right and walked out of the room without looking at me, as if I didn't exist, as if I hadn't just tried to kill him. I got the point: he'd been obliged to brush off a fly. We hadn't known each other for long but we'd learned things about each other and he'd learned I had a streak of pride and was therefore sensitive.

Work, yes.

I let my head fall again, and waited, but the man didn't shout. I shut my eyes and waited again, but nothing happened. He might not be there. *He might not be watching me.*

The median cubital artery runs down the inside of the arm and it's easy to reach at the wrist but the action is obvious, so I took off my shoe and lobbed it up at the light and made sure it missed the bulb before I caught it.

"Stop that! What do you think you're doing?"

Message received.

"It's too bloodly bright," I said, and sat down again on the stool and put my shoe on and turned round to

face the wall and let my head go down. That seemed to
be all right because he didn't say anything. I was to be
watched but not forced to stay awake or face the light.
What had he said? The Serbsky Institute. Where the
clowns worked.

When?

There was nothing in here I could drain into. There
were only the walls and the floor and this stool and the
lamp. I was sitting with my back to him now and I
could fold my arms and let my head go down, heavy
with sleep, until my mouth was against the inside of
one wrist, and he might not see the movement of my
jaws from behind; but once it started flowing there'd be
a gallon and a half and there was nothing to drain into:
he'd see it dripping onto the floor and he'd have time
to come in here and use the pressure point and call for
help and Vader would ask for a transfusion because he
wasn't finished with me yet, he'd only just started. They
wanted to find Schrenk and they thought I knew where
he was.

I could feel the heat of the lamp on the back of my
head. My shadow was clear-cut, swelling and contracting against the wall as I swayed an inch forward, an
inch back, trying to stay awake, trying to think. It became a slow rhythm, and at some time I must have
slept, still more or less upright on the stool, backward
and forward, rocking like an animal in a cage. The
footsteps came out of a dream and into reality, thudding from the distance along the corridor outside my
cell.

Then voices.

I stayed where I was: it was comfortable here against
the wall, with my companionable shadow. This had become my home, my *querencia:* this place, defined by my

shadow's height and my shadow's width, was part of my
identity now. They mustn't—

"Out!"

Mustn't take me away.

"Stand up! Out!"

I hadn't heard them opening the door. I suppose I'd
been asleep, dreaming about identity.

When I looked round I saw Colonel Vader there
with three other men, two of them in uniform. He stood
gazing in at me with that predatory stare for a moment;
then a look of disgust came to his face. "He stinks!
Put him under a shower and find some sort of clothing
for him, and don't be long about it!" He turned and
went out.

He shouldn't have said that.

"Come on, out!"

I went with them along the corridor to the prisoners'
ablutions: a stone floor and zinc basins and open toilets
and a row of showers, the water freezing, hitting me
like a burst of glass fragments, shrinking my head and
roaring in my ears, *he shouldn't have said that,* the
block of abrasive soap scouring my skin, the face
wound burning and throbbing but my eyes resting,
soothed at last after the glare of that blinding light. A
strip of sacking for a towel and my hair still wet when
they took me away and threw me a sweater to wear instead of my shirt: it had been soaked in sweat and that
was why he'd said what he had, correction, that was the
excuse.

My whole body tingling and most of the torpor gone
from my mind, *remember London.* "Come on, in here!"
Back in the cell again, not mine this time: a smaller
one with no window, a slatted bench with one leg at an
angle and bloodstains across the top and repeated on
the wall, the smell of the human animal that had been

in here, *Schrenk?* There was no means of knowing, there were fifty of these cells in the ground-floor block. "Wait here."

No option: they slammed the door and locked it.

I realize, yes, that with my shirt like that I was stinking to high heaven, but he shouldn't have pointed it out. He had done it to humiliate me, crossing the dividing line between men and the area where one is a man and the other has become a pig. It's a critical stage in the business of interrogation, and he had introduced it deliberately, I knew that. But it didn't make any difference.

I walked from wall to wall in the narrow cell, seven paces and back from the door to the window. Drops of water still fell from my wet hair, and I pulled off the sweater they'd given me and tousled my head with it, putting it on again and feeling the dampness against my chest and back. The lamp in here was a naked bulb of low wattage and gave no heat; I began shivering, and walked faster. There wasn't anything else I could do: I could see his eyes every time I moved toward the door, watching from the oblong panel above it.

They came for me soon afterward, three plainclothesmen and Vader, still in uniform and now wearing a greatcoat and peaked cap.

"Is he washed?"

"Yes, Colonel."

"Bring him, then. Hurry."

It was sometime in the night: pilot lamps were burning along the corridors and the big high windows were dark, with a seepage of neon light from the streets along their frames.

"Tell this man where we are taking him, Grekov."

One of them spoke from beside me. "We are taking you to the Serbsky Institute." He was a squat man in a dark coat; I could smell tobacco on him. The two others had an air of higher rank, walking in front of us, one on each side of Vader.

"Tell him he will now be interrogated under extreme physical duress."

"You will now be interrogated under extreme physical duress," grunted the man beside me. But the sense of it didn't get through to me: I was thinking of the other thing Vader had said. The man beside me was armed: I could smell the gun oil. They would all be armed. They walked in step with Vader, but I didn't follow the rhythm. Once, as we passed the main offices near the entrance to the building, the squat man looked down and gave my foot a quick little kick, to get me into step, but I didn't do what he wanted.

"Has he heard of the Serbsky Institute, Grekov?"

"Have you heard of the Serbsky Institute?"

I didn't answer. Vader would have to ask me himself.

"Repeat the question!"

"Have you heard of the Serbsky Institute? Answer?"

They bothered me with their voices; I needed to think. But I had heard, yes, of the Serbsky Institute of Forensic Psychiatry: it's an old granite building with iron gates and armed sentries, containing mostly political wards where those straying from the Party line are submitted to "special diagnosis" and subsequent "treatment." One of the techniques involves wrapping the patient in wet canvas, and as it slowly dries he is asked if he feels ready to change his heretical views, or confess, or reveal whatever he is there to reveal.

I didn't know how Schrenk had held out against that, without losing his mind. Maybe he'd lost it, and it was an animal that had escaped, not Schrenk at all.

"Have you heard of—"

"That's enough, Grekov. He probably doesn't understand the question."

"Colonel."

Then one of the big doors swung back and we went down the steps into the snow. The city had changed since I'd been brought in here: the slate roofs and parapets were white under the black sky, with the greenish neon glowing on it theatrically. The snow was soft under our feet. As we reached the black saloon the man called Grekov opened one of the rear doors and told me to get in. Vader went round to the other side. Another man was right behind me and as I climbed in he gave me a push and got in after me, slamming the door. I was now wedged between him and Vader with the two others in front, Grekov at the wheel. The windows were all closed and the door locks down.

When Grekov started the engine and switched on the headlights the guards at the main gates swung one of them open and we drove through. I could hear chains clinking on the tires: the snow was still falling and Dzerzhinsky Square was covered. There was no traffic. I couldn't see a clock but I was watching for one. The heater was now blowing and the chill of my wet hair began warming.

I had strange feelings about the man beside me. He shouldn't have said that. I knew it was part of the routine but that didn't make any difference: he shouldn't have said it. This comprised most of my feelings about him, but there were other things. I'd seen him as a friendly, cultivated man and as a brute in a towering rage, and these roles had alternated so that my attitude toward him had started to be ambivalent: he'd got closer than he knew to burrowing into my mind while it was half submerged in sleep. I think in another twenty-four hours he would have got me blurting things out between hallucinations. I even believe he might have known how close he'd come to success, but what he couldn't take was the way I'd attacked him and actually got him onto the floor before the guards had come in. It had hit a major nerve in him, deep in the psyche, and all he lived for now was to see me under treatment at the Serbsky Institute, to hear me scream when the clowns went to work. I believe he was that sensitive.

I too am a sensitive man.

One of the chains was slightly loose and kept hitting the underneath of the wing, producing a hollow sound like a drummer tapping for the dead. I could see the gold domes of St. Basil's now in Red Square, and the clock in Spassky Tower—at too sharp an angle to let me read it. The city was beautiful tonight, its floodlit domes and spires and minarets half lost in the veils of falling snow; I was seeing it as I'd never seen it before, like a tourist with time to spare.

Colonel Vader was holding himself away from me as much as he could, and letting me know it. I didn't stink any more but I was still untouchable, the pig thing that had been squatting there in its cage, mired in its own dirt and unable to urinate or defecate without begging permission. That was his picture of me now and he wanted me to know it; he wasn't prepared even to talk to me without using Grekov as a sanitizing intermediary. I didn't mind what he did now: it would be insignificant compared to what he had done, what he had said, when he'd come into my cell. I don't think he realized that.

Grekov drove quite fast, considering the state of the streets; I suppose the snow wasn't deep yet and there were the chains on the tires and he knew his way. It wouldn't have been possible without the chains because the car would have gone straight on with the front wheels locked over. At one stage I caught sight of Vader's face in the fraction of a second, distorting as the rear wheel went over it, but the rest wasn't easily remembered because everything went so fast: I think one of them had a gun out before I reached the steering wheel but there wasn't any shot. The initial move wasn't complicated: I had to hit the back of the seat to produce the necessary momentum and get to the wheel as soon as I could. My right foot smashed into the face of the man on that side and I felt the softness caving in but my main concern was to reach that wheel and wrench it over. My shoulder hit the back of the driver's head and pitched him forward and then the chains bit and the car lurched and lost traction and slid and then lurched again with the chains gouging into the road surface and swinging us halfway round before it rolled.

The speed at this time wasn't much less than the eighty k.p.h. I'd seen on the speedometer just before I began moving, and the roll took us through most of the deceleration phase and lasted until the rear end hit a streetlamp and the windscreen blew out in a shower of glass. Someone had begun screaming and it took me a little time to realize it was the man who'd put a stranglehold on me: I'd broken his thumb to make him release it. It was soon after this that I saw the gun in someone's hand but I wasn't worried, because he couldn't use it: we were in the middle of a storm and the car was still moving fast enough to kill the lot of us if it hit another streetlamp at the wrong angle. It was sliding on its side at this time and the front end was coming round in a flurry of snow as it plowed the surface, and I'd have to wait before I tried getting clear because I could get an arm or a leg trapped between the bodywork and the road. Someone was yelling something about not letting me get away and I used his voice as a guide and found his throat and used a half fist with a short thrust and felt it break the cartilage.

At this stage I began noticing blood, quite a lot of it, shining with an odd purplish color because of the neon lights: someone must have been trapped by the weight of our bodies against the glass of a window as it shattered on impact with the road. It wouldn't be the man who'd been yelling.

Inside the storm of the vehicle there was the storm of Vader's rage: he was in first-class condition and had kept most of his orientation when the car had rolled and he was the worst thing I had to contend with because it depended a lot on chance whether any of us got out of the wreck, but Vader wanted to kill me and he knew how to do it and he knew where I was. Conscious imagery was sporadic and the sequence of events so fast that the brain had to select and analyze as best it could: I'd actually glimpsed Vader's face three or four times but there'd been no particular expression on it until now, when I suddenly saw it very close and immediately above me. Part of my mind was occupied with data to do with the engine, which had been screaming under full throttle with the gears knocked into neutral; the scream was now dying away as the fuel emptied from the carburetor and the cylinders began starving. I could smell the stuff and was alerted: if the car caught fire I would get out without waiting for the speed to decrease. The main cerebral area was occupied with the split-second sight of Vader's face as he in turn saw mine and recognized it.

His was totally animal, as I suppose mine was: teeth bared and the eyes luminous, the nostrils wide and the scalp drawn back, totally primitive. I only saw him for this small fraction of a second before the car hit something again and we were tumbled, all of us, into a different order; but his hands knew where I was and they came for me, working for my throat and doing it so fast that I wasn't ready: I used a four-finger eye dart with both hands but missed and tried again and missed again and felt softness close to me and went for that with one knee and got it right. His hands came away and I waited but he couldn't find me again because the car was rolling for the last time and the rear window burst and sent glass flying against our faces.

There was nothing he could have done to me in any case.

Nothing.

Listen, I want you to understand something: they were taking me to the Serbsky Institute to throw me into another cell and put me through the most exquisite physical and mental agony that has ever been devised by modern neurotic man and I was frightened of that but I wasn't frightened *enough,* because there's always release from agony and it's certain: the organism finally seeks to be insensate, in death. So I don't think the fear of what they were going to do to me was enough to give me the incentive and the speed and the strength and the manic force I needed to take the action I did. It was humiliation, working through rage, that committed me to taking that action in one instant of explosive dementia that had been building up in the psyche since he had come into my cell and said what he did. So there was nothing he could have done to me. I would have stopped him.

He shouldn't have said that.

I think I shouted at him as the car pitched against a curbstone and rolled again. I think I tried to tell him what had happened, that he had said something wrong, that I was a vulnerable man and quick to take offense. I heard my voice shouting something, and it was to him, so perhaps that was what I was saying. Then the car rolled again and I could smell the petrol fumes and feel them pricking against my eyes, so I looked for the space where the windscreen had been. My hands were sticky with blood and they slipped on the edge of the instrument panel as I used it for purchase, but I managed to kick back against the seat squab and get the momentum I needed.

The car was still in motion when I slid across the hood and grabbed the windscreen pillar to save myself as it bounced for the last time and turned over onto its side. This was when I caught a glimpse of Vadar's face again: he'd got out through one of the side windows and timed it badly because of the rolling movement, and went down with his legs still inside and his hands trying to stop the impact as the car turned over on him. His head was just in front of the rear wheel and there was still a certain amount of forward motion. Perhaps he'd been trying to follow me out, I don't know.

I began running through the snow.

11 / SNOWBALL

"I'm getting out," I said, and he stopped dead and stood there watching me under the trees.

"You can't do that."

I came back to him, hands in the pockets of the torn coat, bruises all over me, the blood on my face sticking to the woolen scarf I'd put on under the fur hat, my nerves still on the jump even after ten hours' sleep if you could call it sleep, jerking my eyes open every five minutes because I could still hear that bastard yelling at me from the panel over the door, and now Bracken, trying to tell me what I could do and what I couldn't do. "This isn't my field," I told him, "I need to work alone."

There'd been two signals for me when I'd got back to the safe house, one in cipher, one in code: they'd been worried stiff because I hadn't reported, so I'd called Bracken by silent line at the Embassy asking for an rdv.—that was four o'clock this morning and now it was six at night and I was shaking with bad dreams and no use to London any more, only a danger. He'd have to understand that.

"What do you mean," he asked me, "you need to work alone?"

"There are too many people involved. One of them blasted me off the street."

I'd never seen him so still. In the car last night he'd been like a cat in a sack and I'd thought it was because he was nervous, maybe I didn't know him very well, he wasn't moving a muscle now and he must be half out of his mind after what I'd just said.

"What happened?" he asked me.

I told him about Ignatov and he stood thinking about it while I listened to those bloody children on the far side of the trees: I'd seen them on my way into the park, making a slide on the snow. Their voices unnerved me: it sounded as if they were screaming.

"Ignatov," Bracken said quietly, not really to me.

"He's a Judas. Someone who knows me. You'd better find who he is before he does something else." I wished Bracken would start walking again but he just went on standing there under the black winter trees, appalled. I felt sorry for him: he'd been thrown out here at a minute's notice just as I had and he didn't know half the contacts who were working for him, he couldn't do, this wasn't his field either, he directed penetration operations through the foreign embassies, he wasn't Moscow.

"A *Judas*," he said on his breath.

"So now you know why I'm getting out."

In surprise he said: "Did your cover stand up?"

"No."

"You mean they just let you go?"

"No. They put me into Lubyanka."

He watched me as if he were watching a fuse burning, scared of what I was going to say next. None of this was his fault, it was Croder's: the brilliant and persuasive Croder, chief of the London directorate, *you will receive every possible support,* so forth, I shouldn't have listened to him but he knew how much I was prepared to do for a man like Schrenk.

"You got out," Bracken said tonelessly, "of Lubyanka?"

"No. They were taking me to the Serbsky Institute, but there was an accident." I kept seeing that man's face under the wheel; you always seem to remember the rotten bits. "One of their intelligence colonels got killed, possibly two, so you know what my chances are if I spend any time in the open street: there'll be a full-scale hunt ordered and I've got a scar on my face you can see for miles so it's a dead end, are you getting the message? I want out."

I stood listening to the thin distant screams of the children and the moan of the trams along Soldatskaya ulica and someone saying *he stinks, put him under a shower,* a dangerous thing to have said, the only satisfaction I'd had since I came out of London, his face under the wheel, was this why Schrenk had been "bitter" after they'd put him through the same kind of thing, was it really so impersonal after all?

". . . Ignatov for us."

"What?" I turned to look at him.

"London would ask you to get Ignatov for us," Bracken said. I hardly recognized his voice any more: he was watching this mission being blown right out of his hands and he hadn't begun thinking of the repercussions.

"London's already asked too much," I told him. "They pulled me off leave too soon, I wasn't ready for the stress."

Quietly he said: "Croder mentioned that, yes. And you mentioned it yourself."

"Got a good memory," but it was all I could do not to walk away and leave him the whole bloody mess to look after because he'd used the same tone as Croder had, and looked at me in the same way, wondering if I was getting too old now, too scared. What were they trying to do, push me over the edge?

"We're all of us quite aware," he said in a low voice, "of how much we're asking of you."

"Look, it's no big deal, Bracken, I took on the job when I knew I wasn't ready for it and that was my fault but I need to work alone so that I can be absolutely sure that no one's going to Judas me into Lubyanka without any warning, you can't expect anyone to work like that." I turned and started walking through the trees and he had to come with me; I needed movement; I was frozen stiff standing there picking over the bits of a broken mission. I wasn't used to it and I didn't know how to handle it and neither did Bracken. "I'd agree to get Ignatov for you and pull out afterwards but the streets are too dangerous now: I would have asked you to meet me at the safe house but I'm not even sure it's safe any more."

We tramped together through the snow, the blind leading the blind. The trees were darker here and I felt less exposed.

"I have another safe house for you," Bracken said, and I thought oh Christ he's not going to give up. "I would also guarantee that in future your only contact in Moscow would be myself."

I didn't say anything. I wasn't interested.

"If there's a Judas in the local network," Bracken said, having to make himself say it, make himself believe it, "we have to find him."

"You do. I don't. He's your pigeon."

The snow kicked up from our shoes. Men over there, three men over there, keep an eye.

"You know where to find him," Bracken said. "We don't."

"I can't look for him. Not in the streets."

"Don't you have his address?"

"No." They looked like businessmen, officials of some kind but not in uniform. They were walking toward the frozen pond and I watched them.

"They're all right," Bracken said. "Don't worry."

"Those people?"

"Yes. They're all right." He walked closer to me, protectively.

"You think I'm paranoid or something?" I moved away from him, bloody nursemaid. I'd got the wrong director, I should have been given Ferris.

"If you've just come out of Lubyanka," Bracken said, "under your own steam, you'll feel a bit paranoid for a while. We can accommodate that."

The three men were moving away from us toward the gates of the park. They hadn't even seen us.

"You'll accommodate anything I do," I said, "even if I shit down the chimney, as long as I get Ignatov for you, right?"

"That's right." He moved closer to me, and got into step.

"No go," I said. "You'll have to get him yourself. What I want from you is a ticket home and I don't care what plane it is."

I said it to give him something to think about instead of thinking about Ignatov. He couldn't get me on a plane out of this city: they'd lost Schrenk and they'd lost Kirov and they'd lost one of their colonels and they'd be looking for me under every stone.

"I can't do that," Bracken said. His voice was low

and steady and I'd been thinking he'd got over the worst of the shock but I wasn't sure now: he could be containing it and bulldozing his way to some kind of terrain we could operate in. A man like Croder wouldn't call in someone who buckled at the knees at the first blow. "You have to stay in Moscow," he went on reasonably, "until we can get you clear without any risk. That might not be for some little time." He was walking more slowly. "How do you feel about Schrenk?"

"How do I feel?"

"He was Croder's only argument, wasn't he? You wouldn't have agreed to take this one for someone you didn't respect. You have a lot of respect for Schrenk, and Croder knew that."

I slowed and said: "Not that way."

"I'm sorry?"

"This way. Bloody children screaming."

"Oh. I simply meant," Bracken said carefully, "that I'm going to do everything I can to pull Schrenk out, if it's not too late. We need him out because he's a danger to Leningrad but I don't mean that. I want him out because I respect him too." He waited five seconds. "I thought you'd like to know."

"Oh for Christ's sake, spare me the auld lang syne. I'm going to be lucky to get out of this place alive, let alone take someone else with me. What makes you so sure he's in Moscow anyway?"

"It was in the briefing information."

"Well, the K haven't got him, I know that." There were more children not far away and I hoped to Christ they weren't going to start screaming, like that poor bastard in the cell.

"Repeat?" Bracken stopped dead again to watch me.

"They thought I knew where he was. They offered me an exchange deal."

"Dezinformatsiya?"

"No. They haven't got him, and they want him, as badly as we do."

In a moment Bracken said: "If he's free, why hasn't he reported?"

"I didn't say he was free. I'd say he was dead."

He shut off again for a time. Then: "Killed?"

"How should I know? They chewed him up in there and he just about got away with his skin and then someone did a snatch on him at the clinic in Hannover and it wasn't the KGB and there hasn't been a squeak from him since and that's all I know, it's all anyone knows."

Hit me on the side of my head without any warning and exploded in a white shower all over Bracken and he laughed boomingly and bent down and got some snow and pressed it hard and slung it back at them, laughing all the time, good cover, while I stood there with my nerves screaming through my head, not a terribly good sign, scared of a snowball now, maybe if I could get some sleep tonight, some real sleep without that bastard yelling at me from—

"All right?" Bracken was watching me closely.

"Yes. I'm all right."

"Come on," he said, and began walking the other way. "Look, I'm going to be in signals with London most of the night and I'll ask for a complete screening background on every man we've got in Moscow. If there's the slightest doubt about any of them I'll get them recalled and kept out of here: ours is the only operation we've got running in this field." He was talking briskly, confidently, and for a moment he got me thinking he wasn't worried. "Meanwhile I've got three people working on your last signal, although the present findings are that there are seventeen Pyotr Ignatovs resident in Moscow—not that it means a lot, because if he's a

Judas in our group he'll be using an alias, obviously. One of the ten Natalya Fyodorova's in this city works in a personnel department of the Kremlin, which could match your info; she's described as attractive and possibly a swallow for the KGB. We're still digging, and you'll have anything we turn up." He was walking closer again, nudging my arm sometimes, trying to make contact and pull me out of the aftershock. "I'm going to find out if Schrenk is still alive but first I want to nail this Judas before he can wipe us out in Moscow. But if you feel there's nothing more you can do for us at this stage I can smuggle you into the Embassy and get you taken care of. One of the girls has had nursing experience and of course you—"

"I didn't say I wanted a nurse."

"No, don't misunderstand me—"

"The streets are dangerous," I told him through my teeth. "I don't know how long I could last."

He stopped again, his hand on my arm. "I quite realize that. Why don't you come in for a while and think it over? You'll be perfectly safe at the Embassy. Then see how you feel in the morning."

I looked away. "There's no time to hole up. You know that."

"We could send for someone else to come out." He stood watching me with the light of the city bouncing off the snow and reflecting in his eyes. "We'd quite understand," he said gently, "if you asked us to do so."

Croder had spoken like that. They knew how to keep me running, as long as my feet could move.

"You're risking London," I told him, "if you keep on pushing me, you know that? They're looking for me and they won't stop till they find me."

"We know what the risks are," Bracken said quietly,

"and what we have to do about them." He spoke with confidence, and my mind opened a degree to what he was saying. "But if you could do just one thing for me, we'd all be so much safer. I need to get a look at this man Ignatov, without his seeing me, so that I can tell you whether or not he's working in our cell. Do you think you could arrange that, somehow?"

I stood listening to the moan of the trams at the far side of the park, and the chugging of a concrete mixer where a night crew was putting up a new apartment complex. The voices of the children had stopped; perhaps they'd gone home now. I wished they were still here in the park, even though they reminded me of screaming; they'd taken their innocence with them, and just for this moment I needed it as a touchstone.

Bracken was waiting, his large face patient as he watched me, and this time I knew he wouldn't speak again, before I did.

"I'd need another safe house. And another cover. And another car. I wrote the car off." We began walking together over the snow. "I'd need another coat. This one's too far gone for mending, and it attracts too much attention."

"I can see to all that," Bracken said.

"You'd have to send the doctor from the Embassy. To the safe house." We kept to the path, or what we could see of it, knowing it led to the gates. "To fix my face. Some kind of dressing to stop it bleeding—that attracts attention too."

"That can be done," Bracken said.

I could see the dark hump of his car parked in the shadow of trees outside the park, and had an urge to run there and use its cover. I'd have to get over that.

"If you've got a spare capsule at the Embassy, you can let me have it. Be on the safe side."

"Didn't you draw one?" I suppose he knew it was required procedure for Moscow.

"Yes. I lost it." We were nearing the gates, and the snow took on a chill glitter under the streetlamps. I wondered if I could trust him, and thought I could. I'd never know if I were wrong. "Bracken," I said.

"Yes?" He leaned toward me.

"Don't tell Croder you had to talk me into going on."

"But I didn't," he said, and touched my arm for a moment as we crossed to the car.

12 / TAG

Zoya Masurov: a body like petrified smoke in her black sweater and black thigh boots, her hair blackest of all and drawn away from her pale ivory face, her eyes smoldering in the charred silk of their brows and lashes, taking you in and giving you nothing back, reminding me of Helda, last seen at the edge of a minefield on the East German border, though this woman was harder and would have no mercy, would kill you if you were an enemy and kill for you if you were a friend. But she held most of it in, and it was only when you went close to her that you sensed the undercurrents and felt their pull.

"There is no need to bring a doctor here," she'd told Bracken. "I am a doctor."

She worked on me when Bracken had gone, taking a small black cauldron of boiling water up to the room on the top floor, the one right at the end like the one at Gorsky's place, because we're safest there: it's the required location.

"What should I look for?" she asked me. "Splinters, metal, glass?"

"Glass."

"What contaminants? What was in the glass?"

"Nothing. It was a car crash. Are you the *upravdom* here?"

"Yes." There wasn't much light from the bulb overhead and she was using a big hand lamp that must have come out of a railway sale, her black eyes narrowed as she looked for the glint of glass, swabbing and exploring and swabbing again, never looking at me, looking always at the wound, "I am the *upravdom,* yes, but also a doctor, though no longer in the registry, of course, since they removed my name after nearly thirteen years," the fragments cutting sometimes as she moved the steel probe, her body held perfectly still and only her hands working, the small veins in her temple thrown into relief by the backwash of the enormous lamp, the sweep of one eyelash sending shadow across her brow, "that was at the hospital in Smolensk, the big new one they built after the war. It was there that they found me doing something unforgivable."

The room was warm and this woman was healing me and Bracken had given me his guarantee, no one but himself in the field with me, so I was slowly coming down from the nervous high of the aftershock and beginning to think I had a chance of doing some work in this city and getting out of it alive. But I still didn't know how I could have asked him what I had, to keep it from Croder that I'd needed persuasion. Croder meant nothing to me.

"They found me using American antibiotics," she said. "We didn't have anything at that time for sickle-cell anemia, and they wouldn't allow the import of GH3 because Romania isn't loyal to the master state. But I had a friend at the consulate and he got me the drugs from Sloan Kittering—Kettering, is it?—and I was found using them, and so here I am, the *upravdom* of an apartment block in Moscow with instructions to report on the residents here if they commit any infraction of the rules." She threw the swab into a metal-lined box and prodded again. I winced and she laughed and said, "You can feel it better than I can see it, that's just what I want."

"And a happy Christmas to you too," I said, and she laughed again and had to hold the probe away for a minute. She had sharp white teeth like an animal's, and it occurred to me that if I ever introduced her to the blue-eyed fair-haired Natalya Fyodorova this woman would eat her alive.

"It amuses me," she said deep in her throat, "the way men can't stand pain."

"It's to get sympathy, even when we know there isn't a dog's chance. Did you appeal?"

She broke her laugh halfway. "Appeal?"

"Against the medical brass."

"I didn't know you were listening."

"Oh yes, I was listening."

The place was reeking of alcohol by the time she'd finished, and I stood at the other side of the room from the mirror and took a look; she'd put in a row of new sutures and covered the wound with a long strip of elastic dressing and it didn't look too bad in here, though it wouldn't do for the street.

"Will it start bleeding again?"

"No." She was packing her things together in the big medical bag. "Not unless you open it up again as you did last time."

There was a bloodied swab on the linoleum and I dropped it into the wood stove. "What did they tell you about me?"

"You are for safekeeping," she said.

"What else?"

"Nothing else."

"There's a hunt on," I said, and looked through the grimy window to the lamps in the street below. "They're looking for a man with a scar. If I run out of luck and someone follows me here, are you fully organized? I mean cover, background, instructions?"

"Yes." She swung the bag over one lean shoulder like a knapsack. "But if that isn't enough, I have a sawn-off shotgun and some grenades."

London wouldn't know about that.

"And you'd like to use them, wouldn't you?"

"Yes," she said slowly, "I would like to use them."

As soon as she'd gone I got out the material Bracken had given me. The capsule was in the regulation red tin box and the report was in digraphic code, key 5, using AMBER LIGHT for the first two lines in the grid with *x* separating the double letters; it wasn't new and it wasn't fast but it was almost unbreakable. *Of ten Natalya Fyodorovas in M. one in personnel office Kremlin, 27, attractive, possible part-time swallow, still tracing. Of seventeen Pyotr Ignatovs none linked with intelligence field or police, none suspect, still tracing. No details of subject's arrest though probably in open. Reasons given for application for post of a-i-p his interest in dissident affairs and possibility of his proving useful in that area. No inconsistency seen, since subject is Jewish and has contacts in M. State what link Nat. Fyo. and Pyot. Ign. if any. Destruct.*

I opened the stove and watched it burn. It was about the least informative signal I'd ever received from a director in the field with the operation half blown and the subject probably dead. I think Bracken could have got me a lot more if London hadn't been standing on his hands: I didn't like the way he'd said *we know what the risks are and what we have to do about them*. They shouldn't know any more at this stage than that a Judas had started working through the Moscow cell and blowing the executives one by one, but Croder was running this thing and he wouldn't tell even Bracken any more than he had to know, and I had the feeling that something even bigger than the threat to Leningrad was involved or that in the last twenty-four hours the situation had developed into a threat to something even bigger than Leningrad, something on a vaster scale than an inter-intelligence skirmish.

It wasn't my business. A shadow executive for the Bureau is a ferret and they'd put me down the hole and I hadn't found Schrenk and now they wanted Ignatov, so I'd have to go down the hole again and find him and bring him in for Bracken to look at, and it was a quarter past eight when I put the capsule away and got the secondhand astrakhan coat they'd dug up for me and put it on and went downstairs and through the deserted hallway and out into the lamplit snow.

D.12.145.

I could see the archway of Spassky Gate at one end of the driving mirror. The light on each side of it had gone from red to green as three cars and a plain van had gone through into the Kremlin during the past ten minutes. I was waiting for a car to come through from the other direction: the mud-brown Syrena. She'd said he would come soon after five o'clock and it was now three minutes to the hour.

"Did you tell him my name?" I had asked her.

At one stage she'd broken down and cried. That was last night. "I've told you, I haven't seen him, I haven't seen him!" Shaking against the railings of the apartment block, her face wet and her thin shoulders hunched forward, her small gloved hands gripping the ironwork.

"It's all right," I told her, "but I thought you were lying."

"Why should I lie?" She swung round to face me, furious. "I want you to find him, don't you understand?" She meant Helmut Schrenk. He was all she could think about, and that was what I had to work on. There was no point in telling her I thought he was dead.

Syrena, Spassky Gate. Not brown. Not D.12.145. There were thousands of them all over the city.

The clock in the tower began chiming.

"Why should I give you away to Ignatov?" Blowing into her handkerchief, shaking her hair back, soot on her gloves from the railings.

"Somebody did."

It got her attention and she stared at me in the acid light of the lamps. "What happened?"

"He tried to get me arrested."

"But he's not in the police!"

"No?"

"He's in the transport division, one of the chauffeurs for the Politburo."

"Are you sure?"

"Of course." She wiped her face, half turned away from me.

"You didn't tell me much, you see, the first time we met. All I'm trying to do is find Helmut."

"I didn't trust you, before."

"What makes you trust me now?"

She leaned back against the railings and closed her eyes, exhausted from the anger and hope and uncertainty. After these last months I'd started her thinking about him again and it had disrupted her life.

"I trust you now because I want to. Because I have to."

"They're good enough reasons. Listen, Natalya, I want to find Ignatov. Do you know where he lives?"

"No. We always met at the café, or the skating rink, places like that. But I can find out exactly where he works."

Another Syrena. Mud brown. Not D.12.145. The clock in the tower had stopped chiming. I watched the mirror.

"Can you find out tonight?"

"No. I don't have the keys of the office."

"Is there anyone you can contact, whoever has the keys? Tell them you want to catch up on some work?"

She thought for a moment and then said: "I could ask the security men to let me in with—"

"No, don't do that." I stood closer to her. "Listen, the KGB wants to find Helmut too. Think of it as a race—they get to him first, or I do. It's partly up to you who wins. Keep away from Ignatov and don't change your daily routine. Don't tell anyone about me and don't tell anyone there's a hope of finding Helmut. Try to forget him as much as you can, otherwise you might give yourself away. And him. All understood?"

"Yes." Her mouth was trembling: she was going to cry again but not out of anger this time, but just because she was out of her depth and didn't know what to do, didn't know whom to trust, didn't know if she'd ever see Helmut again. This girl wasn't a swallow, she was just another young Muscovite with a mother and father and friends and a job, and the most clandestine thing she knew how to do was to march with the café crusaders through dreams of freedom in the long night where freedom was dead.

"Ivan was arrested," she'd told me before I left her.

"What for?"

"Handing out leaflets, outside the courtroom."

"Three days. You'll see him again. But keep away from the café, and don't hand out any leaflets yourself. I may need to see you again if I don't find Ignatov."

D.12.145.

Turning to the right as it came through Spassky Gate. I started the engine and moved away from the curb. She'd said he normally took Razina ulica and I turned right and slowed and saw him go across the intersection and turned left when the lights changed and took up the tag with two cars and a taxi in the space between us. The Mercedes 220 was four cars behind.

I knew how good Ignatov was in the street: he'd used his mirror when I'd tagged him before and it had got me into Lubyanka, so this was strictly a red sector I was in. I'd be secure all the time we were on the move but if he stopped anywhere in an open street I'd have to make sure he didn't speak to a militiaman, and if he went to a telephone box I'd have to leave him there and get the Pobeda into some kind of cover. There was no reason why he should suspect the tag: this was a different car with a different number and he'd never seen me closer than a street's width away and this was the rush hour and there were a dozen Pobedas in sight of him at any given minute. But he'd blown me the last time and he could do it again if I gave him the ghost of a chance.

I didn't think he had a transmitter with a concealed antenna because this was the same Syrena he was driving and two days ago he'd had to get out and telephone to trigger the action.

Mirror. The Mercedes was now three spaces behind me and in front of a truck with a high profile and after that I couldn't see anything but if a police patrol wanted to come up on me for any reason he'd overtake the rest and close me in. I could only relax when there was a right-hand street within sight for us as an escape road but this was oversensitive because my image was clean and I didn't think Ignatov had a transmitter. *After Lubyanka,* Bracken had said, *you'll feel a bit paranoid for a while.*

We crossed the first ring road at 5:14 and the second one five minutes later and followed Kazakov ulica eastward with no significant change in the pattern except for some shunting when Ignatov went through the lights on the yellow and I had to get the spacer vehicles behind me and close the distance and then hang back and wait for some new ones to cover me in his mirror. He'd seen me once or twice but he'd seen a lot of cars behind him as we all headed for the suburbs, and the rake of my windscreen was reflecting the streetlamps and he couldn't see my face. I don't think he was going through on the yellow because he'd discovered the tag: Natalya had said he was a chauffeur for the Politburo, so he'd be used to storming along the Chaika lane at the wheel of a government Zil and going through on the red with the policeman stopping the cross traffic, and he must feel frustrated on his off-duty runs in the Syrena.

5:22 and a right turn to take us across the river at the Radio ulica bridge two minutes later. Three spacers, two taxis and a small van, with the Mercedes keeping station behind me. The road surface was fair, with sand across the snow and not too many ruts forming as yet.

This astrakhan coat smelled bloody awful: God knew where Bracken's people had got it from. It reeked of black tobacco and borsht and camphor balls, this week's unrepeatable bargain out of a railway workers' union secondhand store, I'd put it at fifteen rubles. I wound down the window and let the freezing air come in.

Slowing.

He was slowing and peeling off to the right at the fork opposite the park and I saw the pumps of a filling station and slowed with him and took the same turn, because if I went straight on and took two rights I'd come back on him from the opposite direction and he'd get a close look at my face when I passed him; at that point he'd be on my left and the cheek wound would be on the other side but my image was an eighty-eight percent security risk on an inverted scale: I'd made a count while I was waiting for him to come through Spassky Gate and one out of eight men on the pavement had been wearing his scarf as I was, to cover each side of his face against the cold. Ignatov was observant and he'd recognize me if he saw me twice.

He was stopping at the end of the queue for the pumps and I made a half turn and pulled up with a parked truck for cover and waited. At this angle the mirror gave me a square centimeter of critical reflection: the forward half of the Syrena's driving window and Ignatov's head and one shoulder. After thirty seconds he opened the door and got out and I shifted my head to keep his reflection in sight: the back of his dark fur coat and the lower half of his head. Then the image disappeared and I had to risk looking round.

He was going across the tarmac area toward the telephone box.

I watched him.

Bodily changes: sweat, blood leaving the skin, awareness of pulse. Panic trying to set in.

It's a trap. He did this before, when—

Shuddup.

Bloody organism.

We've got to get out of here—

Shuddup.

He went into the telephone box and I saw the dark of his shoulder and the pale blur of his face behind the steamy glass. He knew the number: he wasn't using the book.

The nerves were tingling as the adrenaline came into the bloodstream, and the muscles felt alert. Instinct told me to get out while there was a chance of finding cover and going to ground before the patrol cars arrived, and logic supported this. He'd led me a long way, two days ago, before he'd stopped to telephone, and he'd led me a long way now. I'd performed a model tag from Spassky Gate this evening, but I'd done as well two days ago and he'd seen me and set the trap, just as he was doing now.

So I got out of the car and walked the length of the truck and reached the shadows behind the buildings and watched him from there. The box was in full light under one of the tall gooseneck lamps, the snow reflecting it upward in a wash of radiance; but I could still see only the indistinct image of his face as he stood half turned toward the buildings. I think he nodded, once, before he put the phone back and came out. He couldn't see me in the shadows and I moved the woolen scarf away from my ears and listened to the sounds of the traffic, trying to be selective, trying to pick out a distant siren or the snow chains of a vehicle moving fast.

Ignatov stood looking toward the river, the way we'd just come. He might be watching the lights over there, or the stream of southbound traffic, or the tail end of the Pobeda and its number plate: I couldn't see at this distance. When the queue moved up to the pumps he got back into the Syrena and kept his place, and when the queue moved again and he was alongside the end pump he got out again and stood watching the traffic.

I went on listening. The cold air was numbing to the ears after the warmth of the scarf, and the cheek wound was sensitive. It was seven minutes since he'd come out of the telephone box and his tank had been filled and he was paying the attendant. I could still hear nothing unusual in the traffic's sound. It didn't mean they weren't on their way: with the snow on the streets they'd take longer to get here and there'd be no particular hurry because if he'd given them the location they'd close in from a dozen directions and block my way out.

When he got back into his car I would have to make the decision but the organism was feverish with apprehension: the adrenals were releasing epinephrine and constricting the blood vessels and the liver was releasing glucose for the motor energy; the skeletal muscles were firming and strengthening and the pulse was strong and fast. But it might not be enough to save me if I made the wrong decision.

He was getting back into his car.

I went on listening and heard no change in the traffic sound. The last thing I did before going back to the Pobeda was to feel my waistband under my coat to make sure the small rectangular tin was still there.

Ignatov waited for a slot in the traffic stream and found one and sped up and I followed, watching the mirror and the side streets and the reflections in the windows and bodywork of the cars ahead of me, watching for the first sign of a flashing light. The Mercedes came into the mirror twice before Ignatov led me eastward again, alongside the park; then I lost it for a while. The sweating had stopped but I was chilled with it, and my mouth tasted bitter. The organism was having to deal with the superfluous adrenaline and the muscles were fretting for action. There wasn't going to be any: he'd phoned somebody else.

Who?

His wife or a friend or a woman, anyone, it could be anyone, telling them he was going to be a little late tonight because of the snow. Ignore.

At 5:47 he slowed and took a side street and slowed again and I held back until he turned sharply into the entrance of an underground car park. It was alongside an apartment block and I drove straight past to make a check and then came back and stopped and doused the lights and got out and started walking fast over the snow. Halfway along the street I heard an engine die and a door open as I reached the black mouth of the entrance and went down the ramp, breaking into a run across the dry concrete.

The place was cavernous, with concrete columns standing at intervals, their pattern merging into the darkness. The slam of a car door came but the echoes bounced the sound from wall to wall and I couldn't locate it. Then a flashlight came on and its beam swung and focused on my eyes, blinding me. I began walking into the beam but it went out and I stopped dead, waiting for the dazzling afterimage to clear. I think he was some fifty feet ahead of me, midway between two of the columns; I heard movement but it wasn't distinct enough to get a fix on.

I waited ten seconds, but there was only silence now.

"Ignatov," I said. "I need to talk to you."

He didn't answer. I couldn't tell if he had a gun: it was pitch dark in this area and the click of a safety catch wouldn't necessarily carry this distance. If he had a gun and wanted to hold me off, he would have to put his flashlight on again to take aim. If he decided I was too dangerous, then he would simply fire, but he'd have to use the flashlight even to do that, because the entrance was no longer behind me and I wasn't showing a silhouette.

I stood listening, perfectly still except for my head. I was turning my head to the left, until my right ear was facing Ignatov's last estimated position: the right ear feeds aural input to the left hemisphere of the brain, where the logical analysis of crude sound is made. I picked up nothing at all. After thirty seconds something drove past the entrance along the street, and the sound came into the cavernous dark and set up diminishing vibrations: the acoustics were strange in here, with the concrete columns breaking up the sound patterns and reflecting their remnants.

I thought some kind of movement had been made, when the sound had come down from the street. I wasn't sure.

"Ignatov. We need to talk."

My own voice sounded odd, its echoes overlapping. I went forward, using *tai-chi* steps, long and infinitely slow, keeping my feet slightly tilted to avoid the sound of flat contact, sole to floor. I took ten paces and stopped. I thought he was somewhere between where I stood now and forty feet away: a few minutes ago I'd estimated his distance from me as fifty feet and I'd just moved thirty, allowing for a margin of error of twenty and doubling it. Then he moved and I heard him and spun into the *kukutsu-dachi* stance and waited.

Total silence. I went on waiting. I thought I was close to him now, perhaps very close. In the far distance I could see the rectangular patch of light made by the streetlamps aboveground, but there was no light here. If I could move to one side and work round him in a half

circle I could bring his silhouette in line between me
and the entrance; but he might be trying to do that
himself, and might be succeeding: at any time now the
shot could come, if he were going to shoot.

My scalp was drawn tight and I could feel the slight
lifting of the hair on my head. Ignatov could be within
an inch of me now, and might detect me first. I didn't
know what kind of training he had, whether he knew
how to strike lethally, working by touch alone.

It was difficult to move now with any safety: the dark
itself felt hazardous. A degree of sensory deprivation
was setting in, and my nerves heard movement where
there was none. A few seconds ago I had heard the
faintest rustling to my left, and I had moved one hand
out in the hope of making contact and identifying his
attitude and striking before he could. But he wasn't
there. It wasn't any good listening for his breathing:
he'd be controlling it, as I was controlling mine.

I moved again, with the underwater slowness of *tai-
chi,* and took two paces before *I felt something touching
my elbow.*

It was to my left. If it was Ignatov standing beside
me he would make his move at once so I threw up a
guard and used a very short controlled knife edge with
the left foot and struck solid, bruising it. Flat of my
left hand—yes, a concrete column. I hit the floor immediately, doubling in silence, in case he was close
enough to use the sounds I'd made as a bearing.

I began thinking he must have gone. He wore rubber-
soled shoes: there'd been no footsteps just before he'd
switched on the flashlight. He could have gone far
enough, during the passage of the vehicle in the street,
to move out of earshot. But that was dangerous thinking. I got up slowly, watching the rectangle of light
in the distance in case he moved across it.

Silence.

I took two paces, slowly, undulating, and stopped. Then I heard him draw breath suddenly beside me because of the shock of proximity—I'd come up on him in the total darkness and a grunt sounded as he stifled a shout and I clawed with my left hand to find the shape of the target and felt softness, the curled wool of his coat, all I needed. He struck out with the flashlight and it grazed my head before I brought him down with a crescent sweep and caught him before he hit the ground. He didn't learn anything from this: he thought there was still a chance and tried to unbalance me and I stopped him with a low-power sword hand against the carotid.

"Don't do anything," I told him. "We need to talk."

He didn't say anything. I found the flashlight and switched it on, lighting his face. He was still in shock and his head was lolling, so I helped him upright and he stood swaying a little, dazzled by the light. I moved it down, out of his eyes, but he still didn't seem to understand the position because he jerked suddenly and hooked for my face with his stubby fingers, putting a lot of force into it and getting close before I blocked it with a *jodan* and center-knuckled the medial nerve with enough depth to paralyze.

"Ignatov," I said, "don't do that."

He was quiet again, sagging against me for a time with the local paralysis affecting his system through the nervous meridians. When I was sure he understood the position I raised the flashlight to shine full on his face and looked round.

"Well?" I asked.

"No," Bracken said from the shadows. "I've never seen him before. He's not in my cell. He's not the Judas."

13 / SHADOW

Then who was?

He was very difficult to work with: he kept trying to get away and I had to trip him and catch him before he could hit the ground or the concrete column that was somewhere near us. If I didn't catch him each time he was going to hurt himself because he had absolutely no idea how to fall.

"What did you tell them?" I asked him again.

He wouldn't answer, and that was another thing that made it difficult. I had to ask him everything two or three times and then work on a nerve until he got the message. But even then I didn't know when he was lying. I've never met anybody so difficult.

"What did you tell them, when you went into that phone box?"

"It was to tell my wife I would be late."

"Not *that* time. I mean two days ago, on Wednesday. You phoned the police and they tried to pick me up. What did you tell them?"

"I didn't tell them anything. I—"

"Oh come on, Ignatov!" Used a center-knuckle on the medial: he hated that. *"What did you tell them?"*

I was getting annoyed because someone might come in here and make things awkward. Bracken had gone, five minutes ago: all he'd needed was a close look at Ignatov, and it was too dangerous for him to stay where the action was because he was ostensibly a member of the British Embassy staff and they could throw him out of the country if he came under any kind of suspicion.

Ignatov wasn't answering.

"You'd never seen me before in your life and you went into a phone box and called the police and they came right away, so *what did you tell them?*"

"It was not me."

"What do you mean it wasn't you? *Come on!*"

"I did what I was ordered." He crouched over, hugging his arm because it had needed another jab to get that much out of him. But it sounded interesting. Who had ordered him? *The Judas?*

"Ignatov," I said, "I want you to understand the position. I can do a lot of things to you that would make you give me the answers I want, but it could cripple you for life and I don't see any point, do you?" He was still bent over, trying to get some of the feeling back into his left arm. I'd been leaving his right arm alone for the moment in case I wanted him to drive me anywhere: I didn't know what was going to happen yet. "I'm going to get the answers out of you in any case, so why damage yourself?" He was breathing much too hard for a man of maybe thirty-five or forty, though he was a bit overweight and of course he was nervous. It's harder to make them understand you when they haven't had any training because they've never learned what you can do to them. "Have you any children, Ignatov?"

"Three, yes, three children." He said it quickly because this was where his heart was, in his family.

"All right, do you want them to have to push you about in a wheelchair? You want them to help feed you? Listen to what I'm saying. Use your imagination. A *wheelchair*."

Something went past along the street and a faint rhomboid of light swept across the columns and faded out. I didn't want anyone to come in here until I'd got what I needed from him.

"So we'll start again. Who ordered you to get me picked up in the street?"

I gave him five seconds and then covered him in fast light blows with a lot of control and the focus on the nerve centers so that he didn't even know what was happening. Then I had to wait until he could stand upright again.

"That was nothing, Ignatov. I didn't touch your face and I didn't touch your groin. I'm going to work on those next. *Who ordered you?*"

He whispered a name but I didn't catch it because his system was in shock.

"Who? Say it again."

"Zubarev."

"What was that? Zubarev?"

"Yes." He nodded and went on nodding like one of those dolls with a weight in its head. "Yes."

Some more light came and this time it got very bright and the concrete columns stood out, row after row of them as the car came down the ramp and turned and parked with its nose against the wall, the light spreading and dimming and then going out. I put one arm round Ignatov's throat and left it there while we waited. He got the message this time and didn't try to do anything about it. A flashlight beam came on at the far end of the garage and I watched it bobbing toward the iron staircase in the corner, *but it was promised,* one of them was saying, *it was promised,* very cut up because her boss had said they could have two tickets for the circus if they reached their work goal for the month and he'd broken his promise and now they'd have to spend the evening playing dominoes with the Borisenkos next door, a bloody shame but at least they'd shown me the public telephone in the corner by the staircase, I hadn't seen it before.

"Give me your wallet," I told Ignatov, and he reached inside his coat and I watched his hand when it came out. "Hold this torch." Normal papers plus Party membership card, plus identification as an official driver to the Politburo and a special traffic pass into the Kremlin and "certain designated areas in the City of Moscow" as specified in the 1979 Amendment to the Control of Vehicular Movement. Nothing else in the way of privilege documents but that one would probably rate a salute from a militiaman, yes.

No little book with names in, no sign of any Zubarev.

"We're going to make a phone call," I told him. It was like trying to move a bear: he didn't know which way to walk. He wasn't used to this sort of thing, but that wasn't my fault, he shouldn't have blasted me off the street like that. "We're going to call Zubarev," I said.

Didn't know his number.

"Oh yes you do," I told him, and whipped a very light reverse sword hand against the larynx. "Tell him you're coming to see him, and if he objects, tell him it's very urgent. Insist on it. Do you understand?"

He stood trying to get his breath and I had to wait

for a minute because I wanted him to sound reasonably normal on the phone. I only had one kopeck on me, with a lot of bigger change. "Have you got a kopeck?" I asked him.

He found one, moving slowly, and I watched his hand again when it came out. "He only lets me go there," he said with a slight wheeze, "at prearranged times."

"We're going to prearrange it." I put the two kopecks into the slot. "Ignatov, you gave me a lot of trouble. I don't mind what I have to do to you. Remember the wheelchair." I gave him the phone.

In the close bright light of the torch I watched his face, and his eyes. He was staring at the printed board behind the telephone as if he were reading its instructions, but he wasn't. He was staring at the possibility of saying something to Zubarev that would warn him, and at the possibility of hurling himself at me and throttling me before I could do anything about it. This was natural enough but I waited for him to turn his head and look at my eyes, and in my eyes I let him see without any shadow of doubt that I was the angel of death. He looked away and dialed the number, which I noted and committed to memory.

He asked for a woman first and I reacted and moved my hand in a threat and he whispered that Zubarev never came to the telephone himself.

"Misha," he said with slow care, watching me, "this is Pyotr. I am coming to see him. Tell him that."

I heard her voice: young, strong, husky, positive. She would tell him, she was saying. Was he coming right away?

"Yes. I am coming now." I prodded him and he said: "Tell him it is very urgent, Misha. Tell him I must come."

There was nothing wrong? she wanted to know.

In the light of the torch his flat featureless face struggled with the question, and he managed to get a note of reassurance into his voice. "There is nothing wrong, no. But I must come."

She said she would tell him. Neither of them had mentioned his name. He looked at me and I nodded and he hooked the receiver back. Light swept suddenly across the columns and I turned my back to the entrance as a car came down the ramp and swung at right angles and stopped. I moved Ignatov away from the staircase and talked to him as we walked across to his car, passing a half-seen man and saying good evening to him. When he'd started up the iron staircase I told Ignatov to get into his car on the passenger's side and then I took his scarf and tied his wrists to his ankles and shut the door on him and went round to the driver's side. He hadn't seen me tagging him from the Kremlin and he didn't know the number of the Pobeda but he'd see it if we used my car instead of his, and once he'd seen that number plate he could blast me off the street again the minute he got to a telephone.

He sat awkwardly beside me with his knees drawn up to his chin, his squat body swaying as I turned the car through the columns and pulled up near the entrance and reached across him and opened his door for a moment. "Ignatov," I told him, "if you try to attract attention in the street by shouting out or falling against the steering wheel you might alert a militiaman or a police patrol. If you did that, I'd have to leave you behind, and I'd do that by opening your door like this and giving you a push." I used a fair amount of force so that he rocked half off his seat, then I grabbed him and pulled him back and he sat with his breath hissing out. "You'd hit your head on the road because you wouldn't be able to save yourself, you understand?"

"Yes. Yes, I understand."

"What are the names of your children?"

"Yuri, Irina, and Tania." His head swung to look at me because the question had surprised him.

"You want to see them again," I said, and pulled his door shut and drove up the ramp into the street. "You must take care of yourself."

"Yes," he said, and I heard emotion in his voice, "I understand."

I turned into the street without slowing down too much and he rolled against the door with a thump and rolled back: I wanted him to know how extraordinarily helpless the human body can be without the use of hands or feet.

The evening rush hour was nearly over and the first set of lights was green. "He's at the Pavillon," I said to Ignatov, "is that right?"

"Yes."

I drove northwest along Soldatskaya ulica, feeling the onset of depression. Of all the questions in my head I thought I had the answer to one, and I didn't like it. Ignatov was a professional driver and would have been trained to watch his mirror when he was at the wheel of those big black shiny Zils because the members of the elite Politburo must not be followed about. But he hadn't discovered my tag on the way from Spassky Gate this evening: he had seen the Pobeda several times but hadn't realized it was following him specifically. Certainly I'd taken pains to do the job efficiently, but then I'd taken similar pains two days ago, and he'd known I was there behind him, and there on purpose. It had been daylight then, and this evening it had been dark; but this city was bright by night and visibility was good. So there was an additional factor involved, which had led him to discover the first tag and not the second.

I thought I knew what it was. I had probably known for a long time, right at the back of the mind where we put things we don't want to look at. But it would have to be brought into the light, and looked at; and that was going to be painful. I would almost rather be going to Lubyanka again, in good heart and filled with the fierce animal instinct to fight and survive, than to this place filled with depression and unable to do anything about it. Depression is unreachable, the slow death of the spirit.

"What's your wife's name?" I asked Ignatov. The lights changed to red at an intersection and I put out a hand as he swayed forward again: I'd had to do it several times to stop him hitting his face on the windscreen.

"Galya," he said, and looked at me, wondering why I had asked, and perhaps hearing something in my voice: the depression.

"What does she do?"

"She teaches the ballet, at the Center for the Arts."

The lights went green and he swayed back on his seat.

"Does she teach your children?"

We were almost there, but I wanted this journey to last a long time, and I wanted to talk to this man about his wife and his children and the ballet lessons.

"She teaches our two girls," he said, his voice wary, suspecting some kind of trap.

"Irina and Tania."

"Yes," he said, surprised that I'd remembered. But like most people, I remember most things, and especially those things I'd rather forget.

"I suppose Yuri thinks it'd be sissy for him to learn, does he?"

"Yes, that's perfectly right!" As if I'd discovered a profound truth. But the wariness was still in his voice, the fear that I was building up this little edifice of human intimacy only so that I could knock it down. He didn't have the trust in innocence those children had had in the park.

He was silent, but I saw he was watching my reflection in the windscreen. I think he was beyond trying to do anything to help himself now, or to stop my going to see Zubarev. I'd found his weakness, or his strength, whichever you want to call it. But this didn't mean he wouldn't kill me if I gave him the chance and if he believed he had to, for his children's sake. Or of course for his own.

The lights were green for us at the turning into Baumanskaya and I didn't have to stop, though I would have liked to stop, and turn back, and never meet Zubarev.

The Pavillon block was on our left now and I turned past it and found the car park at the rear, where I'd explored the environment on foot two days ago. The snow was thick here, with the tracks of vehicles making ruts that tugged at the wheel as I drove through the entrance. The building was quite large, with a blank wall facing us and the headlights throwing the shadows of the parked cars against it. A man was walking toward us from the building, going across to his car, and our headlights held him frozen for an instant before I switched them off. He looked transfixed, like a wild creature caught in the dazzle of lights along a country road, and his shadow was enormous on the wall behind him, grotesque and distorted, with one thin shoulder held low like a broken wing and his body twisted to one side.

"Is that Zubarev?" I asked the man beside me.

"Yes."

I watched as the figure moved on again, hobbling toward the car.

14 / DEADLOCK

He looked up at me from the driving seat.

"Oh," he said, "it's you."

I'd gone across to his car quite quickly, to stop him driving away.

He watched me steadily for a moment, his pale eyes narrowed and his small gnome's head slightly on one side. Even sitting down his body was twisted, with the left shoulder held low and noticeably still. He was trying to think what it would be best to do, and I couldn't have helped him even if I'd wanted to. I'd only just got here in time: I think he'd panicked suddenly while he was waiting for us to arrive, and decided to get out in case Ignatov brought someone with him: an example of the type of intuition we develop in the field as a natural aid to survival.

But he couldn't just drive off, now that he'd seen me. There was a question of pride involved. The most he could do would be to pretend he was just popping out for some cigarettes; but he didn't bother. We both knew the position.

"What about a little drinkie?" he said with a sudden lopsided smile.

"All right."

I stepped back to let him get out of the car. He did it clumsily, though he tried not to let anything show, and I looked away in time to save him embarrassment. Perhaps this was why Ignatov had been impressed by my talk of a wheelchair: he'd seen what it looked like to be half crippled.

Dr. Steinberg hadn't told me his patient was as bad as this: he'd just said he "tended to hobble."

He slammed the door of his car. "Is that Ignatov you've got over there?"

"Yes. I'll go and get him."

Schrenk peered across at the humped shape in the Syrena. "Got him trussed up, have you?" He gave a dry snigger. "Leave him there, he'll be all right."

Oh no you don't.

"He'll get bored out here," I said, "with no one to talk to." I went back to the Syrena and got out my pocketknife and cut through the scarf: the knots were there for life. I said quietly to Ignatov: "Don't do anything silly, will you? Remember you want to see the children again, and Galya."

"Yes. I understand." He shook the stiffness out of his legs and came with me toward the building.

"Evening, Pyotr," Schrenk said in Russian. "Where did you find your friend?" Another dry little laugh, totally without humor.

Ignatov said nothing, but stared at the ground as the three of us walked across the rutted snow. Schrenk slipped a couple of times and I remembered I mustn't help him, even if he actually fell. I knew him that well.

Other things were coming back to me in flashes of memory: a plastic chess set on the corner table of the

Caff, where he used to challenge people, waiting there like a spider; a girl with black hair and luminous eyes and an intimate way of laughing, seaweed draped over one naked shoulder on the beach at Brighton; a black Jensen Interceptor with an anti-radar unit, deafening jazz records, an ashtray made out of a piston and stuffed with butts, and the way his fingers moved over the bomb that time, stroking it like a baby rabbit. Shapiro. Schrenk.

Signal Bracken. *I have the objective.*

Not yet.

We went slowly over the snow. I could feel Ignatov's concern that Schrenk might slip and lose his balance and break an arm: he kept close to him, his head turned, looking down. I could also feel Ignatov's awareness that he mustn't help him, if he fell: he had tried to help him before, and been told never to do that, never to do it again. I felt these infinitesimal vibrations flowing between us and carrying their intelligence. Things were sensitive tonight.

I felt Schrenk's rage.

"How's London?"

We always ask that.

"Dockers on strike," I told him.

He laughed again, whinnying softly.

Perhaps when people laugh to cover panic or fright or rage the sound is in some way inhibited, leaving nothing to show but a rictus.

"Good old London," he said, and led us to the heavy metal door in the middle of the building.

His room was on the ground floor at the rear, either because it was the best he could find or because he couldn't manage the stairs and didn't want to get trapped in the lift; or perhaps this was the best he could afford, the London funding having been cut off when he'd left Moscow for Hannover.

Consideration: Steinberg hadn't said his patient was as bad as this. Had they worked him over again, after they'd picked him up in Hannover? I didn't think so. It hadn't been the KGB.

We all stopped, not far along the passage. The number on the door was 15A. Ignatov had seemed to hold back a little on our way from the car park, and I'd let him know I had noticed it and didn't like it. Ignatov had to stay with me until I was ready to let him go: if I'd left him out there he would have got help from the next good citizen to come into the car park and he would have said it was a prank on the part of some hooligans to leave him tied up like this and he would have gone straight to a telephone and blown me.

Leave him there, Schrenk had told me, *he'll be all right.*

Oh no you don't.

He opened the door of his room. It hadn't been locked.

"Hello, sweetheart," he said in Russian, "I didn't go after all—I met an old firend of mine."

She was a plump peasant girl, sturdy and vital and with her skin still glowing from the country air, a girl recently come to the big city to fulfill her dreams of concrete towers and grinding underground trains.

"This is Misha," Schrenk said. She gave me both her hands, warm and damp from the kitchen, bobbing and saying she was pleased to meet any friend of Viktor's.

"Konstantin," I said, "Konstantin Pavlovich."

She bobbed again and then kissed Schrenk on the cheek to show me she adored him, while his bright eye watched me over her shoulder, daring me to judge him for shacking up with a girl like this, reminding me of other times, between missions, when the field executives amused themselves by comparing one another's fortunes: *Christ, old boy, that was an absoltue stunner you were with last night! And where did she get the Bentley?* It occurred to me, in this moment of contemplation as Schrenk's eye stared into mine, that nothing in a girl could be much more stunning than adoration.

Misha smelled of stewed cabbage, and so did the room; she hurried across to the corner and clanked the lid of a black iron pot on the stove, letting out steam.

"What'll it be?" Schrenk asked me. He always spoke to me in English, and to the others in Russian. I don't think he was deliberately ignoring security; I think he felt that security wasn't necessary, because one of us was totally in the other's power and was therefore harmless. It was probably true, though neither of us knew which one would be the survivor, because this was what we were going to have to work out.

"I'll have some beet juice," I told him, and he asked Misha to pour me a glass while he hobbled across to the plywood table under the window and got himself some vodka, waving the bottle to Ignatov, who said he would like a small one, yes. It was all very sociable, though I knew it was far more dangerous for me here in this room than it had been in Lubyanka.

"Cheers," said Schrenk, and tilted his glass. He was having to use so much control that he looked like a half-broken robot going through its mechanical gestures: I couldn't tell whether the slight trembling of his limbs was due to his injuries under torture or to the rage that was in him. The only human thing about him was the brightness of his eyes, but even that was feverish. I thought he wasn't far from the edge of a breakdown.

"Cheers," I said, and we drank together. Ignatov had

moved half a pace and I got annoyed because he'd had quite enough warning. I went across to the door and turned my back to it and looked at him until he looked down, sipping his drink. I didn't want to put a spark to the tension in here by saying anything to him directly, but the fact was that if he tried to get out of this room I'd kill him. I couldn't afford to let him into the street again: the only hope I had of doing anything for Bracken without losing my life was to take other lives first if I had to. They ought to know that; I shouldn't have to keep telling them.

"Like to sit down?" Schrenk asked me.

There was only one small settee, hardly big enough for two people; there was a chair near the window but it was piled with books and magazines and some knitting I supposed the girl was doing—a nice warm scarf for Viktor, perhaps, in the name of adoration.

"I'm all right here," I told him.

He sat down on the settee with a slight twisting motion that he'd become unaware of and no longer tried to cover. Misha moved nearer to him and was going to sit down too but he motioned her away with a little jerk of his head that she understood, even though he didn't actually look at her. She went back to the stove.

"Likes to mother me," he said with a twist of his thin mouth. "I'm a crashed pilot, you understand. Suitable cover for the state those bastards left me in." He drank some vodka.

Lights swept across the window from the car park. It had been from this window that he must have seen me two days ago, checking out the environment.

"She seems a nice girl," I said, "and she obviously looks after you well." I was aware of the clock ticking: it was a small grandfather type, tilted with one side resting on a wad of folded paper to keep the pendulum going. Schrenk had always liked clocks, and of course had used quite a few of them in his work. "Did you tell this man to blow me?" I asked him.

Schrenk's small head jerked slightly: he hadn't been ready to talk business quite so soon, and I suppose at the back of his mind he'd been hoping we'd never have to. He got off the settee with a sudden lopsided movement and stood looking away from me for a moment while he fought for control.

"I had to, don't you know that?" I saw Misha at the stove swing her head to look at him. "Snooping round here like that. I want people to leave me alone." He stood shaking, unable to face me, hating me for making him put up some kind of defense against the indefensible. "I knew you'd be able to look after yourself, wherever they put you. I think you've proved that."

Misha came across the room and took a cigarette from the black-and-yellow packet and lit it and gave it to him, as she must have done so many times: there was habit in her movements.

"Did you tell him who I was?" I asked him.

"No." He drew the smoke in deeply. "No."

"What instructions did you give him? What did he tell the police when he phoned them?"

He couldn't answer right away, though I saw he was trying. He'd wanted me to call him all the bastards under the sun for doing a thing like that, for blasting me off the street as if we'd never worked together or been close to death together, as if we'd never learned to trust each other. I would have made it easier for him if I'd gone across to him and smashed him against the wall, and I think he was still waiting for me to do that.

"He told them," he said at last, "that you were Helmut Schrenk." He tried to laugh but it turned into a coughing fit and he bent over, drawing in smoke with the air and making it worse until the girl went over to him and held his thin shaking body.

I should have thought of that. I should have realized why they'd come at me so fast and with so many men, and why Colonel Vader had been so annoyed when he'd realized I wasn't Schrenk.

"I had to get you out of the way," he said between the spasms of coughing. "I had to get you locked up, so that you couldn't—" He broke off, interrupted by a fresh paroxysm, and lost his train of thought. "But it obviously didn't work."

"Yes," I said, "it worked."

He turned to face me at last, his eyes bloodshot and the cigarette trembling in his hand and his body twisted with the effort of keeping upright.

"What happened?"

"They took me into Lubyanka."

He went on staring at me. "You were lucky. Is that all they did to you?" He meant my face.

Ignatov was moving.

"What is it you've got to do," I asked Schrenk, "that needs me out of the way? And how much is the KGB going to pay you?"

The color was leaving his face. In something like a whisper he said: "You think I'd work for them?"

"If you could do what you did to me, you could do anything."

He crumpled as if I'd hit him. His head went down and his eyes clenched shut and he stood there with his scarecrow body sagging and for a moment I felt the sweetness of revenge coming into me and warming me, and then, when it was over, I was able to think more clearly and remember that this wasn't Schrenk at all; it was the remains of the man they had worked on in Lubyanka.

"Help him to sit down," I said in Russian to the girl. Ignatov moved again.

It seemed a long time before Schrenk was on the settee, looking up at me, dragging on the new cigarette Misha had lit for him. "You think I'd work for *them?*"

"You don't seem to be working for us any more."

"I suppose," he said, and dragged more smoke in, hungry for it, "I suppose you think I blew Leningrad, do you?"

"No. It's still intact."

"That doesn't tell you anything?"

Ignatov moved again and this time vanished behind my field of vision. He was working his way toward the door, behind me. I got very annoyed and swung round with a face-high backhammer fist and he hit the door with a crash and bounced off and brought down a stack of shelves with cheap ornaments on them and I watched them disintegrating on the threadbare carpet while the girl screamed. Ignatov was staring up at me, blood trickling on his temple.

"Don't you ever *listen?*" I asked him.

It was very quiet. There didn't seem to be any noise in the whole of the building. Bad security: I hadn't got any more control than Schrenk.

Misha was hurrying across to help Ignatov, her face shocked as she passed me. One of those coy little Hummel figurines with gold paint on it and its toes turned in toppled off the remains of the shelves and broke on the floor, so I hadn't chalked up a total failure.

"What did he do?" Schrenk asked me irritably.

"Tell him if he tries to leave this room I'm going to kill him. He won't listen to me."

"Pyotr," Schrenk said in Russian, "keep away from the door. And clear up that mess." Then he looked at me again and said in soft astonishment: "Work for *them?*" Apparently it had been on his mind.

"Oh come on," I said impatiently, "it's happened before."

He looked shocked. "Not anyone from our show."

"There's a first time for everything."

Then he was on his feet again, moving very fast considering his condition. *"I tell you I'm not a defector!"*

The veins were standing out on his temples and he was staring at me with the last control over his rage slipping away. *"Do you understand that?"*

In a moment I said: "I don't understand anything, yet. I was hoping you could help me."

Misha went over to him and tried to make him sit down again but he didn't even know she was there: he just went on staring at me, his thin body trembling. "Detsky Mir," he said softly, "Detsky Mir," with his mouth twisting into a hateful smile. Ignatov was looking up at him, his hands full of broken china, and the girl's face had gone blank. I didn't know what Schrenk was talking about either: Detsky Mir was a big shopping center, that was all—Children's World.

No one spoke. I listened to the slow tick of the clock in the corner, and the sounds that had come into the building again. I'd been expecting someone along here knocking on the door because Ignatov had made a lot of noise with the china and Misha had screamed, but nobody came. Family fight.

Schrenk was getting over his rage, but there was something else there just as intense. He stayed on his feet, and he brought the words out with the whole of his body, twisting and crouching over them as if he were whittling them away, one by one, with a razor-sharp knife. His eyes never left my face. "I had time, inside Lubyanka, to think about Children's World. All those soft cuddly animals, and toy trains, and ribbons for little girls. I had a lot of time."

I was beginning to pick up a thread. Children's World is right opposite Lubyanka, in Dzerzhinsky Square. In Lubyanka there are no windows along the top floor, because the top floor is only a façade bordering an open space under the sky, with a machine gun positioned in each corner: it is the exercise yard for the prison. I'd passed Children's World on my way to the prison when they'd picked me up in Red Square.

"I spent a lot of my time," Shrenk said, whittling the words out, "trying to see some *connection*. Some *connection* between those two places. I had more time in there, you see, than you did, and you've got to think of *something,* haven't you, when they start work."

Shrenk prided himself on his ability to survive the most grueling interrogation by the use of practiced and convincing disinformation, Croder had said. *We had him tested at Norfolk, and even hypnosis couldn't break him down. That is the kind of man he is. But we don't know how bad the position is, because we don't know how much he gave away.*

Nothing. He'd given away nothing. Not even Leningrad, let alone London. Now he was here in this squalid little room, staring at me, wanting me to know something important, his maimed body trembling with the remnants of his rage and with something else that I didn't understand. That was why I was listening carefully.

"And finally I got it," he said, "I got a connection going between Children's World and Lubyanka. It worried me, you see. I mean, it's like having one of our prisons with its execution chamber right across the street from Harrod's. Could only happen in Moscow, couldn't it? Typically Russian—slightly short on good taste." He got himself a cigarette before Misha could do it for him, and flicked the match away. "I had to think up a connection, yes. Wandering a bit, am I?"

"No."

Ignatov had finished clearing things up and was squatting on a tea chest near the grandfather clock, watching Schrenk, not understanding a word but listening to the sharp dry sibilants that cut through the silence.

"They're so clever these days, aren't they, at making mechanical toys. I mean that monkey, you know, that beats the two little brass cymbals together when you wind it up—that's old hat now, but I'm not thinking of anything more complicated. Surely they could make a small doll, with trousers and a mustache to show he's a man, and hang him upside down from a kind of trapeze with another doll beside him, also in trousers and with bushy black eyebrows slanting down toward the middle to make him look fierce, and a wooden stick in his hand—you see what I mean? It shouldn't be too difficult."

I think he was trying to laugh, at this point, or the laugh was just coming naturally because of his macabre sense of humor, I'm not sure; whatever it was it ended in more coughing, because of the cigarette smoke. I suppose his lungs were in a pretty bad way, with the ashtrays always full.

"Then," he said when he could, "you'd wind him up and he'd move the wooden stick up and down, beating the bare feet of the doll who's hanging upside down from the trapeze. I'm sure," he said, and the laughter started now, and I hope I never hear a sound like that again, "I'm sure all the little boys would tug their mummies along there to buy one—in this country it'd be a smash hit, don't you think?"

The laughter went on, the strangest sound I have ever heard from a human throat, a kind of soft yelping, like the cry of an animal caught in a trap. I saw Misha staring at him, her plump hands going slowly to her face, while Ignatov watched him with his thick gray mouth slightly open, his eyes bewildered.

Schrenk stood in a crouch as the breath came out of his body in spasms; his eyes were squeezed almost shut, with the glint of tears showing. "You see," he said painfully, "I finally succeeded in making a *connection,* a connection between Children's World and that other world across the square. I could finally believe they existed within a stone's throw of each other. Of course there's always the funny side to these things, isn't there, I mean quite a lot of good citizens are taken inside Lubyanka for interrogation, sometimes for days on end if they prove obstinate, as you well know." Ash dropped from his cigarette and he brushed it clumsily off his jacket. "So you can easily imagine a young mother, worried about the fact that her Jewish husband has disappeared, buying her little boy the funny mechanical toy he's been pestering her for. Then, when he keeps on asking where Daddy is, she can tell him not to worry about him, just go and play with his toy." He began laughing again, in soft little yelps. "Don't you think that's an absolute—absolute scream?" But when he swung his head up to look at me I saw the hatred burning in his eyes with a white-hot flame.

Then I understood. His rage wasn't against me. It was against that jackbooted crowd of thugs in Lubyanka, and the regime in which they operated, and the order of command that structured it from the omnipotent Politburo down to the cocky little militiamen in the streets. Dr. Steinberg had been surprised that I hadn't grasped the most obvious of facts: that when you damage a man as they had damaged Schrenk, with your bare hands and with special implements and with humiliation, you will engender in what remains of him the most murderous hate. *It does, after all, become personal.*

I could believe him now. Schrenk wasn't a defector.

Misha had got him to sit down again on the settee, and for a moment sat with him, her head against his shoulder and her hand cupping his cheek. She looked at me with her face questioning, then withdrew into herself as she remembered what I had done to Ignatov.

"Work for *them?*" Schrenk said bitterly. He shook off the girl and stared at me.

"What does he say?" she pleaded to Ignatov. "What is it about, this *Lubyanka* and this *Detsky Mir?*"

"I don't know," he said broodingly.

"Why did the man hit you like that? Should I get the police?"

"You know better," he said, "than to get the police."

Schrenk patted the girl's hand. "There's nothing to worry about, sweetheart. But your Viktor would like some tea. Would you make some tea for us?"

"There's some in the samovar," she said eagerly, sensing a return to normal.

"That would be very nice."

She hugged him in relief and I saw pain flicker across his face; then she bounced off the settee and ran across to the urn, leaving him staring at me.

"We've got a mission on the board," I said, "and I'm the executive in the field. Guess what they want me to do."

He brushed ash off his knees. "Tell them I'll make my report when I'm ready. I'm not ready yet."

"The objective," I said patiently, "is to get you out of Russia."

"Sorry I can't help you." He drained his glass of

vodka and put it onto the rickety little stool at the end of the settee, getting it wrong and letting it fall to the carpet. Ignatov ambled forward to pick it up for him.

"Leave it there."

"Of course, Viktor."

"I can pick things up for myself, don't you know that?"

"I was forgetting."

We watched Schrenk double over and feel for the glass, his hand swinging like a hook till his fingers connected with the rim; then he put the glass back onto the stool with ostentatious care, though it rattled to the trembling of his hand before he could stop it.

"You mean," I asked him, "you're staying in Moscow?"

"I've got friends here."

"If they're anything like this son of a bitch, then you're welcome to them."

He laughed and said: "He's not too fond of you either. Why do they want me out of Russia?"

"They want to debrief you on the interrogation." I could tell him so much and no more. He was going to lie when it suited him and he was going to do it convincingly, and if I shot questions at him I was going to get as much out of him as they'd got out of him in Lubyanka. All I could do was feel my way softly into the rage, into the silently roaring battlefield they'd made of his mind, and hope to intercept a few signals when he was off his guard, and try to come out alive and get the message to Bracken. "They want to give you some leave. You've earned that, God knows."

"I'll pay my own way," he said, and fumbled in the black-and-yellow packet for another cigarette.

It meant nothing at all. It was just a spark coming out of the volcano. I had to find a way of reaching him.

"Natalya hopes to see you again." At the edge of my vision field I saw Misha turn her head to listen.

"Natalya's dangerous," Schrenk said at once. "Don't forget that." He didn't ask me how I'd got on to her: he knew that when I'd come into the field I would have started by contacting his friends.

"Noted," I said. "But she's got her heart in the right place. They're all worried about Borodinski." It was an oblique shot and I got a hit though he kept most of his control.

"Certainly they're worried about Borodinski."

"D'you think he'll get off?"

"Get off?" No control now. "He'll get life, you know that."

I took it further. "There's a lot of protests going on."

"Protests? They're not protests, for God's sake! There's only one thing those bastards'll listen to." Then he angled his head and watched me steadily. "You're not interested in Borodinski."

No go.

Ignatov moved and I whipped a glance at him, but he was only helping the girl with the tray of tea. The room was full of comfortable sounds: the clinking of cups on saucers and the slow tick of the clock. But the company was wrong. Give Schrenk a few more days in here and he'd wire himself to that clock and blow the whole building apart.

"Thank you, sweetheart," he said, and took his cup from her. "The thing is"—his head turning to me—"I want to be left alone for a bit. I've done enough for London, for the moment, you've said that yourself. I applied for a job here as an a-i-p but you know what happens to an application in that bloody place, it's like a snake trying to scratch its arse, can never quite find it." He sipped some tea. "So you see I don't want anyone coming here, you or Bracken or anyone else. And that makes it difficult, doesn't it?" He didn't look at me when he said that. He wasn't going to enjoy this, and neither was I, but it was something we had to do, had to work out.

Misha brought some tea for me, standing directly between Schrenk and me with her plump country girl's body and whispering. "Who is Natalya?"

"Only an acquaintance," I whispered back, but of course she didn't believe me.

"It makes it difficult," Schrenk said, "because when you leave here you're going to signal Bracken and tell him where to find me. And I don't want that." I noticed the color was leaving his face as he sat squinting through the smoke, and his voice took on a forced quality as he made himself tell me the rest. "The KGB must be hunting you pretty hard if you gave them the slip in Lubyanka. So when you leave here I'm going to blow you as I did before, and there's no way you can stop me." Then his head went down. "Sorry."

15 / PENDULUM

The clock ticked.

We listened to it. No one spoke.

He liked clocks. He liked the measured inevitability of time and the events it would bring. He liked watching fuses burn: I'd seen him do that. He liked mechanics—automatic relays, timed-release units, delayed detonation devices. Even to bridge the philosophical gap between Lubyanka and Children's World he'd had to invent a mechanical toy.

It might be logical, though dangerously mistaken, to think he was therefore predictable, so that one knew what he was going to do next.

Where was the telephone?

He dragged on his cigarette, pulling the smoke deep into his lungs: he needed it more than food; he needed it more than life, because he was dying of it. But he'd got things to do first, and I was in his way.

He'd need a telephone.

Ignatov and Misha were absolutely quiet. They hadn't understood what Schrenk had said to me, but they had seen what an effort it had cost him to say it, and they had seen his head go down like that as he had quietly offered the executioner's apology. *Sorry*.

"There is a way," I said, "I could stop you."

I could leave them both dead and the girl in shock when I left here.

"No," he said, "there isn't. But we don't have to go into that."

Would he need a telephone, though? Ignatov might not be his only contact: he might have a dozen of them, one in the next apartment, one in the apartment opposite, any number of them. There was something he had to do and he might have got a whole cell established to help him do it.

"They're hunting pretty hard," I said, "for you too."

He got up impatiently, twisting his body upright and holding it stiffly for a moment before he started pacing the worn carpet. "But that isn't the position, is it? You're not going to have me picked up—your objective is to keep me out of their hands."

"I didn't mean that. I meant that you might not have much longer before they find you anyway. You must have left a trail and this isn't a safe house—you can get a knock on the door any minute." I tried to forget what this man had done to me and what he was going to do again if I couldn't stop him. "I came out here to get you safely home, and with a bit of luck I can do it. You don't need Moscow any more."

He came up to me quietly, one thin leg swinging slightly more than the other as he tried not to hobble, and looked into my face and said with his eyes bright: "But Moscow needs me."

It was the first indication I'd had that his mind had been affected, that there was more going on inside him than a hurricane of rage. It stopped me dead.

"Come on home," I said. "You're too close to it all. You can always come back if you want to."

"Humoring me?" with his eyes burning.

Oh my God, yes, that fitted too: they hate it when you refuse to believe they're Napoleon.

"Not really," I said.

He watched me with his bright eyes for a moment, his small gnome's head on one side. "You have to go now," he said, and hobbled away from me across the threadbare carpet. "He's leaving," he told Ignatov in Russian. "Don't do anything. Stay where you are."

"Yes, Viktor."

Where was the telephone?

There'd be one in the front hallway, a pay phone. If I went through there I could pull out the wire. But Schrenk knew I'd think of that because he'd think of it himself. This wasn't a half-trained novitiate I was having to deal with.

"I think you're making a mistake," I told him.

"One more won't do me any harm."

"You're relying on me not to get you picked up the minute they arrest me."

Ignatov was halfway between the door and the window, nursing his temple. The girl was over by the stove. I began noting other things, because the trap was closing now and the organism was aware of the need to escape; but I didn't think I was going to be able to do that: Schrenk was a professional and he knew he had the advantage.

"You won't get me picked up," he said, and turned to face me, squinting above his cigarette. "They'd start work on me again and next time they might break me and then I'd have to blow London. I'm perfectly safe in your hands."

Ignatov wasn't moving. He was watching Schrenk,

trying to understand what he was saying. Misha stood rocking on her black strapped shoes, her hands to her face, waiting, watching the man she adored and ready to claw my eyes out if I tried to hurt him.

"You're perfectly safe in my hands," I said, "till they start work on me again and break me and ask me to tell them where you are, as they did before. This time I'll have the answer and I'll have to give it to them."

He said immediately: "That's all right. I won't be here."

We watched each other. We weren't telling each other anything we didn't already know: each wanted the other to know that he knew. The scene going on in this tawdry little room in a Moscow suburb was the exact epitome of the cold war: the war that is kept cold by the ceaseless efforts of the intelligence forces to assure the opposition that nothing can be done in secret, that no attack can be made without an immediate counterattack. The danger cannot be contained simply by finding out what the opposition is doing: *the opposition must be informed that it is known.*

We knew this, and we had to go through the situation point by point in an attempt to contain the danger. We also knew we had to fail. It was going to be his life or mine. He wasn't going to have me picked up: he'd only wanted to know my thinking, and I'd told him. He couldn't risk making a phone call when I left here because it wouldn't give him time to get out when the KGB closed in and found him in the same net.

He couldn't afford to let me leave here alive.

"Give yourself a bit of time," I said, "to think."

"I've done all the thinking."

"There's no special hurry."

"Yes," he said, "there is."

The clock ticked, with a rhythm that was slightly off

balance: it needed a wad of paper a sixteenth of an inch thinner, or a sixteenth of an inch thicker, to equalize the swing of the pendulum. Perhaps it worried him sometimes in the night, disturbing his sense of mechanical precision. Perhaps, every morning, he added a thickness of paper to the wad, or removed a thickness, to equalize the rhythm; it would be like him to do that; I could see him doing it, with his thin body twisted as he crouched at the base of the grandfather clock with Misha watching him, as a mother watches a small boy. I knew him quite well, and this made it so much worse for me to do what I would have to do.

If I didn't do it, I wouldn't leave here alive.

What happens if I find him but can't get him out?

The lamplight sending the rain pattern creeping in rivulets down Croder's face, his dark hooded eyes glancing away as he instructed me, bestowing on me the powers of an executioner.

That would make it easier for you. All we want is his silence.

There was, then, no impediment. I had sanction from on high and there would be no record made of the incident. The file on Scorpion would simply note: *Mission accomplished as per instructions*. Physically there was no problem offered: I could reach him in three steps and use a sword hand to the larynx with killing power and there would be nothing he could do because he didn't have enough speed left, enough strength left, to defend himself. It would occupy perhaps four seconds of my time.

Then I could go home, get out of this bloody place and try to forget. Mission accomplished, *good for you, old horse, you did it again*, and two months' leave on the Sussex coast with Helena, *a dozen gardenias, you shouldn't be so extravagant*, two months to forget the twisted thing on the floor with the black bruise on the throat and the sound of a girl screaming, the comfortable smell of boiled cabbage.

God damn their eyes. This man had done good work for them time and again, put his life in hazard for them time and again, stood up to that hellish assault on his psyche in Lubyanka without breaking, without exposing Leningrad or London, and now they were asking me to leave him on the floor like a bit of rubbish we'd thrown out, *God damn their eyes.*

Mine not to reason why, of course. The ferret in the field obeys orders and goes down the hole and comes up again if he's lucky, leaving behind him those unnameable things in the dark that he had to deal with. Dear God, how long ago was it when they'd said to me: if you decide to go into the field you'll have to bear in mind the fact that you'll be asked to do things you'll find it hard to do, we don't mean dangerous things, you seem all right on that score, we mean dirty things, rotten things that may well give you nightmares afterward . . . We're just giving you fair warning, you understand, so that you'll know what you're going into, if that's what you finally decide . . .

Mine but to do or die, yes, quite. If I didn't kill Schrenk he would have to kill me, I knew that. Things can get very basic in the end phase of a mission. Croder would probably laugh if he knew my thoughts, his rat's teeth nibbling with secret amusement. *My dear fellow, the issue is cut and dried, surely you see that. It's impossible for you to get this man out of Russia if he refuses to go, and if he stays here he'll get picked up again and this time they'll get everything out of him, you've said so yourself. Are you really saying that one man's life is worth the entire Leningrad cell and possibly the security of the Bureau as well? You must be indulging in some sort of sentimentality, and that can be highly dangerous.* The rat's teeth nibbling and the hooded eyes looking away. *Besides, the man's a complete wreck now: we could never put him into the field again.*

Good reason. Good logic. But Lord, hear my prayer, and *damn their eyes.*

He was watching me, squinting through the smoke of his cigarette with an expression I couldn't quite read. He was looking at me almost as if he'd never seen me before, though it wasn't exactly that. Got it, yes: *as if he were never going to see me again.*

How would he try to kill? He couldn't do it himself, and Ignatov was no use to him. He probably had a dozen people not far away, a clique of fanatical dissidents lying low in readiness for a coup. He'd set the whole pack on me once I was outside there in the dark. He seemed very confident.

So I'd have to get in first.

Give him a last chance.

"I was sent out here to find you," I told him, and the tightness in my throat distorted the words slightly. "I was told to pull you out."

"I understand that."

"And you understand why."

"Of course." He began pacing again, one thin leg swinging an inch further than the other, like the pendulum of the clock. That must worry him too, but he couldn't do anything about it. "They don't want me to be put under interrogation again, because next time I might have to blow the whole works. I understand that."

A bit too loudly I said: "Then for Christ's sake give it a minute's thought, will you? Think out the implications."

He looked at me sharply and away again, and went on with his pacing. I wanted him to think this out for himself. I didn't want to have to tell him, the instant before I had to do it.

Final considerations: Reluctance to do it in front of the girl, because she adored him. Possibility of getting her to leave the room, ask her to fetch something, tell Schrenk to send her away for a moment. Other thoughts intruding: *For sale, Jensen Interceptor, only 27,000 miles, fitted anti-radar unit, all refinements. Also 200 classic jazz records (15 Harry James, 12 Duke Ellington) and player.* The plastic chess set would remain in the Caff and the other things like tennis racquets and skis and karate swords would be offered up and down the corridors in off-duty hours: there's usually a jumble sale when someone fails to come back, because we're loners, most of us, and not the kind of people who have relations to leave things to; we're born alone and we die alone and no one really notices. At the Bureau a prerequisite of our service is that we agree not to exist.

"I've told you," Schrenk said, "I've done all the thinking." He brought his pacing to a clumsy halt between the window and the small Victorian writing desk in the corner. "But what you mean is, if you can't pull me out of Moscow you've got instructions to do the other thing. That right?"

"Yes."

He nodded. "Perfectly logical."

I moved at once but the inertia cost me time and he was much closer to the writing desk than I was and his lunge for the top drawer was accurate and he had the gun in his hand and the safety catch off before I was anywhere near.

"Careful," he said.

I looked at his face and stopped dead. The desk was

still rocking on its thin varnished legs and the drawer was sticking out at a slight angle with its brass handle swinging to stillness. There was something else in the drawer but I couldn't see it clearly from this distance; it was just one of a hundred items of data that were bombarding the consciousness and there wasn't enough time to examine it. In addition to this the emotional block was inhibiting reason: *I'd lost.*

"Back off a bit," Schrenk said, "you're too close."

I did what he told me.

"Never carry a gun, do you?" His hand was absolutely steady. "That's a mistake."

Peripheral vision: Ignatov had moved away from the wall where he'd been standing with a handkerchief pressed to his temple; he was looking at Schrenk and waiting for instructions. Misha hadn't moved but I could hear her tremulous breathing: she was a country girl and not used to the big city with its tall concrete towers and the grinding underground trains and men who were ready to kill each other in the warmth of a groundfloor apartment with the comfortable smell of boiled cabbage in the air.

"Sweetheart," Schrenk said, "would you get me another cigarette?" He didn't take his eyes off me.

The girl moved out of my sight and then came back, lighting a cigarette from the crumpled paper packet and handing it to him, taking away the butt of the old one and dropping it into the ashtray. "Will everything be all right?" she asked him, close to tears.

"Everything will be all right, sweetheart, yes. Don't worry."

My left eyelid had begun flickering and without thinking about it I was breathing more deeply. There wasn't going to be any action because things had passed beyond that stage: you can't rush a gun and I wasn't going to try. The only conceivable chance was in getting behind Ignatov and using him as a shield but there was Schrenk behind that thing, Shapiro, not some half-trained amateur. And he wanted me out of his way.

"Had some good times, didn't we?" He drew deeply on the new cigarette. "Remember Rosita?"

I didn't say anything. He wasn't making sense.

"Tenerife? Tell you something. I took her out the night before old Templer flew in. What a gal!" He began wheezing with quiet laughter, his thin body shaking with it. But his gun hand remained perfectly steady. "Poor old Templer. He was going to take her out that night, but of course those bastards . . ." He began coughing but managed to control it: the range was fifteen feet and he knew I could move very fast. "Remember that bloody bomb in the consulate in Cairo? Got the motto out, didn't we?" He giggled again. "Good times. We had some good times." Then he straightened up as far as he could and his tone was serious. "We could do a deal if you like."

I began listening carefully. "What deal?"

I think Ignatov must have moved just at this point, though he was outside my vision field. Schrenk said to him sharply: "Pyotr, stay where you are. If you move any closer he'll try to use you as a shield, can't you see that? Stay *exactly* where you are."

In English he asked me: "Are you interested?"

"I don't know yet."

"Pretty simple. If you agree to abort the mission I'll let you go home."

"It's not on."

"Always so bloody *obstinate,*" he said in annoyance. "Don't you know the alternative?"

"Yes."

"You think there's a chance?" He shook his head.

"I'm not going to have you picked up again, you know that. It's too risky—you might get away as you did before. You know what I've got to do."

He was losing his color, and there was a certain stiffness coming into his body, as if he were readying himself to do something that would need a lot of effort on his part, a lot of determination. I could feel my eyelid flickering again and wondered if it showed: it's always been an embarrassment.

"Spell it out for me," I told Schrenk. "We don't want any misunderstandings."

"You're so right. All I want you to do is to go back to London without telling them where I am, or even that you found me. I want to be left alone."

In a moment I said: "You'd take my word?"

He looked surprised. "Of course."

"You think you know me that well?"

"Oh yes. I'm not risking anything."

I thought about it. "Yes, you are. They could pick me up again and grill me, and I know where to find you."

Concerned, he asked quickly: "Haven't you got a capsule?"

"Yes."

"Then you'd have to use it. That would be part of the deal." He waited impatiently.

I watched him, trying to read the truth in his eyes, in his face, in the set of his angular body, in the steadiness of the hand that held the gun. I believed he meant what he was saying. I was certain he did.

"You know what I'm offering you," he said quietly.

"My life."

"Yes." His face was bloodless now. At least it was going to mean something to him when he finally had to pump that thing and watch my body go reeling back in a series of jerks. I'd at least have an epitaph to go out with: *Someone cared.*

But that didn't have to happen. I could take him at his word and walk out of here and report to Bracken and have the cell move in: there were six of them, fully trained, and they could take Schrenk and get him out of the country and put him back into a clinic and go on working on him, the best specialists, the best attention, until one fine day he could walk without hobbling and stand up straight and go and see that girl in Brighton again, take her out in his Jensen Interceptor and then one day, one day say to me, you broke your word to me that time in Moscow and it's a bloody good thing you did or I wouldn't be here now.

He was half out of his mind and needed protecting from himself: he was mixed up with a bunch of wildcat dissidents planning some kind of protest that was going to land him inside Lubyanka again or flat on his back in the street with his head in the gutter and the young wooden-faced militiamen standing arrogantly over him, kicking him idly with their polished boots until the transport arrived. You have to use *every* means to complete a mission and the object of Scorpion was to get this man out of Moscow and I could do it without any problem, without lifting a finger, yes I accept the deal and you've got my word on it. The rest would be up to Bracken and his team and they wouldn't have any problem either, once Schrenk was subdued and in their care; Croder had lined up support facilities that would get them across the frontier at an hour's notice: Bracken had told me so.

"The thinking," Schrenk said heavily, "is for you to do, not me. But I haven't got a lot of time, quite frankly. I'm going to give you another minute. Sixty seconds. I think that's fair."

The gun was aimed at my forehead. He was a first-class shot and could drop me where I stood without any pain. He was a humane man. Sixty seconds. That was a long time, more time than I really needed. A generous man.

I heard the tick of the clock. We all heard it. The other two hadn't understood anything of what we'd been saying but they could sense what this silence meant: we'd both stopped talking and he was holding the gun perfectly still. I looked at it carefully; it was a 9-mm. Smith and Wesson and would carry eight shots in the magazine. Schrenk would use only one.

Tick . . . tock.

The idea occurred to me that if I remained staring into the barrel of that thing I would perhaps see the nose of the bullet traveling toward me in the final microsecond of life, as young Chepstow had possibly seen it when he'd been sitting at the café table drinking his last cup of coffee in Phnom Penh a couple of years ago, thinking perhaps it was a bee.

Tick . . . tock.

Schrenk was very pale now, and there was something coming into his eyes, a kind of blankness. I suppose he was having to blank out his mind and leave it clear of any philosophical considerations that might finally get in the way of what he had to do, which was to squeeze the first nicotine-stained finger of his right hand by a simple command to the motor nerves.

Tick . . . tock.

How long had he said? Sixty seconds. But he wouldn't fire without some kind of warning. He wouldn't expect me to know when the sixty seconds were up. Perhaps he was counting. Was I expected to count, as well? *Schrenk. Do you want me to count?*

Because it was no go. If I gave him my word I would

have to keep it. It didn't matter if he were half out of his mind and needed protecting from himself, so forth: those arguments were rational but not admissible. It wasn't for me to judge him now. He'd worked damned hard for our people and kept us safe, all of us, Leningrad and London, all of us, while they'd been trying to break him in Lubyanka, and he'd earned our trust, my trust.

Tick . . . tock.

I really do wish you'd get that bloody thing fixed. What I was *not* going to do was walk out of here and tell Bracken I was aborting the mission and ask him to give me safe passage back to London with my tail between my legs. I wish you'd get that bloody thing to tick evenly. It's getting on my nerves. Call it pride, would you, not enough guts to face the fact that for the first time in my life I'm failing a mission, I don't give a damn what you call it, it's none of your bloody business. Must I suppose be up by now, sixty isn't long.

Tick . . .

Flickering. Left eyelid flickering. Sweat running down, wet on the palms. The face wound throbbing, the pulse rate high. Small round barrel and I suppose, I suppose that if in point of fact I finally glimpse the pointed lead nose of the bullet it's going to look quite large, two inches from the center of my forehead, large enough to blot his whole face out of sight.

Tock.

"I'd say that's about it, Q."

Breath.

"All right. No deal."

His eyes widened slightly. "Why not, for God's sake?"

"That's none of your bloody business."

He went on staring for another second or two. "I

didn't think you'd be such a bastard. Making me do a thing like this." His tone had gone dead.

"You should have thought of that before."

In a moment he nodded, and kept the gun on me while he felt for the drawer of the writing desk with his left hand, and found it, and took the thing out, the thing I'd seen before. It was a silencer and he fitted it to the gun.

The distance was still something like fifteen feet, almost the width of the room. The window was obliquely behind him and the door was three or four feet to my left and out of sight. Ignatov was over by the wall and the girl was on the other side near the kitchen area. The only thing in the center of the room was the short velvet-covered settee. There was nothing in the environment I could use for survival in the half second it would take Schrenk to fire. Nothing.

"No hard feelings, I hope." I hardly recognized his voice. He stood there with his body twisted and the left shoulder down, the sweat shining on his thin agonized face as he stared at me—not at my eyes but slightly above them, making no contact, giving me the chilling idea that I was a lifeless object, nothing he could communicate with.

"It's your own conscience," I told him. "That's all you'll get."

"All I expected. Mind turning round?"

"You mean you haven't got the guts to do it while I'm looking at you?"

I seemed to be breathing cold air in the warmth of the room, my lungs gradually contracting, my body shrinking. I didn't watch Schrenk any more: I wanted to forget him, if I could, in the last instant. I watched the heavy shape of the silencer.

"I'm not going to shoot," he said. "I just want you to turn round."

Of course I could refuse but the organism was thinking for itself and I had the instinctive knowledge that if I didn't turn round he'd have to shoot anyway. So I turned round.

"Pyotr," he said.

I heard Ignatov moving away from the wall. "Yes, Viktor."

"Take this gun," I heard the strange voice saying in Russian, "and go outside with him. Keep the gun in the pocket of your coat, so that no one else will see it." The voice stopped, and I heard the effort he was having to make to go on with what he was saying. "This man is extremely clever, and he will take risks, because his life is at stake. You must keep a good distance between him and yourself. Take him out to your car and when he is inside it, shoot him dead." There was another pause, and when Schrenk spoke again there was anger in his voice, as if he had to work up some kind of resentment against me to go through with this. "Drive him as far as the river. If you want to, ask Boris and Dmitri to go with you, but I'd prefer you to go alone. You don't have to use any weights, in the river. All you have to do is to make sure he is found a long way from here. You understand?"

"Yes, Viktor."

A change in Ignatov's voice, too: it sounded strong now, and deeper. He said to me: "Open the door."

The senses had become acute. I heard Misha whispering, so softly that I didn't catch the words. Some kind of prayer? I was quite moved, and had a sudden hatred of Schrenk for doing this in front of her, for being so coarse: he could have sent her out. *Slightly short on good taste,* I thought as I opened the door, and wondered who had said that, where I'd heard it.

"Pyotr. If he makes any attempt to get away, shoot at once, and to kill."

"Yes, Viktor."

Then I heard a long shuddering breath, and Schrenk spoke softly in English. *"Good times."*

16 / SHOOT

He fired six rapid shots at short range into the spine and the impact pitched my body forward in a series of jerks as the chips of bone and cartilage from the shattered vertebrae were forced out through the rib cage in an explosion of blood and plasma. As my face hit the snow I thought *Schrenk you bastard I hope they burn you for this.*

Have to do better. Control the imagination.

I listened to his footsteps along the corridor behind me. I estimated the distance at something like six feet, not nearly close enough to do anything in safety. We kept on walking toward the door leading to the car park at the rear.

He fired directly into the back of the head and the brain matter burst and splattered against the walls in a welter of skull fragments. There was no more time for conscious thought, even of Moira, even of roses: life was simply present, then absent. *Executive deceased.*

Have to do *much* better, yes. A normal reaction to awareness of imminent death with the imagination running wild but it was useless and dangerous: survival possible only through rational thought.

Man in a worn brown overcoat and horn-rimmed glasses.

"Good evening, comrade." Ignatov.

"Good evening. They say it's going to snow again."

"Surely we've had enough!"

A chance, obviously, to move extremely fast and get the man in the brown overcoat between me and the gun, but Ignatov might have fired precipitately and shot him by accident.

"Keep walking."

I quickened the pace a little. He had the gun in the pocket of his coat; otherwise the other man would have seen it. He couldn't take accurate aim like that but it didn't make a lot of difference: at this range he could hit me lethally with three or four shots, shifting the aim according to the visible point of impact. I didn't know if he'd handled firearms before but it seemed likely: Schrenk wouldn't leave me in the hands of an amateur.

"Open the door."

His voice was heavy, its tone entirely changed by his possession of a killing instrument. There had been no power in his voice before, no authority; now there was both, and something else, something like anticipation. I'd pictured the end of the world for him too often, with his three children asking Galya where Daddy had gone, and now he had the end of my own world in his hands and he was impatient for it. Once the eight lumps of spinning metal had gone burrowing into me he would be safe again, and go home to Galya and the children. You could see his point of view.

The night air was freezing after the heat of the apartment. The heavy door slammed shut behind us.

"Over that way."

He was closer, I thought. Or it might simply be that the wall of the building was projecting his voice forward and making it sound louder. I would have to watch things like that.

His mud-brown Syrena was obliquely to our right, not far from the entrance to the car park and facing this way. I hadn't locked it after I'd got him out. The street-lamps cast a sick greenish light across the area and the albedo was high, the reflections bouncing off the cellulose of the parked cars and the blanket of ground snow. Shadows were sharp.

Pyotr. If he makes any attempt to get away, shoot at once, and to kill.

But he was going to do that anyway as soon as we reached his car, so I didn't have much to lose.

He fired into the neck and I felt the spine explode—
Steady.

One, two, three . . . twelve cars. In the corner, a pickup truck. Thirteen objects of good cover, but too far away, the nearest car at least twenty feet from where I was walking: we were crossing an open space. No one in sight. A long way off, the drone of a tram. No sound of other traffic: the evening rush hour was over and in this city by night the streets are almost empty.

What would she do with them?

"Make for the car. The Syrena."

Authority in his tone, the authority of death itself.

Five hundred were an awful lot: they'd fill the whole flat and what could she do with them afterward, change the water every day, sit and stare at them, what pretty roses?

I listened to his footsteps on the snow behind me. I seemed to be crunching more than he was: perhaps he was walking in the hollows I was leaving, putting his feet exactly where I had placed mine. It would look rather comic, like a couple of ducks on their way to the pond, picking their feet up and putting them down at orderly intervals. But there was no one here to see. He would be the last person on earth I was going to see, a dough-faced plodding man with a wife and three little children and a gash on his temple and a gun in his—

"Keep walking."

The sound of his voice jarred my nerves. Why had he said that? Had I been slowing? I must have. Perfectly understandable, as Schrenk would have said, squinting through the cigarette smoke: you don't run to your funeral.

"Which is your car?" I asked him.

"You know which one it is. It's the brown Syrena, near the entrance."

I nodded and walked on.

She was still in Tokyo, filming. Back in two weeks—they'd hold the delivery. No, she wouldn't just sit there and stare at them: she'd go out and get stoned, that was all she'd do. Or she'd take her Lotus up the M1 flat out in the dark with the headlights swallowing up the night and everything she could ever remember of me, and when she got back to the flat she'd just think oh my God what am I going to do with all these bloody roses?

The snow crunched under our shoes. I think one of my shoes was leaking, or some snow had got in over the top: my left foot felt wet. Useless enough sensory data, if you like. I began turning my head very gradually, so that I could trap the sounds from behind me in the auricle of the right ear; his footsteps loudened slightly. I estimated he was still a good six feet behind me, so that there was no chance of turning on him. But I kept my head slightly to one side, exposing the right ear to the auditory source. I could hear his breathing now; he was a heavy man, too well fed by his loving wife.

So in fact the rose thing wasn't really going to work out after all—it was just a grandiose gesture, a juvenile urge to make an impression from out there in the never-ending dark. It would have been subtler to send one rose, one sublime and perfect rose to remember me by, not an ostentatious barrowload. Ignatov, old boy, do you mind if I just phone Harrod's before we wind up the evening?

Something like laughter, a long, long way down in the psyche, a neural reaction perhaps, while the slow cold wave went down the spine and the sweat gathered and ran, the reaction of the beast that smells the slaughterhouse: he was squeezing his finger at every step we took and I could feel the impact and hear the shrill jangling of the nerve system as the organism took the shock.

I believe I've got another thirty seconds to live. But there's nobody I can tell. We're born alone and we die alone and no one really notices.

Headlights swung across the façade of the building opposite and sparked light from the windows. Sound of a vehicle, smell of exhaust gas.

"The Syrena," the man behind me said.

"Oh yes. Sorry."

I hadn't meant to go off course; it was the organism again, not wanting to go near that particular car because it was a hearse. The headlights swung in a half circle and I saw the vehicle turning in from the street, a small dark Moskvich bumping over the ruts with its snow chains clanking and the bodywork rattling—a kind of mad toy that some joker had wound up and sent into the car park to raise a laugh. It obliterated the slight sounds Ignatov was making and of course I couldn't see him because he was behind me, and for a moment the idea came to me that he wasn't there any more, that I'd let my nerves get out of hand to the point where I'd imagined him. It was an enormous relief and I took a deep breath and remembered the reports of people who had come back from the edge of death; they all said the same thing: first you panic, then you try to do something about the situation, then when you realize it's all up you get a feeling of euphoria as the organism anesthetizes the final awareness of death.

But I wasn't at that stage yet and I'd better wake up to the fact that Ignatov was indeed still behind me and all he had to do was stumble a bit on the frozen ruts and his finger would tighten and I'd be finished.

"Ignatov," I said. "You didn't understand what we were saying, did you, Viktor and I?"

"No."

The little Moskvich rattled to a halt a dozen yards away and its lights went out.

"He offered me a deal," I said over my shoulder. "He said he'd let me leave Moscow if I gave him my word not to tell anyone where he is."

"Don't turn round," he said, and I could hear that he meant it. I suppose the Moskvich was worrying him: it might be a friend of Schrenk's or someone he knew, and they might come over for a chat.

"I refused the deal," I said. "But I think that was unwise. I'd like to reconsider." I wanted time.

"The Syrena," he said. There was a note of warning in his voice.

"If Viktor knew I was ready to accept the deal, he'd prefer it that way. We've worked together, you know. He must have told you." More than anything I wanted time.

"He told me nothing."

A man got out of the Moskvich and crunched across the snow. He didn't look in our direction. In the quiet of the night the distant tram went on droning. My senses had become finely tuned in the last few minutes and I was acutely aware of the environment.

"Viktor and I are good friends," I said over my shoulder, "that's why we all had a drink before we started talking. It's just that he thinks I want to stop this little protest he's going to make—you know, about Borodinski. You can quite understand how I feel about it now. I'd like to reconsider the deal he offered me. I want to talk to him again."

My voice sounded odd in the silence of the car park, the voice of a man talking to himself. "Viktor would come down very hard on you if he ever found out I was finally ready to do the deal with him." Time. Give me time.

But it meant nothing, except that a drowning man was grasping at straws, worse, fabricating them out of thin air. Ignatov didn't bother to answer. The Syrena was twenty feet away from me now and I was walking straight toward it. With my head still turned I couldn't tell if he'd come any closer to me; I didn't think so; I think he was still walking in my footprints, hoping to keep the deep snow out of his shoes.

Fifteen feet.

Ten.

The car stood broadside on. The passenger's door was closed, just as I'd left it when I'd cut the scarf from his wrists and ankles and let him get out. The keys would still be in the ignition: I hadn't been concerned about them at the time because I'd seen that the man hobbling across the car park was Schrenk.

"Open the door," Ignatov said from behind me. His

voice faded a little as he spoke: he'd stopped, to keep a safe distance between us when I opened the door.

Thought was becoming rarefied, and reality slipped out of focus: I nearly asked him who was going to drive. The Syrena looked bigger than it had before, a large brown container for the body, snow covering its roof like a white pall and a dead man's face in the window: my own reflection.

Take him out to your car and when he is inside it, shoot him dead.

The night was totally still. I could feel the cold creeping into my left foot, and smell the faint residue of the exhaust gas the Moskvich had left on the air. A long way off I could see the glint of a gold dome: one of the churches, with an illuminated red star at the tip of a spire. Beyond it the sky was black. In the immediate environment I saw my pale reflection in the window of the Syrena and Ignatov's crooked shadow across the bodywork. There was no one else in the car park, so he would have taken the gun from his pocket by now, in order to shoot accurately.

"Open the door," he told me again. His voice was still heavy and authoritative, and there was something else there now, distinct but difficult to define. I think it was a kind of awe: my heightened awareness told me that he had never killed a man before.

I opened the door, and snow fell away.

"Get in."

I did as he told me. He was still six feet away from the side of the car and he wouldn't come any closer, in case I tried to attack him at the last minute. I was right: the gun was now in his hand, and I saw him lift it to eye level and hold it forward so that he could line up the sights.

"Wind the window down," he said. "Hurry."

He wanted to get it done with before anyone else drove into the car park. I turned the cheap aluminum handle and the window went down in a series of jerks, sticking on the rubber flanges and then freeing.

"Shut the door."

The keys were still in the ignition and I tugged them out as I dragged the door shut and flung them hard into his face and kicked away from the door to give me the impetus for a horizontal dive that took me clear of the steering wheel with my right fist punching the horn to provide sound shock and my left hand wrenching at the driver's door handle and the main force of the momentum sending me through the gap as the door burst open and the retaining strap broke and the panel smashed back against the bodywork. The first shot ruffled the sleeve of my coat and shattered the window: he'd shouted something, maybe just a cry of alarm because of the horn, and the soft wet *phutt* of the silencer came an instant afterward. I was into the snow and lurching onto my feet and losing balance and trying to find it again.

If I went underneath the car I'd be a sitting duck, so I feinted to the right with my head and shoulders visible to him through the shattered window and dropped and spun the other way with the sickening rush of a close shot fanning my temple. There was a row of cars immediately behind the Syrena and I went hard for cover and slipped on the snow and crashed down and dug my heels in and went forward again and reached the front end of a snow-covered Pobeda before he loosed the third shot and hit a head lamp and sprayed me with glass and fired again and hit my shoulder before I could use full cover. The 9-mm. Smith and Wesson had eight shots in the magazine and he'd used four and I'd have to remember to go on counting because that could become critical if I lived through the next few minutes.

He was taking it badly. He was a family man and too well fed and I'd been picking away at his nerves ever since I'd got him alone in the underground car park, threatening to pitch him out of the Syrena on our way here, so forth. The work I'd done on his carotid and medial nerves had worried him and the strike I'd used on him in Schrenk's apartment must still be giving him pain. He now knew me well enough to realize that if he slipped on the snow and I got to him before he could aim and fire I might kill him out of hand. A professional hunter would have used this experience to his own advantage and moved well away from the quarry and taken careful aim before putting in the final accurate shot. This man was not a professional hunter: he was afraid of the creature he had to exterminate and his fear confused him. He'd already wasted four shots, half the entire magazine.

But of course he only needed one, even a lucky one, to drop me cold.

I'd lost sight of him and that was dangerous but he wouldn't know that. I was crouched under cover of the Pobeda and all he had to do was lie flat and take aim and smash one of my ankles to subdue me and stop me running but he hadn't thought of that: because of his fear he was thinking more about being attacked than attacking me. I was beginning to know him.

Then I saw his face and as the gun flashed my shoes slipped and dug in and I went sideways and then forward, hurling myself toward the car immediately behind and feeling the bite as a bullet scored the neck muscle and smashed into the bodywork of the car alongside. I ran hard but it was open ground and my feet were slipping as the cold air pumped into my lungs and froze the neck wound as I lunged for the pickup truck in the corner and slipped again and hit the front wing and went down with one foot dragging and my back exposed. I could hear him following and I think he slipped once and went down because his breath grunted out and there was a scuffling sound; then I was behind the truck and moving toward its rear, backing and facing the way I'd come.

I couldn't hear him now.

Blood was seeping into the collar of my coat from the neck wound. The shoulder had been oozing and filling the sleeve but there was no artery hit or I would have weakened by this time; my left arm was still usable and there was no other damage. I stood in a half crouch, listening to the silence. He would be close to the truck, on the other side: from here I could see the open ground I'd run across and he wasn't there. He had two more shots left in the magazine and he might be aware of that: he wouldn't like it but he'd now have to stalk me at close range and make sure of a lethal hit when he fired next. I didn't want to lie flat and sight for his feet underneath the truck because I'd be too vulnerable if he rushed me; I had to rely on auditory cues alone for information but they wouldn't be very strong: his breathing and the brittle sound of the snow when he moved. For the moment I heard nothing; the night was grave-quiet.

The snow was fresh in the lee of the truck and I scooped it into my hands and compressed it, making a snowball, kneading it until it was heavy and iron-hard. I would need to blind him or hit the wound on his temple if it were going to do any good but there'd be no time to aim before he fired and he wouldn't fire until I was securely in his sights: he had learned from

the uselessness of those six shots. I waited, with the
snowball melting gradually through my fingers.

He was moving now: I heard the faint crunching of
snow from near the front of the truck. It was a risk but
I dropped flat and sighted along the underside of the
truck and saw his face and the blossoming flash of the
shot and heard the fluting rush of air against my jaw
as I twisted over and reached for the tailboard and
pulled myself up with my left hand slipping because
of the blood, my shoulder flaring with sudden pain as
I flexed it: the bullet had lodged there close to the bone.

Seven. But I was scared now because he was getting
close and he knew he'd have to make it for certain with
the last shot. I lowered my feet to the snow again because he wouldn't shoot to maim at this stage. The
snowball was resting on the surface and I picked it up
and pressed it harder and put it on the metal footrest
below the tailboard and stopped and made another one
and held it ready, listening.

He didn't move. I thought I could see the top of his
head, a dark patch in the corner of the truck's windscreen; but I was sighting through the rear window of
the cab and the image was indistinct: it could be the
driving mirror or the corner of a roof in the distance.
The whole truck was sliding to one side and then lifting
silently—*watch it*—and I fell forward against the tailboard and took a deep breath until the scene steadied,
losing more blood, much more blood than I'd thought,
getting light-headed. I tried to drop flat again to see
where his feet were but the scene started rocking badly
and I straightened up and held the snowball against the
neck wound to slow the bleeding.

Something below me and I looked down. Blood on
the snow, purple in the acid light of the streetlamps.
Nothing else to attract the attention, no sound from

him. *He mustn't know.* He mustn't know about the blood because I couldn't do much to stop it until I was out of range and all he'd have to do was to wait it out until it left my brain, quietly draining, while the scene shifted and swung and turned over on me and I hit the snow and he came to stand over me, *phutt . . . finis.*

I would have to make him fire again for the last time. He hadn't moved yet, or I would have heard his shoes on the dry snow; he would be waiting for me to move first, waiting and listening. He was right-handed and if he moved he would circle the truck anticlockwise with his gun hand leading; but he didn't move. It worried me. I made another snowball, a bigger one, purple and white in the green unearthly glow of the streetlamps, blood and snow, pressing it harder, the dark stain spreading across its surface as the truck tilted and went down, dipping and rising and *oh Christ I'm leaving it too late,* steadying, a deep breath, I would have to find him in the next sixty seconds while there was enough blood left to feed the brain, *Ignatov where are you,* the pain flaring again in the shoulder as I fell flat and stared into the narrow gap between the truck's chassis and the snow.

He wasn't there.

The ball of ice freezing my hand, the scene shifting again as I got to my knees and then to my feet. He wasn't there, that was all right, I could go now and try to get someone to look at my—*watch what you're doing and think for God's sake think because he's—*

Towering over me, stark against the streetlamps with his feet on the step of the cab and the gun coming into the aim at short range, *snowball,* all the strength I had left and it flew upward against the flash and struck his face but I was spinning round and going down again hitting the snow and bouncing with the pain bursting in the shoulder and the truck's angular shape rocking against the sky and the blood coming into my head again and bringing consciousness back, scaring me because there were sudden intervals of amnesia and I couldn't remember if that was the seventh or the eighth shot, but he didn't fire again and I managed to grab his foot as he dropped from the metal step and tried to start running. He came down full length and I put him out with a neck strike that would leave him alive because all I had to do was to stop him going to the nearest telephone before I could get clear.

The keys of the Syrena took a long time to find in the snow, two or three blackouts, the shoulder burning alive, but found them, the keys, all right.

I called the Embassy from the underground garage and got Bracken direct at Ext. 7. Speech code for Schrenk, Apt. 15A Pavillon, Baumanskaya, told him they'd have to be quick. And pick me up.

Then I walked through the concrete columns and up the ramp and found the Pobeda where I'd left it, got in and sat waiting, might hit something if I drove any more. I hoped they wouldn't be long, blood on the phone down there, whole trail of it, someone might notice. Dizzy and getting thirsty, singing in the ears, dark coming and going. Hurry.

17 / MIDNIGHT

"For God's sake leave me alone," I told them.

"He's all right," a voice said.

"Who is?" I hit out and felt an arm and heard something crash onto the floor.

"Steady," someone said. It sounded like Bracken.

"Open your eyes." This was in Russian, a woman's voice. I'd heard it before somewhere.

"Eyes?"

Then I saw her, swaying from side to side, leaning over me, melting into some kind of shadow and taking shape again. I remembered her now.

"Can't you keep still?" I asked her.

She laughed, deep in her throat.

Raging thirst.

"Can he sit up?" I saw Bracken now.

Place stank of chemicals.

They helped me, but only on one side. The other side was peculiarly numb. "Am I in *bed*, for God's sake?"

"Take it easy," Bracken said.

I let them pull me upright and when they weren't ready for it I swung my legs over and stood up and they caught me as the wall swung round and hit me full in the face.

"When was that?" I asked them.

"An hour ago." Bracken was trying to sound cheerful. He was sitting hunched on a brown-painted crate below the window, his big blunt face lit by the streetlamps outside and the glow of the stove. The woman was leaning against the wall watching me with her arms folded, black sweater and slacks, raven-black hair, eyes like slow coals, Zoya, *you are for safekeeping*, a lot of it was coming back.

"I've got a thirst like a camel."

She laughed and swung a jug over a glass. The room looked like a hospital ward, bowls and towels and instruments all round the bed, a sickly stink in the air. I drank three glasses of tepid water and lay back again and then the whole thing hit me.

"*Bracken*. Did you find him?"

He shook his head slowly. "No. But then we didn't expect to."

I shut my eyes and something inside my head kept saying *all that for nothing, all that for nothing*.

"Why not?" I asked him.

"You phoned at eight forty-two. I got three men there by eight fifty-seven. He'd had fifteen minutes to get out, quite long enough."

"*Shit.*"

"You did your best."

My eyes came open. "Time for epitaphs, is it?" There were half a dozen pillows and a couple of them rolled onto the floor but I kept moving and got my legs over the edge of the bed. She came at me fast but I said, "Leave me alone for Christ's sake, I'm all right now." My left arm was in a sling and I couldn't feel anything on that side. It didn't interest me; all I could think about was that *bastard* Schrenk. I'd nailed him at his base and now we were about as close to him as we'd been when I'd first got into Moscow.

Why had I let him reach that gun?

Because I hadn't wanted to kill him. I'd been holding off, taking things right to the brink, chancing my own life and trying to save his. Sometimes you learn things the hard way.

"Take it easy," Bracken said, and got off the crate to hold me up.

"Time is it now?" I asked him, and wobbled about, leaning on him when I had to.

"Nearly twelve."

"Twelve what? Oh. Night."

"He must rest," Zoya said angrily. I suppose she was waiting for me to fall over, going to be right out of luck. Two lumps of metal lying on a bloodied swab in one of the basins. I said: "What are those?"

"They both went into the same shoulder," Bracken said. The woman began clearing the stuff away, obviously not prepared to speak to us any more.

"Did you find Ignatov?"

"No."

"What about the girl?"

"What girl?"

"There was a girl there. Misha."

"The apartment was empty when our people got there." He steadied me as I moved my feet. Weak as chewed string, bloody infuriating.

Someone was outside the door and we all froze by habit and Zoya opened it, standing close in the gap. A man spoke in Russian and she nodded and went out, shutting the door.

"Croder's on his way here," Bracken said, and I jerked my head to look at him.

"Croder?"

"Things have been moving. Look, why don't you sit down for a bit?"

"How did he get into Moscow?"

Patiently he said: "You mean Croder?"

I let him lower me onto the crate and I put my head back against the wall and waited until the throbbing eased off. It was the first time I'd ever heard of a control coming right into the target area from London and now it had to be Croder and he was going to find his executive in the field looking just about as useful as something the cat had coughed up and there was nothing I could do about it.

"What's he doing in Moscow?" I asked Bracken.

"Going to help us out. Want another drink?"

"You don't need any help, for God's sake." He'd pulled me off the street and got me into the safe house at a minute's notice, even Ferris couldn't have done any better. "Fill me in, will you?"

"I've been in signals with London for the past twelve hours. They—"

"Did you know Croder was coming out here?"

"Yes."

"Uninformation, Jesus, I—"

"His orders. They blew Gorsky, by the way." He didn't want to talk about Croder.

"Gorsky?" The man at the first safe house, a good man, reliable. "Did Schrenk think I was there?"

"Presumably. The KGB raided the place an hour ago."

Schrenk wasn't going to leave me alone. That was all right. The next time I'd follow instructions. *All we want is his silence.*

Do it for Gorsky.

"Mind getting me some water?"

"Coming up."

I was drinking it when the door opened and Croder came in, a thin scarecrow in the heavy military coat, his skull's head catching the light from the corridor and then darkening in shadow as he moved further into the room, picking his way through the cluttered furniture as if through a minefield, halting in front of me at last and staring down with his black hooded eyes.

"What happened?"

"Schrenk tried to kill him," Bracken said.

"Where is Schrenk?"

"We lost him again."

The skin drew taut across the pale pointed face and the hooded eyes blinked once. It was like watching a lizard, but I felt a strange sensation of comfort: with someone like this here, cold-blooded and totally dedicated, we wouldn't make any more mistakes.

He heard the door click shut and turned with a quick swing of his shoulders; it was Zoya coming back. He looked at Bracken again. "How many do we have left in the cell?"

"It's still intact. Six of them."

"How are they deployed?"

"Two are watching Schrenk's last known base and two are watching an apartment block where Schrenk's lieutenant lives with his family. Pyotr Ignatov. One mobile liaison, one signals."

Croder swung back to look down at me. "I assume you're not operational."

I was so annoyed that I got onto my feet before Bracken could try to help me. This time it didn't feel too bad. "I'm short on protein, that's all. There wasn't time to eat."

"He lost blood," Zoya said in thick accents. "I could not make any transfusion here, of course. He is weak."

Croder looked at her. "Are you a doctor?"

"Yes. There were two bullets, and a third wound. He needs to rest. He came out of general anesthesia an hour ago."

"Can he handle protein yet?"

"Perhaps, in liquid form. But you are taking risks. He has lost blood, quite a lot, and so he is weak. The conditions were sterile but I cannot guarantee there will be no infection."

"Have you any liquid protein?" Croder was into fast fluent Russian.

"I have chicken broth, yes."

"Give him some, if you will."

I sat down on the crate again, sliding my back against the wall and feeling the left shoulder gradually coming to life. The room spun slowly for a while and then Croder came back into focus, perched on the end of the bed. Zoya went out and he asked Bracken: "What's security like in this place?"

"As good as you'll get," he said, "in Moscow. She even keeps weapons here."

"We don't want those." Croder looked back at me. "I don't wish to press you, but I'd like your report on Schrenk. Just give me the salient points if you feel up to it."

There was still some fog in my head but I thought I could work out a summary. I took a minute and then said: "He's gone half out of his mind. They roughed him up too much in Lubyanka. And he's Jewish. He's made some friends among the dissidents. He's out for revenge and he's rationalizing it, thinks he's crusading for the cause. Just my impressions."

I had to wait for a bit because I was out of breath. Croder watched me, still as a reptile, his black eyes brooding.

"Don't hurry," he said.

"He blew me off the street. H said he had to get me out of his way, didn't want anyone to know where he was, wants to be left alone." I tried to remember what else Schrenk had said, with the cigarette smoke curling past his narrowed bloodshot eyes and his body twisted to face me. "He said there's only one thing the bastards will listen to, by which he meant it was no good just protesting against oppression. I'd say there's something he wants to do, and very badly. I'd say he's becoming a dangerous fanatic." I stopped again to get my breath. "Something else. He said 'Moscow needs me.' I was trying to talk him into pulling out with us, and that was his answer. Degree of megalomania, I suppose."

"Do you think so?" asked Croder.

I thought about it. "It's hard to say. I mean he's still a very capable operator. He could do a lot of damage if he wanted to."

"Quite so."

Then the door opened and we all looked round. It was Zoya.

"Bracken," I said. "Does Schrenk know this address?"

"No. Don't worry."

All very well. Schrenk had just blown Gorsky's safe house and if he knew about this one he'd send in the KGB and there'd be nothing we could do: they'd get the London director, the director in the field and the executive all in one bag. It didn't bear thinking about.

Zoya had brought me a can of self-heating soup, U. S. Army issue, God knew where she'd got it from. She poured it into a thick white cup and gave it to me.

"Would you say," Croder asked in his cold thin tones, "that Schrenk has got a cell together?"

"Possibly. There's this man Ignatov, and he mentioned two other people, Boris and Dmitri. It's either a cell or some kind of wildcat group of revolutionary dissidents."

Croder said nothing for a moment, then began speaking in formal Russian to Zoya. "You did a splendid job with this man's injuries—I should have mentioned it before. I'm most indebted to you, Doctor."

"It was good to work again."

He gave a slight bow. "Now if you'll excuse us, we have to debrief him."

"I understand." She looked at me critically as she turned to leave. "Take care of him, please. He is still weak."

She took away the self-heating can and quietly closed the door. Croder sat with his head half turned, listening to her footsteps growing fainter along the passage. Then he swung round to look at me. "I want to get a picture of Schrenk in my mind, as clearly as you can give it. Would you say he's totally unbalanced by his experiences in Lubyanka? Do you feel his imagination has run wild and that he sees himself as the shining liberator of oppressed Russian Jewry, that sort of thing? Or would you on the other hand say that he's still in full possession of his professional expertise and capable of mounting a sensitive operation with the help of an organized cell? Please consider carefully, because this is important."

They were both watching me in the silence, and I leaned my head back against the wall and shut my eyes, remembering all I could of Schrenk: the ravaged face and the crippled body with its rage contained like a furnace, that strange laughter that had led to those fits of coughing when the force of his hate had threatened to choke him, the chilling diatribe about Detsky Mir and its mechanical toys. When I felt ready I opened my eyes and said:

"I don't think he's unbalanced, in the normal sense. I think he's been given a direction. I've never seen such hate in a man, and he's turned it into a driving force—which is typical of him. I'd certainly say he's in full possession of his talents and could get a cell together. I don't believe he sees himself as a shining liberator, but I'm pretty sure he's capable of liberating Borodinski, for instance, by leading an armed raid on the courthouse and getting him out." I left it at that.

Croder wrinkled his thin brows. "Did he mention doing such a thing?"

"No. It was just an example."

"I see." He studied his skeletonic hands. "I don't think he's interested in Borodinski, but the rest of the picture you've given me ties in with the information we've received—that he means to assassinate the Chairman of the Presidium of the Supreme Soviet, Leonid Brezhnev."

I got off the crate and onto my feet. Bracken came to help me but I said, "No, I'm all right." I took a few steps, keeping close to the wall, and began feeling stronger. The thing was, I couldn't just go on sitting there. Not now. I went on shuffling between the furniture, making quite a lot of progress, and when I turned round I saw that Croder was standing up now, watching me. He said thinly:

"You think he can do it. Don't you?"

"Yes."

"You didn't hesitate."

"No."

Croder looked at Bracken. "What do you think?"

"I think this is all we needed."

Croder said to me: "I should explain that we've had various information coming in, some of it to Bracken, some of it by signal to London. That's why I decided to fly out." He was standing perfectly straight and perfectly still, I noticed; he didn't need to pace up and down or light a cigarette to transfer his tension: he could handle it internally. "The information we had was from fairly reliable sources but the informants weren't close to Schrenk, as you have been. Frankly I was hoping you'd tell me that he was half out of his mind and a broken reed. Since your considered opinion is quite otherwise, then we shall have to take action." He looked at me very directly, as he'd looked at me at the airport in Berlin. "You say you tried to talk Schrenk into pulling out of Moscow and that he refused. Is that correct?"

"More or less."

"Is it correct, or isn't it?" Standing perfectly still, his shoulders hunched in his oversize military coat, his black eyes fixed on me.

"Yes." And I waited for it.

"Then why didn't you follow my instructions?"

Bracken looked away.

I couldn't tell him the truth: that I'd been going to do it. *Three paces and a sword hand to the larynx, a matter of four seconds.* I couldn't tell him that because it'd sound like a lie.

"I still thought I could talk him into pulling out."

"Did you indeed? And what happened?"

"He got to a gun."

"You let him do that?"

The room had begun swinging slightly and I found my right hand on the back of a padded chair. Croder stood facing me with that eerie stillness of his, and I wanted to go and smash his face in.

"You weren't there," I said to him, "were you?"

"It makes no difference, surely."

"Oh yes it does. If you want to know what the execu-

tives are up against why don't you come out and do their bloody job for them? You'd learn a lot."

The echoes seemed to go on for a long time. In the silence I heard Bracken clearing his throat, but he didn't speak.

"The fault," Croder said icily, "is partly mine. I know your reputation. You're ready enough to do dangerous things, even foolhardy things; but you're not ready to do *unpleasant* things. When will you learn that in our trade a conscience is a luxury?"

I held on hard to the back of the chair, thinking out what I'd say, that Schrenk wasn't expendable, that in the Army he would have got the VC for holding out as he had in Lubyanka, that killing in cold blood is not the same as killing in a rage. Other things crossed my mind, but in the end I said nothing, because I knew Croder was right in principle and was now proved right in fact: we hadn't got a crippled lunatic on our hands, we'd got a man perfectly capable of assassinating the head of the Russian state.

Something I wanted to know.

"Are you suspending me?"

He looked me over. "If you think your services can be of any further value, I'd appreciate your staying in. If there's anything unpleasant to be done, I shall do it myself. That is why I'm here." He turned away.

"Come and sit down," Bracken told me. "Get your strength up. Might need it."

I got across to the painted crate without much bother, but the shoulder was really coming back to life, a good sign but a bloody nuisance. "Give me some information, for God's sake," I told him. "Fill me in." I'd been out cold for three hours and he said he'd been in signals with London the whole time.

He glanced at Croder, who nodded. "Our information," Bracken said, "had been coming in for quite a time, and from more than one source. We—"

"Quite a time?"

"Some few weeks," he said awkwardly. "That's why it was decided to send you out here. One of the reports said that Schrenk faked his abduction at the Hannover clinic with the help of his friends: he meant us to assume the KGB had got him back inside Lubyanka, so that we'd give up and leave him alone. I wasn't told of this until today, but—"

"The first reports," Croder cut in, "weren't directly from our own people: they were from the underground dissident faction and passed to London for raw intelligence analysis. The dissidents believed that Schrenk was acting officially and with the backing of the British secret services—revolutionary fervor always has an element of insanity, as I'm sure you know."

I began going cold. "If I'd been given this information," I said, "I would have eliminated Schrenk the minute I found him."

Croder wheeled on me. *The instructions were already there.* I told you specifically in Berlin that all we required was his silence."

"Perfectly true."

"Thank you."

There was still some of the chicken broth left in the cup and I finished it.

"Feeling all right?" Bracken asked.

I managed something like a laugh. "How would you feel?"

"Don't worry. We'll find him."

I looked at Croder. "I suppose you've considered warning the Soviets?"

"Of course. It would be suicidal. The situation at this moment is that an attempt on Brezhnev's life might be made and might succeed. If it succeeds, the interests of Russian dissidents will suffer unimaginably in terms of reprisals, since some of the action group are bound to be caught. But if we even leaked a warning to Russian security the repercussions could be disastrous, not only for the Jewish dissidents but for East-West relations, even if no attempt were made at all." His feet had come together and he was standing perfectly still again, his black eyes brooding. "Those two possibilities are unfortunately not the worst. The worst possibility is that Schrenk might make the attempt, and succeed, and be discovered and identified as a Western agent." When he stopped speaking the room was intensely quiet. "Not long ago, when it was known in the United States that Oswald had offered his services to the KGB shortly before he assassinated President Kennedy, the KGB themselves were terrified that one of their number might have instructed him to do so, and that the Americans might find out. I can imagine few situations that could push us closer to the brink of world war, and that is the situation we are now faced with here in Moscow."

The intense quiet came back into the room. The shock of what Croder was saying had left my head strangely numbed, and I didn't have any particular thoughts, except perhaps: *This is an awful lot to handle, even with Croder running things in the field. An awful lot.*

"When do you think this idea began," I asked Croder, "in Schrenk's mind?"

Bracken was turning his head, but not to look at me.

"That's hard to say. He'd applied for the post of agent-in-place a few months ago, so it seems he was then involving himself with the dissidents. I would think that his experiences in Lubyanka not only left him outraged but determined on taking revenge, and finally

the Jewish dissident cause provided him with the necessary rationale."

Bracken and I both had our heads turned to listen,
and now Croder heard it too. Someone was coming
along the passage outside and we waited, our eyes on
the door. It would of course be Zoya. It had to be Zoya
because if it were anyone else we were wiped out. It's
always like this in a safe house: you'll stop with half
the toothpaste on the brush or your shoelace half tied
while you listen, facing the door; but tonight our nerves
were strung tight because we were the three major components of a mission cooped up together in one small
room and we wouldn't stand a chance in hell if we got
raided.

Knocking on the door. I sensed Bracken jerk his
head a degree but he didn't speak. It was Croder who
spoke, his cold voice perfectly steady.

"Who is it?"

"Zoya."

"Come in."

She opened the door and I heard Bracken let out his
breath. I suppose he was closer to this thing than I was:
he'd been in signals with London and London would
be panicking; he'd also had Croder on his back, and
the knowledge that unless we could do something the
life of the Soviet chief of state could be running out.

"There are two men," Zoya said.

"Did they give the parole?"

"Midnight red."

"Please have them come up."

"They are English," she said. Croder nodded and she
went out.

"We have six people," Croder told me, "to support
you in the field. I have asked two of them to come here

for briefing. They are Shortlidge and Logan. Do you know them?"

"No. Not by those names."

"Logan was an a-i-p in Bangkok," Bracken said, "liaising with the Embassy when you—"

"Yes, got him. Have any of them worked in the field?"

"No."

"Combat-trained?"

"Three of them have been through Norfolk," Bracken said. "They're contact and liaison, outside of their post duties."

"They can tag."

"Oh yes."

"Fair enough."

"I guaranteed you full support," Croder said.

"I appreciate it." The bastard meant that he hadn't sold me short despite the fact that I'd let him down by neglecting to kill Schrenk. Or perhaps he didn't mean that; perhaps I was being paranoiac, because of the size of this thing we had to handle, and because of the time factor: we had no idea of the deadline, and Schrenk could be going in at any minute, including now.

Then they came in, Shortlidge and Logan, both typically non-descript men with quiet voices and poker-face reactions to what Croder told them. All he missed out was the bit about the Chairman of the Presidium of the Supreme Soviet: he used the word "coup" every time.

"The situation, then, is that we have no idea when the coup is planned to take place, and we have no idea where. What we have to do is to find our way in, and our target for surveillance is of course this man Ignatov." He looked at Bracken. "How many are watching for him?"

"Two. The other two are watching the Pavillon building."

"They never left there, I assume."

"No, sir."

"Shortlidge, you can join them and make inquiries after a woman named—"

"Misha," I said, and described her.

Then Croder went through the whole of the briefing again and we repeated paroles, countersigns and contact modes until we'd got it right. We were to dispense with signals through the Embassy: he gave me an Ultravox walkie-talkie and told me that Bracken and the six members of the cell would keep in contact by that medium alone, using speech code only and using the air with extreme discretion.

On street mobility Logan told me: "We've got most of the blood off the inside of your Pobeda and she's tanked up. We didn't have time to find new plates, so we've altered the old ones and rubbed some mud on. Don't forget to lose your papers."

Bracken told us he'd be based here at the safe house, since he wouldn't be able to enter or leave the Embassy without surveillance. Croder and I would wait here with him until we got a signal from the field.

"What was the street like?" I asked Logan.

"Looked clean enough. Three cars this side of the intersection, all facing toward it. Truck outside the warehouse opposite with a lot of snow on it. Nobody moving. The militia work east and west across the intersection and their nearest phone is a hundred yards west of there."

It was 1 A.M. when he and Shortlidge left us. By that time I felt ready to eat solids and Zoya brought me some goat's-milk cheese and black bread.

"Is there some pain?" she asked me.

"Yes."

"That is good."

"And a happy birthday to you too," I said, and she laughed because it was becoming our favorite joke. The left shoulder was throbbing to the rhythm of the pulse but it was only muscle and tissue pain: Ignatov hadn't hit bone. "If I don't see you again," I told Zoya, "you did a great job and I want to thank you."

"Of course you'll see me again," she said, and left us.

Bracken was getting increasingly nervy and couldn't keep still. I did some walking about myself and tried out the arm for movement as far as the sling allowed; the shoulder flared up but the pain was confined to that area: the nerves and muscles through the lower arm to the fingers were unaffected and I'd be able to drive a car with the sling off.

Croder stood still for most of the time, keeping clear of the window and taking a few short steps occasionally and coming to a stop with his feet together and standing still again, his thin neck buried in the collar of the military coat, his dark eyes impassive. Sometimes we heard sounds from inside the house, and turned our faces to the door. The stove began losing its heat after a while but we didn't put any more wood on.

I went over the street scene as Logan had given it: three cars parked this side of the intersection, a truck in the other direction, so forth. I went over the briefing pattern, contact modes, signals, the whole thing. I was getting thirsty because of the anesthetic and the saltiness of the cheese, and kept going to the tap over the basin and coming away with the taste of chlorine in my mouth. We didn't talk much, though Bracken began voicing his nerves after a while.

"I don't see how he can expect to do anything on that scale and get clear."

"I don't imagine for a moment," Croder said thinly, "that he can get clear. What concerns me is that he might reveal his identity. If he is discovered to be a London agent I hesitate to consider"—he stopped and in a moment said so quietly that we barely heard him—"but we've already gone into that."

I thought about Schrenk. "He won't want to live, once he's gone in."

Croder turned his head. "You don't think so?"

"He was quite an athlete, before. Tennis champ, good-looking, lots of girls. Now he's a wreck. This is a suicide run."

In a moment Croder said bleakly, "So we have that aspect to contend with too."

I didn't say anything. There wasn't anything we could do about it: a potential assassin who means to get clear after the act will take a lot of care and might finally balk at the risks, but a *kamikaze* will go right in for the kill with nothing to lose.

We grew quiet again, and every five minutes Croder took his few short steps and halted again, his death's head staring at the walls. Bracken lit a cigarette and then began chain smoking.

Just before three o'clock we got a signal.

18 / ZIL

Driving was more difficult than I'd thought. The left
arm worked all right with the sling off but I was still
feeling the loss of blood and I got into three front-end
skids over the snow because of partial blackouts before
I reached the rendezvous. Within ten minutes of leaving
the safe house I passed seven militia patrol cars, one of
which made a U-turn and followed me for five blocks
before it peeled off, presumably in answer to a radio
call. The whole environment was strictly a red sector
because the number plates of the Pobeda weren't legible
and traffic was so thin at this time of night that I was
liable to get pulled up by the police just to relieve their
boredom. The operation could blow at any given minute and Croder knew that but all he could do now was
run the whole thing into the ground if he had to, because of the time factor: we didn't know when Schrenk
was going in.

The signal had specified a warehouse in Losinous-
trovskaya ulica alongside the main rail line between
Belokamennaya and Cerkizovo stations and I reached
there at 3:21 and slid the Pobeda across the ruts into

the shadow of the building and cut the engine and wound the window down and waited, checking for sound and movement. It wasn't likely to be a trap but if Schrenk picked up my trail he'd come for me himself instead of leaving it to Ignatov, I knew that.

There was a train rolling somewhere, north and west of the warehouse, and its sound made a blanket for aural cues in the immediate vicinity and that was dangerous: I would have preferred to leave the car and get into more flexible cover but the contact had to show himself first and it was a safe principle, so I stayed where I was, listening to the train and trying to pick up closer sounds. Something was changing in the visual pattern on the other side of the car and I watched it: a door along the wall of the warehouse was coming open. Someone was standing there but I did nothing until a torch was flashed on and off three times, one long and two short; I got out of the car and walked across the snow with a trickle running through the spine because a night rdv. is always risky: a signal can be intercepted and you can find yourself walking straight into an ambush.

"Midnight red."

I countersigned and he flashed the light briefly over my face and then his own, and I recognized Shortlidge. He led me into the warehouse and shut the door, then switched on the torch and swung the beam across piles of broken crates and sacking and loose timber until it focused on the black Zil limousine.

"Okay?"

"Yes," I said. "Fill me in."

"I was watching Area 1 and saw Ignatov's car come up. Two men got out and went into the apartment block—one of them could have been Ignatov but I'd only got your verbal description. One of them came out in about half an hour—not Ignatov, too young and too thin, a dark chap. We—"

"How was he walking?"

"Walking? Quite normally."

"He wasn't crippled. Hobbling."

"No."

"All right, go on."

"Two of us tagged him here and he stayed fifteen minutes and then left. Logan's still on the tag and we're reporting by radio. I was told to stay here and show you this lot."

I gazed across at the brilliantly polished Zil. "Did you see what he was doing in here?"

"No. He locked the door after him."

"How did you get in, afterward?"

"Picked the lock. It's a tumbler."

"Did he bring anything with him?"

"Nothing too big for his pockets."

"Take anything away?"

"Not that I saw. He wasn't carrying anything."

He was moving his feet up and down, his hands stuffed into his pockets. There was no heating on in this place and a freezing draft was blowing across the floor. The building was old and looked abandoned; above our heads there was a gap of light where the roof had started caving in under the weight of the snow, and the whole place creaked. Various smells were distinguishable: rotting timber, damp sacking, sour grain, petrol, and rubber.

I went on staring at the big black limousine, not comfortable with it. "All right," I told Shortlidge, "I want you to keep watch outside. I'll be here about an hour. Where's your car?"

"Round the back."

"Can I use this torch?"

"Help yourself."

"There's one in the Pobeda glove pocket, if you want one. Listen, if you can't see the door to this place from your car, sit in mine. I want you to warn me if anyone comes, but keep out of the action if anything starts, understood?"

He considered this, moving his feet up and down. "What about if you're up against it?"

"I'll look after myself. Your job is to get a signal back. Croder's instructions."

"Okay." He left me.

I stood listening to the creaking of the building, feeling the cold draft numbing my ankles as I stared at the big black Zil. It was probably going to be all right, but even Schrenk was human and could make a mistake, and it was a minute before I was ready to go across to the thing and start work.

Long wheelbase, four doors, Central Committee MOII number plates, immaculate bodywork and chrome. I shone the torch through one of the windows. Brushed vinyl club seats, thick dark blue carpeting, two telephones, built-in tape deck, air-conditioning vents and controls, cocktail cabinet, wood-grain paneling, dark blue nylon curtains at the rear windows, a thick glass division between the front and rear seats separating the passengers from the chauffeur and escort.

I began underneath, fetching some sacking from a pile near the wall and spreading it on the dirt floor and sliding inward on the flat of my back with the torch in my right hand. The general layout was massive but clean, with cross-braced box section chassis members and two enormous exhaust silencers running half the length of the car. I checked ledges, niches, and junctions, inching my left hand along the topside of every component, the sweat beginning because the organism was confined and wouldn't be able to help itself if anything went wrong, wouldn't even know about it except for a microsecond of cataclysm.

Careful, old boy. Don't touch the wrong thing. Amusement in his tone as he watched me, his eyes narrowed against the smoke of the cigarette.

Bugger off.

I went over the rear axle casing, propeller shaft tunnel, flywheel housing, crankcase flanges and trays while the building creaked and the draft chilled my bones and the bastard began laughing softly with that awful laugh of his that turned to coughing because of the cigarette smoke.

You're taking a chance, old boy, I suppose you know that.

Yes, I knew that. He was human and he might have lost some of his cunning when they'd half killed him in that bloody place and I couldn't be sure that my hand wouldn't at some time touch a badly assembled trip mechanism or set off a too-sensitive rocking device or break a circuit when I opened a door and triggered the interior lamps. Taking a chance, yes, and I couldn't get his voice out of my head.

I stopped after ten minutes and lay listening, with the torch switched off and the stink of oil in the air, the draft shifting and fretting and freezing the skin. Four vehicles had gone past the warehouse and each time I'd switched off the torch because this building wasn't light-proof. Five minutes ago a train had rolled slowly alongside, its vibration setting up a buzzing in one of the Zil's head lamps.

You're pushing your luck, old boy. You—

Shuddup.

I wiped my hands on the sacking and got out from underneath and opened the driver's door, doing it quickly because there was a Russian roulette factor in play: Schrenk was working in foreign terrain and he couldn't be a hundred percent certain of his components or materials, however competently he assembled them.

In twenty minutes I was finished with the interior, lifting out the seat cushions and the carpets, checking the cocktail cabinet, telephones, tape deck, air-conditioning vents and the tip-up seats. Most of this time was spent in checking the recess behind the dashboard in the forward compartment, working with extra care among the wiring, terminals and fuse boxes.

There's only one thing those bastards'll listen to.

A bomb.

He was so good at them. I'd watched him rigging a bang more than once, sitting over the bloody thing and crooning like a witch, his thin nicotine-stained fingers stroking and fondling and fiddling, the pliers paring the insulation and making the loop in the copper cable, his fingertip spinning the brass terminal free as if he were playing with a toy, his pale eyes bright and his mouth touched with a faint Giaconda smile.

"Anyone would think," I'd said to him once, "it was a baby rabbit."

He'd looked up quickly. "That's all they are, old boy. Baby rabbits." A soft chuckle. "Until they go up, of course. Then they're tigers."

I pulled the hood lock and went through the engine compartment, taking nearly half an hour because of all the subsidiary tanks, reservoirs, chambers and small boxed components; a lot of them were labeled but I had to identify the rest by following the cables, pipes and linkages to find out which system they served. Then I shut the hood and opened the trunk and checked the spare wheel, the first-aid box and emergency tool kit.

The torch battery was running low by this time but I'd almost finished now.

Didn't find anything, old boy?

It could of course be packed inside the upholstery or the roof lining or the door paneling, anywhere like that, but a major search with tools would take time and at this stage I'd prefer to report to Croder and get his instructions; until we knew the overall picture we didn't necessarily want Schrenk to know we'd found the Zil and we didn't necessarily want to immobilize it: he could have alternative procedures planned.

I started on a final check before the torch was too dim, covering the areas behind the radiator grille, inside the wings, and under the bodywork valances. Another freight train was rolling through but the warehouse was a sound box and when the door creaked I froze and waited, concealed by the Zil.

Light flashed from a torch.

"You there?"

"Yes."

"Someone coming."

I went over to the door. "Keep inside and stay hidden," I told Shortlidge. He moved for the pile of crates and I shut the door and got behind it and waited. The train was still rumbling but I could hear footsteps over the brittle snow outside and then a key in the door. It was turned sharply twice: he was surprised to find it was already unlocked.

I'd have liked a final word with Shortlidge because I didn't know whether he'd follow my orders and stay out of the action or decide to get mixed up in it and risk two deaths and no signal to base, but he was a fully trained a-i-p with a Curtain-country post and I stopped worrying and watched the door. It opened cautiously and a man came in and snapped a light on and I used the right hand and searched him for weapons while he was still out and then got some snow and packed his face with it till he came to. Then I began asking questions.

The rdv. was for the road bridge over the Jauza where Stromynka ulica crossed it from east to west, and Croder was waiting for me when I got there, Bracken and another man with him, a black Mercedes 220 parked in the cover of shadow.

"This is Fenshaw."

"Good evening," I said.

They made room for me in the car and Fenshaw stayed behind the wheel looking edgy. The 220 was facing south but there was enough room to make a one-point turn and get out north if we had to. The river flowed past us under the streetlamps; I could see the glint of broken ice drifting.

On the radio I'd asked Bracken why we had to meet in the open and he said Croder wanted to keep within short-distance radio range of three points: the safe house, the warehouse, and Area 2, where they were watching for Schrenk at the Pavillon apartment block.

"Where is Ignatov?" Croder asked me now.

"Shortlidge took him to his base, blindfolded. Did you contact Logan?"

"Yes. He and Marshal are guarding the Zil."

"All right." I had to make a lot of effort to sort out what I had for him because sleep was trying to black me out. "They're setting up a high-explosive action timed for six o'clock tonight inside the walls of the Kremlin. I checked the Zil as far as I could without dismantling anything and when I left there it was clean, superficially. This could tie in with what Ignatov told me—that the explosive hadn't arrived yet."

"Do you think he was lying?"

"No." I'd had to work on Ignatov's nervous system again but I don't think that would have been enough without additional persuasion, so I'd reminded him what his wife and children would feel like when they heard he'd been found dead.

"Is he to drive the Zil?"

"No, a man named Morosov, also a Central Committee chauffeur. I don't think Schrenk would trust Ignatov with the end phase: he's not a professional. Schrenk plans to radio-detonate the charge himself, two minutes after Brezhnev goes aboard the Zil at the steps of the Grand Palace, where the Presidium will meet. The car is to be handed over to Brezhnev's personal chauffeur ten minutes beforehand, ostensibly following a maintenance-check road test. The chauffeur's not in the act, and is down for sacrifice."

I was trying to get the whole report into order but there were memory gaps and I was aware of them and knew they'd have to be bridged.

"This man Morosov," Croder said. "What's his motivation?"

"He's a dissident. They all are, except Ignatov. I think Schrenk is blackmailing him into cooperating, judging by his subservience."

"Blackmailing him?"

"He's a trusted functionary. He'd only have to steal a tankful of petrol for his own car to get ten years in the camps. I'd say Schrenk caught him out in something."

"The rest of them are dissidents, you think."

"Yes. The Borodinski trial's created a lot of anger and they're coming out into the open now." I shut my eyes and tried to remember other things, but the dark came tiding over me and I jerked my head up.

"Take your time," I heard Croder's voice.

Bracken opened a door to let the cold night air come in. I could hear the river now, and the discordant ringing of the ice floes as they touched together on the surface.

"There's a four-car motorcade when Brezhnev travels. He always goes in one of four Zils, with two motorized units of the Guards Directorate leading and following." My mind switched. "Have you got any closer to Schrenk?"

"A little. We have a contact."

I sat up straighter. "Oh really?"

"We can now stop the Zil operation," Croder said carefully, "but the danger is that the moment Schrenk knows we can do that, he might switch to an alternative plan. We must therefore conceal the fact that we're on to the Zil for as long as we can."

"Not easy, from the moment he starts missing Ignatov."

"Precisely. Our main target, then, remains Schrenk himself."

Bracken asked: "If we find him, is Quiller to go in?"

Croder let a couple of seconds go by. I don't think he was hesitating: I think he was deciding how to phrase it. "No. I shall expect him to help us locate and subdue Schrenk, but I shall not expect him to do anything more than that. Schrenk," he said with a note of warning, "must be considered strictly expendable. I trust that is understood."

The smell of the river came through the open door, the smell of dead fish and diesel oil and rotting wood. *Drive him as far as the river,* Schrenk had said in front of me, as if I hadn't been there, as if I were already dead. *You don't have to use any weights, in the river.*

All you have to do is to make sure he's found a long way from here.

"Do you have anything more for us?" Croder asked me.

My head jerked up. "What? No. Yes. There's a reception at the American Embassy"—this was *bloody* important and I'd nearly missed it out—"and three other Central Committee people are going there with Brezhnev from the Kremlin, by separate motorcade. Kosygin, Andropov and Kirilenko."

"What's his idea?" Bracken asked. "If he doesn't hit Brezhnev he'll at least hit one of the others?"

Croder turned to me. "What type of explosive were they going to use?"

"Composition C-3 plastic in sheet form: four rectangular slabs to fit under the cushions of the Zil. And twenty-five kilograms of steel ball bearings, distributed between the plastic and the cushions."

"My God," Bracken said quietly. "This is Schrenk, all right."

"Yes. Bloody great military grenade. If the four of them came down the steps to their cars together after the meeting, he could hit the whole lot."

I shut my eyes again and let my head sink down. I'd told them all I'd got out of Ignatov and I wanted to sleep and let Croder and the rest of them take over.

"Did you ask him if there was any alternative plan ready to go?" Bracken wanted to know.

"Yes. He said he didn't know of any."

"Was that the truth?" Croder asked.

"I think so."

Listen, you tried to blow my head off out there in that car park, you think that doesn't mean anything to me? You start lying and by God I'm going to leave you here for dead.

I'm not lying. I want to see my children again.

The broken sheets of ice touched together on the river's surface, bringing the sound of muted bells. "I think he was telling the truth," I told Croder, "but that doesn't mean Schrenk hasn't got an alternative operation planned."

"Precisely. Is there anything more you have to tell us?"

I took my time to think, in case I missed anything. "No."

"Very well." He nodded to Bracken and they both got out of the car. "Take him to base," he told Fenshaw, "and ask the woman to look after him. Then I want you to come back here and pick us up."

Periods of waking and sleeping, the smell of wood smoke and antiseptic and the rough woven blanket. At one time the sound of metal on metal and I was half-way out of the bed before I was fully awake, something crashing onto the floor.

"It is all right." She came over at once and held my arms with her strong fingers, looking into my face. "I was just putting some more wood on the stove."

"Oh. Good of you." The room was cold.

"How do you feel?" She picked up the beaker of water I'd knocked over.

"I was dreaming, that's all." The big black Zil going up, bursting like a chrysanthemum.

"You should be in hospital," Zoya said, leaning over me. "I am worried about infection."

"You worry," I said, "while I sleep."

At some other time I saw the cold gray light of the new day frosting the grime of the window, and had a run of coherent thoughts for the first time since Fenshaw had brought me back here. It was possible that everything would be all right, provided we could find Schrenk. Croder could stop the Zil operation at any time he chose. Logan and Marshal were guarding it at the warehouse and could smash the distributor or pour dirt into the carburetor whenever they got the instructions. Ignatov was also under guard. If Schrenk hadn't got an alternative lined up, there was a chance that everything was going to be all right.

Dreams again, with the soft discordant chimes of the ice on the night-running river, the soft wet *phutt* of the silenced gun, blood on the snow.

Then later I woke to find Bracken leaning over me, speaking softly and with the fear of God in his voice.

"They've shot Logan and Marshal," he said, "and taken the Zil."

19 / SCARECROW

5:41.

The winter night had come an hour ago, and the sky was starless. Snow had started falling again before noon, and was now beginning to settle as the evening temperature dropped below zero.

C-Charlie . . . Heading west on Sucharevskaya ring road.

I checked the time again. C-Charlie was Croder.

There were seven of us out: four of the original cell with Croder, Bracken and myself making up the number. Logan and Marshal had died instantly in the shooting and an ambulance had picked up their bodies after an anonymous telephone call from Bracken. That had been at 6:39 this morning, nearly twelve hours ago. Since that time Croder had kept the whole cell working to locate Schrenk and had failed. Nothing had been seen of the Zil.

I picked up the set.

A-Able . . . Going east on Krasnocholmskaya, now crossing river bridge.

The snow came out of a black sky, hazing across the

taller buildings and covering the roofs of vehicles until they began blending with the background. Traffic was easing as the rush hour neared its end. A few trucks were using chains again, and sand crews had just appeared at the major intersections.

Croder had said: "If we haven't found either Schrenk or the Zil by five o'clock this evening we shall begin patrolling the outer ring road in the hope of sighting the Zil on its way in to the Kremlin." His face had been pale, and his head sunk into the collar of his overcoat. "We shall maintain constant radio contact and A-Able will be prepared to go into action if we sight the Zil. What action he may take will depend on the circumstances and his own discretion, but whatever happens we have to realize that the Zil may explode without warning at any time. It may be triggered with a timing device, or Schrenk may choose to detonate the charge by radio beam, sacrificing the driver. We don't know. This is a last-ditch stand, and I expect every conceivable effort to be made to avert disaster. I've already pointed out to you that the disaster we have to avert does not simply concern the explosion of a motor-car in a crowded city, but concerns the explosion of a totally unpredictable situation on an international scale. Thank you, gentlemen, that is all."

I'd asked Bracken later if they were going to reconsider the idea of warning the Guards Directorate by an anonymous phone call a few minutes before the four leading members of the Politburo got into their motorcades. He'd just said, "God knows. That's up to London, not us."

We knew that Croder was in signals with London hourly through a timed system of public phone box calls to the Embassy. We also knew that Croder was personally against the risk of exposing a plan to assassinate the Soviet chief of state by warning his security forces in time, without making "every conceivable effort" to block Schrenk on his run in and get control of the Zil.

"There is, of course, the other thing," Bracken had told me privately. "That Zil might already be inside the Kremlin. If it is, there's nothing we can do."

With the bridge behind me I watched the mirror for a few seconds longer than normal because a militia patrol was coming up fast and I started looking for an immediate right turn. The Volga stayed in the mirror for ten seconds and then overtook and left me behind. A minute later I caught up with it again at the Kamensciki street junction, slowing behind a mess of vehicles trying to make their way past some sort of accident by the Metro station: I saw a stove-in radiator with rusty water blowing out of it and a Moskvich draped halfway across the curb. Sirens had started up from the opposite direction.

The surface was tricky in places now because the ruts were getting lost under the new snowfall and you couldn't use them to steer with. I was keeping my speed down to a little below the limit and checking the mirror the whole time: there shouldn't be any tags but if I missed sighting the Zil ahead of me I might see it in the mirror and send out a fix on the radio.

"We shall expect it to be crossing the ring road," Croder had told us at the briefing, "toward the Kremlin. But that doesn't mean it might not have to make a right turn onto the ring road itself and follow it for a time until it can turn left. Watch for that."

I hated Croder and I pitied him. I pitied him because he'd run a reasonably effective mission up to the point where I'd failed to kill Schrenk, and in less than twenty minutes it could be blown out from under him through none of his own fault; and I hated him because the fault was going to be mine and he'd taken pains to let me know it. All right then, not hate. Guilt.

5:43.

G-George . . . I'm making west along Samotocnaya, just passing the circus building.

Shortlidge. He was keeping station a mile behind Croder, who would now be moving south and west, somewhere near the planetarium.

Calling G-George. Repeat signal.

Radio reception was strengthening and fading as we circled the center of the city, the new steel-braced constructions affecting the signal. We'd been told to mention a landmark when we could, as well as the street's name. We knew them by now: we'd spent two hours with the maps.

Shortlidge was repeating. His voice sounded dead. He was the one who'd found Logan and Marshal; he'd known them for three years and had worked closely with Logan on the Yugoslavian spy-bust thing when half the foreign a-i-p's in Moscow were being smoked out of their holes. Logan had a wife, a young ice skater working her way up through the city championship teams, and Shortlidge was going to have to tell her what had happened.

I used the set again.

A-Able . . . I'm going north, leaving Narodnaya with the Kotelniceskaya Hotel on the left. Where is F-Freddie now?

No one came on the air for almost a minute; then Croder began asking for a signal. We didn't get one.

Calling F-Freddie. Location please.

No answer. Croder went off the air. F-Freddie was Wilson and either his set was out or he'd skidded on the snow or the police had pulled him in for something.

At 5:44 I saw a black limousine half a block ahead of me and the set was in my hand a couple of seconds later but I didn't signal yet: it could be a Chaika. I pulled out and got past some of the traffic in front of me with the front wheels shifting across the ruts of packed snow and the rear end breaking away and correcting and breaking away again until I had to start slowing for the lights, Chaika, finding a slot in the right-hand line of traffic and pulling over, it was a Chaika, not a Zil.

B-Bertie . . . Proceeding south and west along Bolshaya just past the Gorkogo intersection, the Hotel Peking on my right. Did we lose F-Freddie?

I checked the time at 5:45.

A-Able to C-Charlie . . . This is the deadline.

Croder came back straightaway.

C-Charlie . . . We continue until further orders.

The lights in front of me went green and I got going again. The deadline was 5:45 because Ignatov had said the Zil was to be handed over to the chief of state's personal chauffeur ten minutes before Brezhnev was to board the car outside the Grand Palace, and it was a five-minute run from the ring road to the Kremlin at this time of the evening. The pickup time was six o'clock. So this was zero and the seven of us were circling the target area and the radio was silent and I was beginning to sweat because Schrenk was a professional and had enough hate burning inside him to carry this thing through to the final blast and if he succeeded the headlines would carry the shock around the world.

Because I had failed to carry out the instructions.

5:46.

Zero plus one and too late.

E-Edward . . . Going north on Ckalova and just crossing Karl Marx.

The snow drifted out of the dark sky, eddying in the slipstream of the car ahead of me. It was becoming mesmeric, and I wound the window down and let the freezing air come in, taking deep breaths of it. I'd slept for nearly four hours after I'd got back from the warehouse but the blood loss was still a problem. In less than a minute the left shoulder was numbed by the draft and I put the window up again but went on breathing consciously until the haze went out of my head.

5:47.

If I'd been given this information I would have eliminated Schrenk the minute I found him.

But the instructions were already there.

The snow whirled against the windscreen. There was of course a chance that Schrenk had made a mistake or the stuff hadn't arrived in time or the Zil had come unstuck in the snow but he was highly talented and they'd crippled him and he knew what he wanted to do and it wasn't particularly difficult with that amount of feverish dedication driving him: history was liberally punctuated with successful assassinations and he wasn't trying to do anything new.

This was why I looked to my left at every intersection, sometimes seeing the glow of a golden dome through the snow haze. That was where we would see the column of smoke going up, a few minutes after six o'clock.

The traffic was thinning now as the city's population flowed from the factories and offices to the apartment blocks in the suburbs.

5:48.

D-Donald . . . I've got a Zil.

C-Charlie calling D-Donald—give your location.

I'm heading north and coming up to Ulyanovskaya.

The police let him through on the red light. The Zil is moving west on Ulyanovskaya now and going fast.

Did you see the number plates?

No. It was broadside on when it went past.

Did it have any kind of escort?

No. It went through the lights on its own.

C-Charlie calling A-Able. Where are you?

I hit the button. *A-Able: I'm at Obucha and the lights are red. There's a left-turn arrow and I'm waiting for it now.*

Two seconds went by.

From your present location, can you intercept the Zil before it reaches the Kremlin?

The map had been open on the passenger's seat since we'd started patrolling and I looked at it now. *It depends on what speed he makes. I can't go across the lights as he can. But I've got a chance of cutting him off at Solanka intersection.*

The left-turn arrow went green and I gunned up and took the intersection in a controlled slide across the ruts and got the Pobeda straight and settled down.

A-Able moving west toward the boulevard ring, light traffic. Orders?

Stay on the air and report progress. C-Charlie calling all other stations . . . All other stations remain listening but do not signal unless emergency repeat do not signal unless emergency. Break pattern and head for A-Able with all speed.

I was coming up on two taxis and a truck and pulled over to pass but the ruts were deep and I lost the rear end as the steering dug in and the momentum set up a swinging action, left to right, left to right until I changed down and put a lot of power on and broke the rhythm, one of the taxis using the horn because I'd swung too close.

Croder dropped the call sign now: from this point there'd only be his voice and mine on the air.

What is your direct route to the Kremlin?

Due west by Podkolokol'ny, Solanka, and Razina.

Present location?

Crossing the boulevard ring.

The trees stood on either side, white with snow against the iron sky. The lights were changing to amber and I kept my speed constant and crossed over and gunned up a little because they'd put sand down here. The inner boulevard signal was at red and I switched my headlights full on and kept going and crossed the intersection and heard a whistle blow.

I am now on Podkolokol'ny. Traffic police alerted because I crossed on the red, but my rear plate is illegible.

Acknowledged.

I hadn't intended to take the intersections on the red because the police would use their radios and I'd be initiating a collision course with the nearest mobile patrol but the Zil would now be curving northeast across Ustyinsky Prospekt and heading for the major fork at Solanka and it was the only chance of my cutting him off because if he got there first I wouldn't be able to catch him and there were no other oblique streets where I could gain on him by using angles.

Location . . . Podkopayevsky on my right. I'm passing the junction now.

Acknowledged.

He would want to say more than that, but he left the air clear for my signals. He would want to say that I should make every conceivable effort to reach the Solanka fork before the Zil because that was the only hope we had left. He would want to say that there was a red lamp burning at the top left corner of the board for Scorpion in London and that the lamp must go out when the mission had succeeded, not because it had failed.

A taxi was pulling away from the curb and doing it too wide and I touched the brakes and got nothing, so I used the wheel and angled the front end out of the ruts and straightened again, overcorrecting and hooking the rear bumper of the taxi: I watched it in the mirror, sliding against the curb and bouncing and coming to a stop with the front wheels locked hard over.

Location . . . Passing Ivanovsky on my right and approaching the fork at Solanka.

Acknowledged. C-Charlie to all other stations. Keep heading for A-Able at the Solanka fork as fast as you can. If necessary ignore traffic lights.

The nearest to me would be E-Edward, last locating south of me on the ring road at Ulyanovskaya, and he would have made an illegal U-turn and come back to the intersection and turned right to follow the Zil. D-Donald had been farther to the north and would have turned west and south and would reach the Solanka fork soon after E-Edward. Bracken had last signaled from the other side of the ring road and would be coming east and rounding the walls of the Kremlin, but he had more distance to cover. In five minutes from now the Zil could be in the center of three or four converging cars and it wouldn't be heading for the Kremlin at this time unless it had the explosive on board and that could be dangerous: Composition C-3 was relatively insensitive to impact but if the Zil crashed it could false-trigger the detonation device. If I sighted the Zil I'd need to make a signal.

Location . . . Solanka fork, approaching fast, lights at red.

I could hear a siren somewhere. I'd run the red at the

boulevard intersection and hit the taxi soon afterward and the policeman who'd blown the whistle could have walkie-talkied the network to put a car onto me; or it could be F-Freddie in trouble after his failure to acknowledge or it could be just an accident somewhere on the icy streets and nothing to do with us.

The lights were still at red and I took the Solanka fork on the low side of fifty k.p.h. with the front end stable enough in the ruts to take me close along the nearside curb with a chance of bringing the wheel over hard if I had to, putting the Pobeda into a front-wheel skid and breaking the ruts to slow the momentum if anything came through on the green from the main fork road to my left. I wasn't risking a broadside collision because the fork road had the only right-of-way and the traffic would merge at forty-five degrees, but I flicked the headlights to full again and started watching the left-hand outside mirror.

Crossing Solanka, lights at red.

The Zil wasn't there.

We began hitting the cross-ruts and the front end lost its line and cocked over and wouldn't come back but the wheel had some resistance left and I waited and then hit the brakes as we plowed into the loose sand alongside the curb and the Pobeda shook itself straight as the nearside rear wheel hit and bounced and got traction as I gunned up and settled down again with a No. 55 bus a hundred yards ahead of me and nothing this side of it but a taxi. It was no go.

No sign of the Zil. I'm across the—

Mirror.

Zil.

Correction, I've got the Zil now, I've got the Zil.

It was behind me, crossing the fork on the green with its headlights full on and coming up fast.

Croder's voice came faintly through bad static but with a lot of control.

Repeat, please. Repeat signal.

I hit the button again. *I've got the Zil behind me at fifty yards and closing up on me fast. Listen, I want the others to hold off, tell them to hold off, we can't risk crashing the Zil—it's a live bomb.*

I switched to listen and heard him acknowledge and then start telling all stations to support the scene but keep clear of the Zil. He repeated and asked for acknowledgment and the others began coming in as the siren started up again from somewhere in the immediate area, another one joining it: the network had been alerted to something and the patrols were closing in.

The bus was moving slowly in the nearside lane and I checked the mirror and pulled out in the path of the limousine behind me. In this city the Zils and Chaikas normally drive on full headlights for the police to let them through the intersections but this one began using the horns when it saw me pull out. According to Ignatov it would have the Politburo chauffeur Morosov at the wheel and he wasn't used to other vehicles getting in his way and tonight he was running two minutes late and his rendezvous was ultra-priority.

I began slowing.

There was still a clear lane on my offside and I waited for him to take it. The Zil was massive and could break through the ruts of snow and keep its steering stable enough to make a lot of speed through streets like these and if I let him go past me I'd lose him without any chance at all of catching him again: this was strictly a one-time operation because he now had a straight run to the Kremlin and the police would let him through every light. Through the snow haze ahead of me I could see the bright gold domes of St. Basil's Church at the south end of Red Square: we were less than a mile from the Kremlin now and time was running out.

The Zil was shaping to overtake, its dark mass filling the mirror. Its horns were still blaring and its headlights blinding and I had to use my left hand as a shield against the window glass while I kept on slowing and watched the shadow of my own car on the road ahead of me: if the Zil pulled to the left or right I'd see the angle change. When it stopped hooting I could hear the sirens again, their howl loudening as they neared the area. I hit the tit.

I've still got the Zil behind and I'm blocking it. We're approaching Razina ulica. Several sirens going, they've been getting nearer.

The Zil began using its horns again and I saw the angle of the Pobeda's shadow change, shifting to the left as the limousine started pulling out to the right lane in another attempt to get past. I pulled out too, blocking him again and bringing the speed down to less than forty k.p.h. We were past the bus now but there were two taxis and a truck ahead of us on the far side of Razina ulica, the major street that ran at right angles across our path. At this point I was moving into a situation that looked strictly shut-ended: if I kept on across Razina the Zil would turn left and head directly for the Kremlin; but if I turned left onto Razina it would keep straight on and use the left turn at Kuybysheva and reach the Kremlin that way.

Whichever I did, the Zil could peel off and get clear.

Morosov was an experienced driver and would know every minor turning if I tried to cut him off. The Zil could go through every light and the instant its image was seen by the guards at Spassky Gate they would change the signals to green and let him through. So I would have to stop him in the next thirty seconds and I'd have to do it without making him crash because there was enough explosive on board to wreck half the block.

Location Solanka and Razina intersection. I'm going to try stopping the Zil.

Its massive shape was right behind me with its horns strident and its lights dazzling as I made three rapid feints to the left, right and left as we reached the intersection. Morosov reacted instantly, swerving to the right, left and right to overtake, and as he swung to the right for the last time I gunned up and went for him, nosing across his front end and forcing him to slow and then throttling into a rear-wheel slide and coming back across him and feeling the Pobeda tilt suddenly as the weight of the limousine made oblique contact. The horns had stopped now because he was having to use both hands on the wheel, and I heard the sirens again.

There was sand on the surface here but the snow had packed into ice underneath it and for a moment I lost the Pobeda as it reacted to the impact and swung full circle and hit the curb and came off again still swinging; but I was still on the right side of the limousine and got enough traction back to nose across its path and this time Morosov braked too hard and started sliding, the black polished bodywork veering across my windscreen as it corrected and slid again with its huge momentum taking it in a series of swings that sent it glancing against the Pobeda three times before it lost the surface and swung full circle, its speed gone and its rear wheels spinning as Morosov tried to find traction and failed.

The Pobeda was down to crawling speed and I hit the door open and got out and began running, pitching down once on the gritty ice before I got to the Zil and wrenched at the driver's door. The sirens were coming in and a dazzle of light flooded the street as the heavy door swung open and Morosov brought a revolver into the aim and began firing too late and too high: the explosions hammered against my eardrums as I used my right hand in a rising fork strike and got the gun clear and hooked him off balance onto the roadway. He tried to get up and I chopped twice and dropped him and climbed into the Zil. The engine was still running and I slammed the door and found the throttle and teased the rear wheels into motion as a black patrol car came in from Solanka with its siren going.

The Zil was on the move but the surface was tricky and I had to keep tapping the throttle to use the power of the huge engine to take me in a series of swings before I could straighten up and give it the gun. I'd rammed the radio into the pocket of my coat when I'd abandoned the Pobeda but there wasn't time to use it as the limousine got up speed and I swung left at the first intersection and brought the power on and settled down. The mirror grew bright but I'd got a hundred-yard lead and swung left again to work my way back to the ring road and away from the Kremlin.

Time check: 6:07.

I began thinking about Schrenk. He couldn't be far away.

I tugged the radio out of my pocket and hit the button.

A-Able to C-Charlie . . . Location approaching Solanka fork road from south. I am now on board the Zil. Has anyone seen Schrenk? Has anyone seen Schrenk?

The lights were still in the mirror but there was no siren going.

Calling A-Able. You have three of us in your imme-

diate area. Anyone identifying Schrenk report imme-diately.

I watched the mirror. The car behind me wasn't try-ing to close up. It was probably D-Donald or E-Edward but it could be Schrenk.

Who is behind me? Who is behind me?

Schrenk had planned to radio-detonate the charge and the only way he could do that was to join the Zil on its way in to the Kremlin and then peel off and circle the area and wait for the Zil to come through Spassky Gate. But Schrenk was a man to cover his risks and he would have done that.

D-Donald calling . . . I'm following the Zil.

I acknowledged and turned right and headed for the boulevard ring. Sirens were loudening from the left and a flood of light came into the limousine as I crossed the intersection.

Schrenk would have covered his risks and made sure the Zil would blow, even if something stopped him do-ing it by radio beam. I knew that. I knew him well.

The ruts of snow were sending the big front wheels too far to the near side and I brought them out and felt the rear end go and had to throttle up and break the ruts to get any bite from the treads; my speed was a rising sixty k.p.h. and there were two vehicles ahead of me in the nearside lane. A patrol came in from the left and its lights filled the interior again; its siren was wail-ing and I throttled up to clear it as the driver tried to cross my bows near the Solanka fork road.

There was no time to think but I'd have to. Schrenk would have covered his risks and the only way to be quite sure the Zil would blow would be to time the charge. And he would have timed it for five or ten minutes after six o'clock, when the Soviet chief of state would be on board.

Time check: 6:08.

The sweat broke out on me and I had the urge to slide the limousine into the curb and get out and run for my life but I couldn't do that because I wasn't certain of the facts and if I abandoned the Zil and it didn't blow, it would remain an appalling danger on the open streets of the city.

I would have to blow it myself.

Calling D-Donald . . . D-Donald . . . The Zil could explode by timer at any minute. Keep your distance.

My scalp was shrinking and my palms were wet on the wheel. I'd have to blow it myself and that meant crashing it and I was trying to remember where I'd passed the construction site on the way from the ring road.

D-Donald acknowledging.

C-Charlie calling all stations. Keep your distance from the Zil.

I'd passed the big construction site not far from the boulevard ring, after turning onto Obucha ulica and heading west. I made for there now.

The night was full of sirens wailing as other police patrols began focusing on the area. I saw two cars going fast across the inner boulevard ring and a third in a controlled slide coming from the south and turning in my direction. It was past me before the driver recognized the image of the Zil behind my headlights and the note of the siren died away behind me.

Two cars now in my mirror: D-Donald and a smaller Moskvich, possibly Schrenk. He would have been looking out for the Zil and once he'd seen it he'd track it by cutting through some of the minor streets and my scalp contracted again because he'd come out of Lubyanka half crazed and if he realized I'd taken over this thing from Morosov he might use his radio beam to detonate in a final access of rage.

I crossed the outer boulevard ring at close on seventy k.p.h. and saw a group of cranes poking into the night sky over to the north. I was going too fast for the intersection but the surface had sand on it and I brought the speed down and swung left at the next side road and straightened up with lights moving into the mirror again and the sirens loudening. The patrols hadn't got an accurate fix on me yet but it'd be a matter of minutes now before they found me and closed in.

Red lights and I ran them and cut it close and had to lock over to avoid a patrol car storming through on the green but the front wheels of the limousine went into a skid and the offside wing clouted the patrol car and sent it spinning full circle across the intersection with its headlights sweeping the buildings and flashing once across my eyes before I got the Zil straight and saw the construction site coming up through the haze of snow.

Lights came into the mirror again and stayed there, closing on me. I tilted the glass to cut the dazzle.

Who is behind me? Who is behind me?

It wasn't a police car: the sirens were still some way off.

Who is behind me?

The light continued to flood the interior of the Zil.

All stations, Croder's voice came. *Who is following the Zil?*

There was no answer.

Then it could only be Schrenk.

He had picked up the Zil near his planned rendezvous point and lost it and come up on it again and now he was sitting there. Either he was aware that I'd taken over the wheel or he was wondering why Morosov had gone off course away from the Kremlin. I think if he'd thought Morosov was still at the wheel he would have started using his horns by now, signaling the Zil to stop. He wasn't doing that. He wasn't even flashing his lights.

A-Able calling . . . I think Schrenk is behind me now. I'm at Obucha going north from the outer boulevard ring and trying to reach the construction site. I'm going to crash the Zil in an attempt to detonate the charge. Keep your distance. Keep your distance.

The lights were still behind me.

Calling C-Charlie . . . There's a car on the tail of the Zil and it must be Schrenk. Watch out for him.

I couldn't increase speed on this surface and the building site was too close now for me to use the side streets in the hope of shaking him off. He was sitting there watching the big shape of the Zil, his gnome's head on one side and his thin body twisted against the seat, his eyes narrowed in the backwash of the headlights. What was in his mind?

Old times . . .

Sitting there watching me take the dream out of his hands, the grandiose dream of making a statement in the name of the oppressed and in the name of the man they'd taken inside Lubyanka and half destroyed. *This is what you have done to me. Now I'll show you what I can do to you.*

He was watching me now with one hand on the wheel and the other on the radio detonator. *Old times . . .*

What else could he be thinking? There was nothing left for him to do now but turn his rage on me. And nothing I could do to stop him.

Time check: 6:10.

If Schrenk had timed the charge he wouldn't have left it later than 6:10, because the American Embassy was a ten-minute run from the Kremlin, so this was zero and he didn't even have to squeeze his transmitter: all he had to do was wait. When the Zil blew, he would go too: he was well within range and he knew that. But this would be the way he'd choose.

Nothing I could do.

The black cranes grew against the snow haze and the headlights swept across the rubble this side of the excavation crater as I put the Zil at the truck ramp and gunned up again with the wooden safety rail dead ahead. I waited until the speed rose as the rear wheels got a grip on the rough terrain and then I hit the shift into neutral and pushed the door wide open and dropped and rolled and sensed the weight of the huge car sliding past me toward the crater as I went on rolling with a blaze of pain burning in the left shoulder and the snow flying up before I hit rubble and crashed to a stop and got up and began running.

I heard the Zil going through the rail and breaking it up as it reached the crater's edge and tilted over, and for an instant I swung round and saw its headlights filling the hollow as the dark figure of a man began moving across the wasteland from the car that had come in alongside.

Perhaps he thought he could get to the Zil and disarm it in time, because he'd worked hard on this and he didn't want to see it all come to nothing; or perhaps, like a small boy who couldn't keep away from fire, he'd come here to watch the tiger. I don't know, nor will I ever know. He was still moving toward the crater at a hobbling run when the night broke into thunder and in the blinding shock of light I saw him silhouetted for a moment against the fiery curtain of snow, his small shape flung upward by the blast like a scarecrow in the wind.

I turned and threw myself down and felt the shuddering of the ground under me as the air roared past in a heated wave, tearing at my coat and bringing a hail of debris whining through the night. The steel shrapnel was now moving outward from the crater, crackling across the façade of the buildings opposite and smashing windows.

Then headlights swung in from the street and a car neared me, its wheels bouncing across the rubble. I got onto my feet and a door came open, and I heard Bracken calling to me to get in.